1 2 3 4 5 6 7 8 9 10

OAKBRIDGE
K021024
ISBN 9781739549671 (paperback)
ISBN 9781739549688 (eBook)
A CIP catalogue record for this book is available from the British Library

Black, Peter Jay
Murder at Hadfield Hall / Peter Jay Black

London

RUTH MORGAN INVESTIGATES...

MURDER
at Hadfield Hall

PETER JAY BLACK

1

Ruth Morgan's grandson sat bolt upright in the front passenger seat of her motorhome, eyes wide, cheeks flushed. "I told you we were going the wrong way." Greg, built of gangly limbs and teenage angst, tugged on his seat belt as though contemplating making a run for it.

"Don't be absurd. The guy at the main gate let us in." Ruth squinted through the windscreen. "How is this my fault?"

"But after the gate," Greg murmured through tight lips, "that sign said turn right to Hadfield Hall, not left."

Ruth furrowed her brow. "What sign?" She couldn't recall any helpful roadside directions, let alone one so vital.

"The white sign." Greg looked at her with incredulity. "You could not miss it, Grandma. You really couldn't." He gestured with his hands. "It was big." He moved them farther apart. "Massive." Farther apart still. "*Colossal*. And . . ." Greg swallowed. "This is worth repeating." He fixed her with a hard stare. "It. Was. White."

"Hmm. Interesting. With black letters?"

Greg nodded.

"They were large too?"

Greg nodded again.

"And you think I shouldn't have missed it? The sign?"

Greg ground his teeth and faced forward.

Ruth had perfect vision, even at sixty-five years young, so she couldn't blame her eyesight. She thanked a robust habit of munching raw carrots, plus her fortunate genetics. "Well, clearly, I overlooked it." Although Ruth still wasn't sure Greg hadn't imagined this mythical sign. After all, the lad was prone to exaggeration during times of stress.

He pinched the bridge of his nose. "This is so embarrassing."

"Nonsense. Stop being dramatic. Anyone could have made the same mistake."

Greg glared at her. "Seriously? You're saying after the thirty-foot-tall yellow dog, and the windmill, you didn't suspect something could be amiss?" He thrust a thumb over his shoulder. "You are telling me, you still did not for one moment think the dragon, with its glowing red eyes and smoke coming out of its nostrils, was a big enough clue we were going the wrong way?"

Ruth shrugged. "Okay, so almost anyone could have made the same mistake." She grinned at him. "Where's your sense of adventure? This will be something to tell your grandkids."

Greg folded his arms and muttered, "If I live long enough to have any."

The smile slipped from Ruth's face. "Don't tell your mother." Her ears still rang from the last scolding she'd received from her daughter over the Finsbury Flyer shenanigans.

Someone outside shouted, and Greg jolted.

"Ah, here we go." Ruth wound down her driver's side

window. "See? This gentleman is here to help us." She leaned out. "Good afternoon, sir."

"What in the blazes are you doing?" the man screeched. He wore a dark blue shirt, trousers, and a matching cap with the word SECURITY emblazoned across it in important-looking stitchwork. He glowered up at her.

Despite the apparent wash of negativity flowing her way, Ruth offered him her best smile. The one that said, *Oopsie daisy. Silly me. Mistakes happen,* but the security guard didn't seem particularly dazzled by this, nor subdued.

Ruth cleared her throat. "We appear to have taken a wrong turn."

"Wrong turn?" His voice rose several more octaves, enough to strip paint from surfaces, or sonic-weld metal parts together. "Wrong turn?" The security guard stabbed a finger in the direction they'd come. "How did you get past the fence?"

"Fence?" Ruth's eyebrows shot up. "There was a fence?" She looked over at Greg. "Did you see a fence?"

He sighed and nodded.

"Really? Oh." Ruth refocussed on the security guard. "I'm terribly sorry if I caused any trouble for you. I merely followed the road."

"This isn't a road," he snapped. "It's a path. A footpath. For people. Pedestrians. *Guests.* Not this . . ." He flapped his hands at the motorhome. "*Thing.*"

"Not a road, you say?" Ruth squinted through the windscreen. "Are you sure?"

However, she conceded he could be on to something.

Ahead, hundreds of people milled about the place. Some gathered in groups, laughing and pointing at Ruth's gigantic tin palace, others wrestled kids into pushchairs, while yet more lined up for their turns at various attractions.

There was a riverboat ride that promised an enthralling pirate adventure, several roller coasters, bumper cars, a giant Ferris wheel, plus a pendulum ride where all those strapped to it appeared to be reevaluating their life choices. And those rides were in the immediate vicinity, let alone what the rest of the theme park had to offer.

Ruth's gaze shifted back to the irritated security guard. Veins now pulsed in his neck, so it was time to get moving.

"Can you see us out, please?" She batted her eyelids.

He, however, murmured something not befitting a family-friendly environment, and then waved several of his colleagues over. After receiving barked commands that may or may not have had some English words thrown into the mix, they corralled the throngs, ushering park guests to a safe distance.

"Right." The security guard nodded to Ruth and stepped back. "Reverse the way you came."

"Reverse?" Ruth's eyebrows almost touched her fringe, and she glanced at her grandson again. "Now there's something I've not tried before."

Greg rolled his eyes, unfastened his seat belt, and slid behind Ruth's chair. He leaned out the driver's window to address the security guard. "That won't work. Reversing all the way back there? We'll never make it. Grandma is the worst driver in the world."

"Hey." Ruth frowned. "How dare you."

She would've insisted he take the wheel instead, but despite his grand old age of nineteen, Greg had not yet learned to drive. For one, he'd never shown much interest in cars, and secondly, he was off to Oxford University later in the year, and a motor vehicle would've been an unnecessary expense.

"She'll have to turn around." Greg pointed to a gap between a giant magician's hat and an ice-cream stand shaped like a Tudor house. "There."

The security guard hesitated, glowered at Ruth for a few seconds more, but then must have realised arguing was pointless, so he barked a new set of incoherent orders at his underlings.

Once the crowds were farther back still, with hundreds of phones now raised into the air in eager anticipation, Ruth wrestled the gear stick into first. "This should be fun."

As it turned out, there was barely an inch to spare on either side of the motorhome as they pulled into the gap, and then Ruth had to reverse out.

Greg lifted his feet onto the chair, buried his head between his knees, and squeezed his eyes shut.

"Assuming the brace position?" Ruth asked.

"Tell my family I loved them."

"I'm your family," Ruth said. "Do you love me?"

"Not right now."

After almost backing over a ten-foot-tall plastic bunny, and a very grumpy man in a sparkly unicorn costume, Ruth finally navigated onto the path again, and headed the way they'd come.

She glanced into the side mirror as the unicorn made a rude gesture. "Charming." Ruth gripped the steering wheel. "Ah, this must be the fence our security friend mentioned."

Greg opened his eyes and tutted.

Sure enough, a section of the fence ahead was absent, but in Ruth's defence, she hadn't done that. It sat to one side, ready for someone to replace it.

Speaking of which, three workmen in yellow hardhats—

perched on upturned crates and drinking coffee—wore passive expressions as the motorhome trundled past them.

Ruth gave the men a jaunty wave and continued out of the theme park.

Greg slumped in his seat. "That was a nightmare." He wiped sweat from his brow and pointed at a giant white sign with black lettering. "Told you."

Ruth ignored the road sign, again, *apparently*, and she followed the lane as it swept to the left.

Their current destination in the northeast of England had been tricky to locate, so far from the nearest motorway, but Greg hadn't recognised her navigational prowess in getting them this far.

Another mile along the road, a gate loomed before them, barring further progress. Ruth pulled up to it. A mass of decaying ivy wound in and out of the wrought iron and across the walls of a tumbledown stone gatehouse.

A dull glow flickered within.

Greg rubbed his hands together. "This will be amazing. From their website, Hadfield Hall looks incredible. One thing, though . . ." His face turned serious. "No mysteries."

Ruth inclined her head. "Whatever do you mean?"

"You know exactly what I mean, Grandma. No investigating anything, right?" Greg waved a hand at the gate. "This is only supposed to be one of your food consultancy gigs." He'd agreed to travel the country with her during his gap year. However, judging by Greg's current sour look, he now regretted that decision. "Stay out of anything dangerous," he warned. "Nothing reckless. And no weird stuff."

Ruth crossed her eyes and poked out her tongue. "But, Gregory, *weird* is my middle name."

"Truth," Greg muttered, and glanced through the windscreen again. "How about I make a bet with you?"

"Such as?" Gambling had never been Ruth's strong suit. She'd once put a lot of money on a horse that had literally run the race backward. It was quite impressive, actually. If she'd only bet on that outcome, she would've been a multi-millionaire by race end.

"Go the whole weekend without getting neck-deep into things that don't concern us." Greg cleared his throat. "Then I'll buy dinner for the next week. Mum finally paid me for the Christmas work at Morgan Manor."

Sara ran the family cat-breeding business.

Ruth rubbed her chin. "Out of interest, what happens if I do get neck-deep into a mystery or two?"

"Two?" Greg fixed her with a hard stare, and then a mischievous smile twitched the corners of his mouth. "We just got a sneak peek of Marsh Park. I suppose that could be a sign. One even you couldn't miss."

This tickled Ruth's curiosity bone. "Go on."

Greg motioned through the gates. "This mansion house we're visiting is also part of Marsh Park estate, yeah?"

"Same owners. There's also a zoo. It has—" Ruth's face dropped. She didn't like where this was heading. "Why? What are you suggesting?" And she didn't like the way her once sweet grandson now smirked at her.

Penguins and giraffes Ruth could handle; anything with metal tracks and lots of screaming was a hard pass.

Greg waggled an index finger in her face. "If you so much as investigate a missing teaspoon, you agree to go on a roller coaster with me." He thrust out a hand. "Deal?"

Ruth's chest tightened. Not only would her cleithrophobia go bananas about being strapped to some death wagon on rails, she'd also throw up in spectacular fashion. Speaking of which— "Hold on. You get motion sickness."

Greg fished a bottle of tablets from his pocket. "Still have these." He shook them. "The ones Mr Finsbury gave me. I'll be fine." Greg winked, pocketed the tablets, and held his hand back out to her.

Ruth found the wager hard to ignore. "Fine." She shook his hand. "But not a roller coaster that goes upside down."

"Too late. No going back. I get to choose, and you must do it, so I suggest you keep your nose out of other people's business."

Ruth huffed.

Margaret, her sister, had hooked her up with this latest paying gig at a year-round haunted getaway. Marsh Park, which they'd just had an uninvited glimpse of, was famous enough, but the adjacent Hadfield Hall even more so.

The spooky-themed mansion doubled as an exclusive hotel where guests enjoyed a fright or three. All in the name of fun, of course, with nothing too gruesome, or any jump scares. In fact, devotees of the more macabre side of life had been known to hold wedding receptions at the unusual venue.

Movement drew their attention to the building as a man in a dishevelled travelling cloak and a top hat appeared at the doorway. He held a lantern next to his pale face. Lank white hair stuck to his cheeks, and the rest hung to his shoulders. He stepped from the threshold, walking with a stoop, dragging his left foot through the mud.

Ruth leaned out her window. "Good day."

The man's sunken gaze moved from her to Greg and back again. "Invitation?" he said in a low drawl.

"Oh yes, of course." Ruth pulled an envelope from under the bare-bottomed garden gnome she'd wedged in the corner of her motorhome's dashboard, and slid out a card. "Here you go."

On it, written in red ink by a neat hand, were the words,

Mrs Morgan,

We summon you to Hadfield Hall, where spirits dwell and creatures crawl. Tortured souls wail all night, while beneath crooked spires bats take flight. Ravens caw upon the eaves, and ghostly hands bring a chilling breeze.

Enter if you dare, and be careful what you believe, for nothing good can ever leave.

WM & CM.

The hatted man took the invitation and held it close to his gaunt face. Then he stepped back and raised the card above his head. The invitation burst into flames and vanished in a puff of smoke.

Ruth clapped. "Brilliant. Utterly brilliant. Did you see that, Greg?"

The man did not react to her applause. Instead he shuffled back to the hut, then slammed the door behind him.

"I think you're right," Ruth said. "We'll have a lot of fun here."

Greg nodded. "Hands down, best job you've ever had." He pointed at the iron gates as they swung inward with a loud, high-pitched squeal. "I'll keep an eye out for any more road signs."

"You do that." Ruth edged the motorhome forward and bumped onto a gravel driveway flanked by dark forest. Some trees had glowing eyes that followed them.

She shuddered and wound up her window. "Delightfully terrifying."

Margaret and her husband, Charles, had been friends with the owners—Clarence Marsh and his sister, Winifred —for decades. So, when Margaret had put the famously reclusive Marsh siblings in touch with Ruth, requesting a visit to their hotel kitchen—to give her opinions and advice where necessary—she'd leapt at the chance.

For Greg's benefit, if nothing else.

Although, with their recent side bet in place, Ruth was beginning to regret her decision.

The forest ended, and the driveway opened to a Jacobean mansion house; four storeys tall—not including the basement—constructed of red brick, with giant leaded windows, and spired towers stretched skyward on either side.

Ruth circled a lawn and parked to one side of the mansion, as per the instructions she'd received along with the official invitation.

She'd leave the keys in the ignition, allowing a valet to move the motorhome to a preferred spot, so as not to ruin the haunted house aesthetic.

"Good luck to them reversing out of here." Ruth switched off the engine. "Hope they don't back over anything valuable." As far as she was concerned, it took immense driving prowess and unrivalled concentration to steer the metal behemoth. Not an experience for the faint of heart.

Ruth unfastened her seat belt, climbed from the driver's side, and found Merlin—her glorious midnight-furred Burmese cat—up on the back of the sofa, peering out of a side window. Ruth smirked. "I think he approves of our destination."

"Makes sense," Greg muttered as he headed to his bedroom. "I bet he'd love to snatch a few souls and drain a few necks, given the chance."

"What's the nasty boy say about you?" Ruth cooed as she lifted Merlin from his perch. "You'll be pleased to know you're coming with us. No kitty hotel for you this time, my lad." She set him on the cushion inside his custom box and closed the hatch.

Greg fetched their suitcases, and he seemed eager to get into the mansion.

"Now remember." Ruth pulled on a long black coat, pink scarf, and pink beanie. "No matter how many attractive ghosts you see, no marrying a corpse bride. Got it?"

He frowned at her. "I have a girlfriend."

"You're right. Silly me. I forgot. It's been a whole five minutes since you last mentioned Mia." Ruth hoisted Merlin's box by the brass handle. "Let's go." She descended the stairs and stepped outside to a brisk northern breeze.

Keen not to remain in the open long, they jogged toward the house, up the front steps, and into a covered porch. Ruth knocked on a giant oak door fifteen feet tall, the knocker carved into the shape of a human skull.

While they waited, she looked about, and a gazebo in the garden to their right caught her eye. Someone had threaded fairy lights in and out of the trellis, and filled the interior with hundreds of white roses.

Ruth recalled her husband had tried a similar gesture once, but with candles. Two minutes into their romantic date, Ruth had knocked over one of them and almost burned down the park and surrounding woodland.

A full minute went by, and Ruth was about to knock again, when the front door to Hadfield Hall swung inward with a low groan.

A slender man stood in the doorway, wearing a black suit, black shirt, and bloodred tie. He'd slicked his dark hair to his head with enough oil to lubricate a battleship, had alabaster skin, and sharp features. "Velcome to Hadfield . . . Hall." He also had a mock Transylvanian accent, but it came out more like Arnold Schwarzenegger. His deep brown eyes locked onto Ruth.

She chuckled. "Hello, Vlad." When this received a blank stare in response, Ruth added, "You know: Vlad the Impaler. Dracula?"

A flicker of a frown crossed his features. "My name's Liam." The accent had momentarily gone, but then it swiftly returned as he motioned at the floor, where a black granite threshold stone resided. "Enter of your own free will."

"Thank you. Don't mind if I do." Ruth hopped over the granite block with a flourish.

Greg hesitated on the doorstep outside, a suitcase in each hand, swaying.

"What's wrong?" Ruth asked. "Sc—Sc—Scared?"

He glowered at her and stepped over the threshold.

The door swung closed behind them, slamming shut, and they both jumped.

Ruth and Greg found themselves in a grand hallway with a marble floor and a flight of stairs sweeping up to the next level. Old portraits hung on the walls—their occupants barely visible behind years of grime.

Hadfield Hall reminded Ruth of her sister's house, only far grander in scale, and dusty. A tatty crystal chandelier dangled lopsided from the ceiling, burdened by cobwebs.

Liam led the way across the vast hallway to an oak reception desk with claw marks, as if a giant beast had once had issues with the room service bill.

"Wait here. I shall inform Madame Marsh of your arrival." Liam shuffled round the counter and through a door at the back of the reception area.

Ruth turned on the spot, taking in the creepy elegance. She pointed high above their heads to a dome with bats flying in circles. Of course, the bats had to be fake, suspended by fishing wire on motors, but it was still an impressive effect.

Several guests milled about the place, smiling, laughing, and clearly having a great time with their spooky-themed surroundings.

Greg set the suitcases down and peered into a glass cabinet with a dummy wizard inside. He wore a dark blue robe and hat, complete with crystal ball in front of him. "Fortune-teller machine." Greg fished into his pocket, pulled out a pound coin, and slid it into the slot.

The wizard sprang to life: his eyes glowed, his arms moved, and his jaw worked as he spoke. "Listen closely, friend." He waved his hands over the crystal ball, and it filled with smoke. "Ah, yes. Yes, I see. Something's coming through . . ." A card slid from a slot in the front of the machine. "Good luck. *Ha, ha, ha.*"

Greg snatched the card and angled it in the light. "Today is looking bleak." He screwed up his face. "I paid a quid for that?"

Ruth nudged him out of the way. "Let me try." She was about to hunt for a pound coin in her purse when the wizard inside the cabinet spun round to reveal a haggard old witch in his place. Ruth shrieked. "That's horrible." She cringed and leaned in to examine the witch's wrinkled features, along with the bulbous wart on the side of her grotesque nose. "Ghastly." Ruth shuddered. "Kind of reminds me of Margaret."

"In what way?" a sharp voice asked.

Ruth shrieked again, louder this time, genuinely terrified, and spun.

Her older sister, Margaret, stood behind them, wearing a long coat and her best scowl.

2

Ruth's heart thumped against her rib cage at the sight of her sister.

Under Margaret's coat, she wore a dark purple dress with silver stitchwork, and matching high heels. Her sharp features and cold, dead eyes meant she fit perfectly with Hadfield Hall's aesthetic. "I suppose you think you're funny, Ruth."

Ruth clutched her chest and panted. "What are you doing here?" Her eyes then narrowed with suspicion. "Checking up on me?"

It wouldn't be the first time her sister had done such a thing. Once, when they were kids, Ruth had been at the local pool, having swimming lessons, when Margaret showed up unannounced. No doubt to make sure Ruth didn't embarrass her by doing anything idiotic, like drowning.

Ruth had been midlength, heading to the deepest part of the pool, demonstrating an impressive stroke somewhere between a doggy paddle and a one-winged butterfly, when she'd spotted her sister watching from the stands . . . and had almost drowned.

Margaret sniffed. "I have far better things to do with my day than bother myself with any concern regarding whether you'll show up to an appointment." She said all that without taking a breath.

Ruth was fairly certain her sister was a vampire and didn't need to bother herself with such trivialities as breathing. "Tell me one time I didn't show up." She furrowed her brow. Sure, Ruth was late on occasion, but it was never her fault, and she always made it to her destination eventually, along with oodles of apologies.

"Our father's ninetieth, for one example." Margaret examined her nail polish. "Among many, many others." She then arched a pencilled eyebrow. "Remind me, Ruth. Where were you that time?"

"It wasn't my fault," Ruth said through clenched teeth.

Margaret clucked her tongue. "It never is."

"Cars break down. Completely out of my control."

"Apparently so," Margaret said. "Seeing as you smashed through the wall of some poor old lady's sitting room."

Perhaps wanting to defuse the situation before it got to name-calling and eye-gouging, Greg stepped forward and gave her a hug. "I'm glad you're here, Aunty Margaret."

"Great-aunt," Ruth muttered.

Greg looked about. "Where's Uncle Charles?"

"He has business in a nearby town." Margaret appraised her great-nephew. "So, I hailed a taxi and had the driver drop me here. Wanted to surprise Winifred and Clarence with a brief visit." Margaret's forehead wrinkled. "Clarence refuses to see anyone. I'm terribly worried about him."

Ruth knew little about the owners.

Margaret's expression glazed over. "Clarence has always been reclusive, but I've never known him this withdrawn. Odd behaviour. Something's clearly bothering him." She snapped out of it. "On top of that, his assistant tells me he has pneumonia, of all things. Poor Clarence. I offered to fetch medicine, but the doctor has apparently got it all taken care of."

Ruth winced. Pneumonia was dangerous at any time of life, but at Clarence's advanced years, it could easily turn deadly.

A maid in a black and white uniform hurried past, and into the back office.

"Well . . ." Margaret buttoned her coat. "I'm off." She held up a hand before Ruth could jump in with her usual, *Yes, you are*, jibe. "Goodbye, Ruth."

Ruth gave her a double thumbs-up. "See ya, Sis."

"You're not funny."

Ruth poked out her bottom lip. "Am to some people."

"And yet we're still unable to find a single one." Margaret shook her head at her younger sister's antics. "You are exhausting." She then pecked Greg on each cheek.

"Can't you stay for a drink?" he asked.

Ruth's stomach clenched.

"I'm afraid not," Margaret said.

Ruth's stomach unclenched.

"I need to get back to Charles." Margaret kissed Ruth's cheeks with a little more force than Greg's, and then she glided to the front door like a swan on ice skates. As opposed to Ruth's gait, which resembled a one-legged duck on a seesaw.

Ruth murmured, "That's why we haven't seen any real ghosts yet, Gregory. My sister scared them all away."

Despite her jibes, Ruth loved Margaret very much.

Beneath the prickly exterior, Margaret had a soft, gooey

core, and was always there when Ruth needed her most. Ruth made sure that kindness went both ways.

Thirty years ago, when someone murdered Ruth's husband, Margaret had been at her side within hours.

She'd been a shoulder to cry on, helped with all the horrendous funeral arrangements, made sure Sara still got to school on time, and even tried to convince Ruth not to involve herself with the investigation.

Unfortunately, Ruth had duly ignored that advice.

Frustrated by the lack of progress in her husband's murder case, and despite being warned several times by her superior not to interfere with an active and deeply personal investigation, Ruth did, and he'd sacked her for it.

Despite once being a police officer, and still having a huge amount of respect for the force, Ruth supposed she'd wound up a little cynical.

Her husband's unsolved murder fuelled her desire to solve mysteries, but at the same time made Ruth wary of official investigations and their lack of resources.

Raised voices behind Ruth snapped her out of her thoughts.

The door to the back office stood open, and a man and woman in their late twenties faced one another, cheeks red, fists clenched.

The girl—wearing a Victorian-style parlour maid's uniform consisting of a black dress with a lace collar, a full-length white apron, and a matching mop cap—then waggled a finger in his face. "You snuck off again. I know you did. You can't tell me otherwise. Why don't you admit it?"

The man wore a long dark coat with gold cuffs and collar, a white shirt, black tie, and a hat to match the coat, complete with a wide gold band. Obviously, a porter. And, like his companion, he wore white and grey makeup to give him a spooky, undead appearance, in keeping with the hotel's theme.

"Nadia, please." He folded his arms. "You're imagining it."

"Am I? That was your excuse last time. Stop gaslighting me." Her face twisted with a mixture of anger and pain. "You told me you were visiting your mother, but Kelly spotted you in the village. She said you acted suspiciously. Went into Gracie's Florist." Her bottom lip trembled. "You can't deny it, Mike. You've been up to something for the last month. I know you have. Admit it." Her voice quavered. "You're acting strange. Hardly talking to me. Distant." Tears now welled in her eyes. "What's going on? Talk to me."

Mike turned to leave, but she grabbed his arm. She let go. "Sorry." And then her voice softened. "Please, just tell me the truth. What were you doing earlier?" She motioned to the front door. "Where did you go this time?" Nadia studied his cold eyes. "You promised we'd leave this place, get that cottage near your dad's house, and start a family." When Mike still didn't respond, the tears flowed freely, tumbling down her cheeks. "Why are you so cruel? What have I done to deserve this?" Her shoulders drooped. "You're seeing someone else, aren't you?"

Ruth tried to turn away, did everything in her power to resist the urge, she really did, but it was impossible. Instead, she lifted her chin, and said in a loud, clear voice, "He's not seeing anyone other than you. You needn't worry on that score."

Greg squeezed his eyes closed and murmured, "Here we go again. Sticking your nose into other people's business. That lasted ten seconds."

"This doesn't count," Ruth said through the corner of

her mouth. "What would you have me do? Watch the poor girl suffer?"

"Don't watch at all. It's got nothing to do with us."

In the back office, the porter and parlour maid both stared at Ruth.

"W-What did you say?" Nadia dabbed her eyes with her sleeve.

Ruth leaned against the reception desk. "I think you can trust him." She examined a brass bell and tried to sound casual, as though commenting on the weather or some interesting TV program she'd watched recently. "He's not playing around. Well, at least I think he's not." She eyed Porter Mike, and he gave a tight shake of his head in reply.

The two spookily attired hotel workers seemed taken aback by the uninvited interference into their personal lives. However, if the pair of them wanted it to remain a private disagreement, they should've waited until they were outside, after work, or at least have closed the office door.

Ruth gave her grandson a sidelong glance. "This doesn't count as a mystery either, only an unsolicited intervention of the caring kind. Don't look at me like that. It's an entirely different thing. I'm helping them."

Greg sighed. "Sure."

With a thoroughly confused expression, Nadia the maid looked at Mike the porter, and then back to Ruth the busybody. "Sorry. Who are you?"

"I'd say now is as good a time as any." Ruth gave Mike a meaningful look. "How about you? Agreed? No point delaying any further. Wouldn't want to lose her."

Nadia clenched her fists and glared at him. "Who is this lady?"

Mike lowered his gaze, and addressing Ruth, he mumbled, "Can't do it now."

Ruth softened her expression. "I think it's clear she can't wait much longer. The poor girl looks about ready to bop you on the nose." She smiled. "Can't say I blame her. How about we cover for you? I'll get my grandson to invent a convincing story if anyone turns up."

Greg shook his head.

The phone in the office rang, and Mike answered. After a moment he said, "Yes, madam," and hung up. Mike hesitated, squeezed Nadia's shoulder, mumbled an apology, and then left the office, closing the door behind him.

Ruth caught one last glimpse of the poor girl's dumfounded expression.

Sheepish, Mike walked round the reception desk. "Madam Marsh is running late. She asked me to see you to your rooms." He reached for Merlin's box.

Ruth pulled back. "I'll take this. Thank you. Merlin doesn't like strangers carrying him." She handed the box to Greg.

The porter extended the handles on the suitcases. "This way."

They followed him to an elevator, the doors opened, and he motioned for them to step inside.

Ruth's chest constricted. "Do you mind if I take the stairs?"

Right about now was when people would usually ask if she feared enclosed spaces or had something against elevators in particular. Then she'd have to explain cleithrophobia to generally blank expressions.

However, Mike didn't appear interested in any elaboration or past panic-stricken examples. Instead, he looked from Ruth to the elevator, and then he stepped inside. Mike held the door for Greg.

"That's okay." Greg shifted his grip on Merlin's box. "I'll go with Grandma."

"Two floors up." Mike let go of the elevator doors, and they slid shut.

"I think you've really annoyed him," Greg said.

"I'll make sure to leave a big tip on our way out."

"It's your tips and meddling that gets us into trouble." As they headed up the stairs, Greg added, "And I don't get it. What just happened between him and that girl?"

"Promise not to force me onto a roller coaster, and I'll tell you." When this received a hesitant shrug, Ruth's lips twitched. "Our new friend Mike was about to propose. Sweet, no?"

Greg's eyebrows arched. "How do you figure that?"

"Spotted the gazebo on our way in," Ruth whispered. "He's decorated it. So romantic." Her thoughts returned to her late husband. John had been a caring man, putting others' needs above his own, and he'd often surprised Ruth with romantic gestures. Albeit most of them were slightly odd, whacky, or even outright dangerous.

In fact, one time in particular stood out: in the North Atlantic, somewhere off the coast of Shetland—a Scottish archipelago.

John had convinced Ruth to board a rickety fishing boat that looked about ready to sink, and then they'd travelled ten miles into the middle of the ocean, where they had abruptly stopped, donned wet suits and scuba equipment.

At this point, all hopes of a romantic meal on a remote island had evaporated, and Ruth should have refused to go any further. However, curiosity, as it so often did, got the better of her.

Thirty feet below the ocean surface, they boarded an underwater research laboratory consisting of three interconnected cylinders. The middle of which John had prepared with a picnic, complete with tartan blanket, a hamper bursting with sandwiches, pork pies, and scotch eggs, plus a bottle of fine wine. How he'd arranged permission to do all that was still a mystery.

But despite her best efforts, Ruth had only managed approximately ten minutes down in the steel tomb at depths no human should venture, because her cleithrophobia had turned her right around and she'd swum back to the fishing boat.

It was the thought that counted.

Although John knew of her phobia, he never really figured out it wasn't about confinement; the cylinders were large—well, as far as underwater cylinders go—but it was the fear of being trapped with no quick escape.

Many of their adventures had resulted in such cleithro-phobia-inducing scenarios.

Ruth sighed.

She still missed John terribly.

"Wait." Greg stopped on the first landing, breaking her reminiscences. "How do you know it was him? That porter guy who decorated the gazebo?" His eyebrows knitted. "I mean, could be anybody. For any reason. Perhaps it was one of the guests."

Ruth gave him a grandma-knows-all look. "Deduction and sound reasoning, dear Gregory."

He stared at her. "You mean, you're guessing."

"How dare you." Ruth held up a finger. "First of all, from their conversation, it seems Mike has been sneaking about for a while, and keeping things from his beloved Nadia."

"Like with the florist's?"

"Exactly." Ruth huffed out a breath and ascended the next flight of stairs. "However, he isn't pulling away from their relationship. His body language told me that. He's nervous about what he's about to do, and whether she'll say yes." Ruth held up a second finger as she reached the next landing. "And about that florist." She panted and waved in the direction of the front door below. "That gazebo outside is filled with fresh flowers. Fresh. Bought recently." She held up a third finger, took another deep breath, and continued up the stairs. "Next clue was the mud on the side of his otherwise shiny shoes, and the hem of his immaculate trousers. He'd been outside recently, and in a hurry. Hadn't had time to change or clean them. Probably decorated the gazebo in his tea break, ready for when they knock off work."

Greg shrugged. "Still don't get how you know he was about to propose."

When Ruth reached the top of the stairs, she caught her breath, and held up a fourth finger. "I spotted something his lady friend hadn't."

"Which is?"

"The distinct outline of a ring box in Mike's right-hand pocket."

Greg gaped at her, and then he laughed. "You could've led with that observation, o wise and all-seeing one."

"Where's the fun in that?" Ruth winked.

Mike the porter waited for them farther along the landing. He opened the door to a spacious double bedroom with soft furnishings, a desk, faux fur rug, and a view overlooking the grounds—which included a hedge maze and a stone fountain: things any self-respecting manor shouldn't be without.

The porter placed Ruth's suitcase next to the wardrobe, while Greg set Merlin's box on the floor and opened it. However, the cat remained inside, curled up on his cushion.

"Is he all right?" Mike asked. "Does he need anything?"

"He's fine," Ruth said. "Likes to do things in his own time. Merlin will venture out when he is good and ready."

"Or when he wants to murder something," Greg said.

Ruth slid the litter tray from the base and filled a bowl with water, then she backed from the room and closed the door.

The next bedroom along was identical, and once Mike had placed Greg's belongings by the wardrobe, he turned to Ruth.

She held up a hand. "First of all, I'd like to apologise. It was none of my business. I'm sorry. I overstepped my bounds."

He hesitated and then let out a breath. "I've been putting it off for months."

Ruth inclined her head.

"Oh, I don't mean I've been having second thoughts about proposing," Mike said. "Only that I wanted to find the right way to do it." He glanced over his shoulder and lowered his voice. "I thought about taking her somewhere romantic, a nice restaurant by the river, but Nadia loves this place. So, I asked Madam Marsh if I could propose here, and she agreed." He straightened. "Speaking of which, I've been instructed to show you to the kitchen. Madam Marsh will meet you there."

"Very well." Ruth fetched money from her purse and tipped Mike well, despite his protests, then gestured. "Lead the way."

"I'll stay here." Greg dropped to the sofa.

Ruth offered him a wry smile. "Calling Mia?"

"What if I am?"

"Well, it's been an hour since you exchanged texts," Ruth said as she followed Mike out. "Must seem like an eternity."

"What are you on about? I texted Mia as we were walking up the stairs." Greg gave Ruth a sarcastic look as she closed the door.

She headed down the stairs with Mike, and vowed not to get involved with anyone else's private business during their stay at Hadfield Hall, but Ruth had a feeling that might be easier said than done.

3

Hadfield Hall's sprawling kitchen boasted high ceilings adorned with intricate cornices. Light streamed through mullioned windows, casting warm hues across the tiled floor.

Copper pots and pans hung from an immense wrought iron rack suspended from the ceiling, dominating the middle of the space. Assistants busied themselves performing various tasks, one toiling over a giant pot set upon a range cooker within a brick hearth.

The kitchen layout struck Ruth as practical and inviting, seamlessly merging a Victorian-era cooking feel with a modern working environment. While the heart of Hadfield Hall's kitchen remained aesthetically old, a twenty-first-century heart beat within.

Workers loaded and unloaded dishwashers with china and silver cutlery, while up-to-date appliances lay concealed within original cabinetry.

At the far end of the kitchen, a door stood open, leading to a vast pantry, its shelves bursting with fresh produce.

Ruth paused on the threshold, breathing in the scent of

freshly baked bread mingled with the sweet aroma bubbling from a nearby pot. "Heaven."

A woman in her eighties, though she could easily have passed for a decade younger, swept into the kitchen.

She wore a tweed jacket and a pleated skirt that reached her ankles. She'd styled her long silver hair in a loose bun. A pair of tortoiseshell glasses perched on her nose, lacking a safety chain.

Winifred Marsh extended a hand. "Ruth Morgan, I presume." She possessed a posh lilt, a blend of high society and country living.

Smiling, Ruth shook her hand. Her attention was drawn to a brooch fastened to Winifred's lapel. It depicted a peacock with long feathers, its plumage encrusted in jewels. A single diamond representing the magnificent bird's eye glinted in the light. "Beautiful."

"A gift from my grandsons. My birthday was a couple of months ago." Winifred's expression faltered. "I apologise my brother Clarence isn't here to greet you in person. Refuses to come down from his ivory tower." Her face brightened again. "Did you catch your sister earlier?"

Ruth's stomach tightened. "Hard to miss her."

"I'm so glad Margaret put us in touch. We have been itching to upscale the dining experience, and Margaret has always spoken so fondly of you." Winifred glanced about. "We'll have you for the rest of today, and most of tomorrow, Friday. Late afternoon, the guests, and most staff, will depart the hotel. Shall we say leaving at six o'clock tomorrow? Will that give you enough time?"

Ruth had already agreed to spend one night and set off before Friday evening, though she wasn't sure why the guests and staff also had to leave Hadfield Hall.

As if reading her thoughts, Winifred added, "Every year

around this time we close the hotel to the public for a weekend, and the shareholders have a little get-together." She
rolled her eyes. "Clarence's idea. We've done it for the last
twenty years. A bonding experience, apparently. Though
not much of that goes on, I'm afraid. Quite the opposite."
She lowered her voice and leaned in. "Although, seeing as
four of us shareholders are related, and the remaining two
are close friends, I fail to see how much bonding we
require."

Ruth tried to imagine running a business with Margaret
as a partner but could only picture arguments. She
motioned around the kitchen. "Impressive. Really impressive." And that was an understatement.

Winifred smiled with obvious pride. "I had a lot of input
during the renovation. We run a tight ship, of course. Like
clockwork. Everything in its place."

Ruth's gaze shifted to a row of spice jars lined up along a
narrow shelf beneath a window, each labelled in elegant
calligraphy. "I can see that."

"Let me show you about." Winifred led her to the
assistant stirring the largest pot on the cooker with an oversized wooden spoon.

The assistant produced a miniature silver ladle from her
apron pocket and handed it to Winifred.

Winifred tasted the concoction. After a few seconds
spent staring at the ceiling and smacking her lips, she
nodded her approval. "Five more minutes." She passed the
ladle back to the assistant. "A smidge more cinnamon. Just a
dash, mind."

"Yes, Madam Marsh."

Winifred beckoned Ruth past more assistants busy
chopping, rolling, baking, and cooking. "We have several
cooks and chefs on our rota. When I told them of your

visit, I had them prepare a list of things we'd like you to look at."

"Happy to." Ruth was glad of the warm welcome. When stepping into someone else's kitchen, it wasn't always a given. Her gaze fell upon an intricately cut arrangement of tomatoes and carrots shaped like flowers.

Since starting as a freelance food consultant, everyone she'd worked with had been friendly and accommodating, happy to share their enthusiasm, and eager for any constructive feedback. Even so, Ruth always entered these jobs with a touch of apprehension, especially when hired by the owners of the establishments, rather than the chefs themselves.

Winifred stopped at a rustic farmhouse table surrounded by mismatched chairs. She picked up a binder and held it out to Ruth with a look of pride. "We've highlighted recipes we feel need updating. We also have regular health and safety inspections alongside the rest of the hotel, but it couldn't hurt going through some of that too."

Ruth took the binder, and her eyes widened at the weight. She set it on the table and flipped the cover to reveal page after page of recipes, all highly detailed in their processes and exacting ingredients.

Mrs Beeton has some competition with this hefty tome.

The recipes included everything from hors d'oeuvres and starters to desserts and petit fours. She continued to riffle through the pages—some had pictures too.

A cook with red hair, a kind round face, and a wide smile approached. "I'm Blanche." She wiped her hands on a tea towel before offering one to Ruth. "Glad to have you with us. We've been very much looking forward to your visit."

They shook hands.

Winifred nodded to the binder. "I'll see you in the morning, Mrs Morgan, and you can tell us how you're getting on. Shall we say eight o'clock in the dining room?" She motioned to Blanche. "We'll discuss your suggestions over breakfast." After a nod of confirmation from both, Winifred strode from the kitchen.

Ruth watched her go. Winifred Marsh brought back memories of her late husband's mother. She'd had the same presence—a grace that filled any room, no matter how large, and a strong, commanding personality that never failed to draw attention.

"How did you get into this line of work?"

Ruth snapped out of her thoughts and turned to Blanche. "Oh. Someone murdered my husband."

Blanche, who up until that moment possessed a warm aura that seemed to extend beyond her physical presence, visibly deflated. "Really?"

Ruth smiled by way of an apology for her bluntness. "What I mean to say is, after my husband died, I changed careers. Started in catering, and then moved to this line of work." She opted to leave out the years spent working sandwich vans and struggling to make ends meet.

Blanche's face brightened again. "It's wonderful, isn't it? The culinary arts. I simply love working here. This is my eighth year at Hadfield Hall."

Ruth checked the time on her phone. "What time is dinner?"

"Six."

It was a little after two, which gave Ruth four hours before dinner. She refocussed on Blanche. "I'll see what I can get done with this today."

"I can't wait." Blanche's expression left no doubt about her sincerity.

When people were receptive to her advice, it made

Ruth's job a whole lot easier. She glanced around the kitchen. "We'll work through the health and safety tomorrow afternoon, and I'll make any recommendations then."

Due to its sheer vastness, the kitchen could benefit from a couple more fire blankets, an extra extinguisher or two, and the relevant signage, but everything appeared well within legal limits.

Ruth hoisted the binder. "Mind if I work on this in my room?" She'd be in the way sitting at the table amid the organised chaos.

Blanche pointed to the far side of the kitchen. "You can use the office, if you like. It's small, but quiet."

"My room is fine. Thank you." Besides, having Merlin curled up on Ruth's lap while she worked was one of the many upsides of self-employment.

After a few more pleasantries, Ruth left the kitchen, clutching the heavy binder, and headed back toward the reception area.

She turned a corner, but raised voices stopped Ruth in her tracks. A door to an office at the other end of the hallway stood ajar, revealing a bright room with a bookcase and an aquarium filled with colourful saltwater fish.

Winifred Marsh sat behind a desk, her palms flat on its surface, as a man in his forties, dark-haired, slender, and well-dressed in a fine shirt and sports jacket, paced in front of her.

He clenched and unclenched his fists, his eyes blazing as he glared at Winifred, who met his gaze with calmness.

"Haven't we been over this a thousand times?" she said without a hint of anger.

"Why did you give in to him?" His accent was similarly posh.

Winifred's eyes crinkled at the corners as she studied the younger man. "Sit down, darling. You'll give yourself an aneurysm."

He hesitated before sinking into a worn armchair. "I can't believe you did it, Grandmama. He'll never change. No matter how much money you throw at him, he'll gamble it away. He's a degenerate."

"You know your brother as well as I do." Winifred's gaze drifted to a photograph on the bookshelf—it showed two boys, no older than eight and ten, standing in front of a fountain. The younger beamed at the camera while the older scowled. "Always reckless. Acts without thinking." Her attention returned to the man before her. "But what would you have me do, Ray? You know the trouble he gets himself into."

"Whatever you've bailed him out of, it was his mess to solve," Ray said through gritted teeth. "Not yours. If you keep helping, he'll never learn. He will keep gambling until he has nothing left." His attention shifted to the photographs. "Until none of us have anything left. Would that make you happy?"

"Of course not. What a thing to say."

Ray faced her. "And yet you're happy to see the business fail because of your shortsightedness."

Deciding she'd eavesdropped far too much, Ruth turned to leave, but a shadow moved to the left of the office door.

Darting out of sight, she peered around a potted plant.

Liam, the butler who'd answered the front door earlier, listened to their conversation, oblivious to Ruth's presence.

Winifred sat back and interlaced her fingers. "Orlando's heart is in the right place. He needed a lifeline. So, I gave him a portion of his inheritance early." Her expression softened. "You'll get yours when my time comes, don't you worry."

Ray gripped the arms of the chair. "It's not about the money, Grandmama. It's the principle of the thing."

"Not about money?" Winifred's eyebrows rose in disbelief. "Really?" She let out a breath. "Are you sure about that?"

A woman stepped behind Liam in the hallway and grabbed his shoulder. "What are you doing?" she hissed.

He jumped and faced her. "N—Nothing."

Ruth gauged the woman to be in her late thirties, with auburn hair that fell to her shoulders. She looked past Liam toward Winifred's office. "Listening in? Are you serious? What if you get caught?" She shook her head, and then her gaze met Ruth's.

Ruth stiffened, offered a quick wave, and hurried away, embarrassment burning her cheeks.

Later that evening, with the kitchen binder two-thirds complete and vowing to rise early to finish it, Ruth sat in a comfortable armchair by the window in her suite. Merlin was curled up on her lap, and *Mrs Beeton's Book of Household Management* lay open on the arm of the chair.

Ruth had read through the hefty 1901 tome several times over the years, but it still impressed her with its brevity and dated ideas, not to mention more than a smattering of unusual, some would claim dangerous, recipes.

Publishers had added to and embellished this copy of *Household Management* numerous times since Mrs Beeton's untimely demise at the tender age of twenty-eight.

Many of the recipes and guides had been lifted from

other works, their original creators given no credit. Even so, Ruth considered the battered tome her most prized possession.

Today's curio was . . . *beef tea*.

Now, Ruth loved tea in all its many forms, from Earl Grey to Darjeeling and the millions of other varieties between. But a good old-fashioned British-style breakfast tea with a gallon of milk and a bucketful of sugar was her favourite.

She had to confess that beef had never crossed her mind as a viable alternative.

Surprisingly enough, there were twelve recipes for beef tea, including one with egg and another involving oatmeal, but her standout choice had to be *Beef Tea Custard*.

Yum.

The simple recipe included half a pint of good beef tea —made from two ounces of lean, juicy beef; two table-spoons of cold water; and a pinch of salt—plus two egg yolks, one egg white, and more—you guessed it—salt. Left to stand for two hours. Then one would simply strain the resulting juice and season to taste.

High blood pressure be damned.

To elevate this humble beef tea into a custard, the culinary scientist would be required to beat the egg yolks and white together, pour them into the prepared beef tea and add more seasoning.

Next was to pour said mixture into a well-buttered cup, cover it with buttered paper, and stand it in a pot of boiling water. Twenty minutes later, you had Mrs Beeton's blessing to turn out your amazing *Beef Tea Custard* and serve it either hot or cold to hapless guests.

So, less of a tea, more of a thick gravy in both design and nature.

"Interesting." Ruth vowed to try it out on Greg and was about to mark the page when movement at the corner of her eye drew her attention to the garden outside.

Moonlight illuminated the hedgerows and lawn. Winifred Marsh hurried along a path, heading toward a gate in the wall.

Ruth glanced at the clock on the mantelpiece—11:32 p.m. —and then returned her attention to Mrs Beeton and her avant-garde ideas.

The next morning, having dedicated another two hours to the glorious Hadfield kitchen binder and making plenty of what she hoped were constructive suggestions, Ruth sat at the breakfast table in the dining room with Greg.

Many guests had already finished their meals and left the hotel, while porters had lined up twenty or so suitcases as the remaining visitors finished their breakfasts.

Meanwhile, Ruth, having polished off her bread and jam, watched in rapt silence as Greg worked his way through a second full English. He'd already had three rounds of toast and a bowl of chocolate cereal.

Ruth checked the time on her phone—8:35 a.m. Winifred Marsh was late. Running a hotel had to be a tough job, and Ruth wasn't surprised she'd been waylaid.

Wiping her mouth with a napkin, Ruth said, "I need a few hours to go through the kitchen's health and safety and answer any questions Blanche may have about this." She hefted the binder from the table. "What are you doing today?" Ruth studied her grandson. "After you inevitably spend an hour on the phone to Mia."

Greg swallowed the last of his bacon and eyed a Danish

pastry on a nearby cart. "I thought I'd explore the grounds. I fancy tackling that maze. Apparently, there's a prize if you reach the middle."

Ruth smiled. "Do you remember—"

"Don't say it." Greg's expression darkened.

Ruth kept her smile in place. "All I was going to point out is that you should take your phone this time. Then if you panic—"

Greg knocked back his glass of orange juice and stood. "How come you've got a photographic memory for all the bad stuff that happens?" He stormed across the breakfast room.

Ruth trotted after him. "I don't have a photographic memory. I simply recall the most hilarious happenings. It's a grandma thing."

Greg muttered a few swear words, drawing the attention of Liam behind the reception desk, then spat out a "See ya later" to Ruth and headed upstairs.

"Remember, Gregory," she called after him, "if you get lost in the maze, don't cry this time. Just call me, and Grandma will come save you."

"I was six years old," he snapped back.

Ruth giggled and hurried away before he could find a suitably hefty object on the landing to throw at her.

The kitchen was a hive of activity, with everyone busying themselves tidying away the breakfast things.

Blanche approached, her eyes locked on the binder in Ruth's arms. "I can't wait to see what you've come up with." She bounced on the balls of her feet.

Ruth handed it over. "Minor suggestions." Truthfully, the basics were fine, and her tweaks were mainly recommendations on how to jazz up a few meals. "I've added more recipes I think will complement what you already have."

Blanche led Ruth to the kitchen office, and together they spent the next thirty minutes going through the ideas, with Blanche making extra notes.

Once they were done, she closed the binder and sat back. "You know, I used to work in a truck stop diner. It was in England, but done up like an American one. That's how I got my start."

Ruth cocked an eyebrow. "You did?"

Blanche's expression turned wistful. "It was all about fried breakfast, fried lunch, deep-fried dinner." She refocussed on Ruth. "I tried adding vegetables to their plates, but the workmen and drivers wouldn't touch them." Blanche leaned forward. "So, I decided to sneak some broccoli into their mashed potatoes." She shook her head. "The next day, I received an anonymous note that said, 'Dear Veggie Fairy. Please stick to chips, and stick the broccoli where the sun don't shine.'"

Ruth laughed.

"Now I make vegetables optional." Blanche sat back. "Is your grandson a chef?"

"Greg can't boil an egg without needing to call the fire brigade." Ruth snorted. "He's off to study archaeology and history later in the year."

Blanche's eyebrows lifted. "He should look at the ruined church. It's been on the grounds for centuries. Built long before Hadfield Hall. I can show—"

Liam burst into the room, sweaty and out of breath. "Have you seen Madam Marsh?"

"No," Blanche said. "Mrs Morgan and I would like to show her this." She tapped the binder.

Ruth turned in her seat. "Winifred was supposed to meet me at breakfast. Never showed up."

Liam's shoulders slumped. "She's not in her office."

"Her rooms?" Blanche asked.

Liam shook his head. "Bed still made from last night."

"Well, she must be somewhere." Blanche frowned. "Can't have left the estate. Madam Marsh doesn't drive."

Liam turned to leave.

"Hold on," Ruth said. "I saw her last night. She was in the garden."

Liam turned back, his face a mask of worry. "What time?"

"Around half eleven. I spotted her from my window."

"Can you show me where?"

"Of course." Ruth stood, and addressed Blanche. "We'll go through the health and safety when I get back."

Blanche rose from her chair. "I'll ask some staff to check all the downstairs rooms."

As Ruth followed Liam from the kitchen, she pressed her phone to her ear and called Greg. "How's the maze?"

"I'm just about to go down."

"Small detour," Ruth said.

There was a short pause. "You're not sticking your nose in somewhere it doesn't belong, are you?"

"Meet you at reception."

He groaned.

A few minutes later, Greg came down the stairs. "What's going on now?" He looked between Ruth and Liam.

"Missing person," Ruth said. "Winifred Marsh."

Liam led the way out the front door, down the steps, and around the side of the house.

Once there, Ruth glanced up at what must be her hotel bedroom and then got her bearings. She pointed down a path that led through a gate in the wall. "She went that way."

The three of them hurried through the gate to where the

path forked. The left-hand side headed down the hill, whereas the right cut through a forest.

Ruth motioned to the higher path. "You go that way. Greg and I will take this one. Come back to this spot in ten minutes."

Liam marched through the trees.

Ruth and Greg followed the sloping path past a flower garden and came out at a river. They stepped onto a wooden bridge that spanned it, six feet above the water, with railings a little over waist height.

Lying on the boards in the middle was Winifred's jewelled peacock brooch.

Greg bent to pick it up, but Ruth grabbed his arm.

"Leave it." Her chest tightened, and by the look on Greg's face, he had a bad feeling too.

They crossed the bridge and followed the riverbank in the direction of the fast-moving water, all the while Ruth's heart grew heavier with each step.

Greg stopped dead in his tracks and pointed.

As the river swept to the right, there swayed a cluster of reeds. Among them lay a woman's body, facedown, her hair shaken from its usual bun and spread across the surface of the water in silver-grey tendrils.

4

B ack at Hadfield Hall, Ruth sat opposite Inspector Jane Harlow and Sergeant Nick Pierce at the kitchen table.

The lunch in their room had done little to ease the solemnity that had settled over them. Greg sat rigid in his chair next to Ruth, stunned into silence.

The image of Winifred's lifeless form among the reeds played in Ruth's mind like a recurring nightmare. Her voice sounded distant even to her own ears as she provided the officers with details: her full name, address, the nature of her work, and the peculiar life she led travelling the country with her grandson.

Then, with a heavy heart, she described the morning's search—their walk through the grounds and over the bridge, the discovery of the peacock brooch, the unsettling journey along the riverbank, and finally, the terrible sight of Winifred's body. Ruth confirmed that Winifred wore the same clothes as the previous night.

The whole time, a pale-faced Greg stared straight ahead, his hands clasped so tightly that his knuckles stretched white.

"What prompted you to search by the river?" Inspector Harlow asked, her voice abrupt and professional.

Ruth shifted in her seat as the memory of the previous night flickered through her mind. "I saw Winifred in the garden before I retired for the night. I was reading by the window." Winifred had moved with purpose, and her silhouette disappeared into the darkness beyond the gate. "This morning, as I might have been the last to see her, I offered to help in the search."

"What time did you see Mrs Marsh?" Sergeant Pierce's pen scratched across his notepad.

"Half past eleven. Perhaps a little later." Ruth closed her eyes, seeking any detail that might prove useful. "I couldn't see her face, so I can't say if she seemed agitated or not." She opened her eyes. "Winifred walked briskly, but not panicked. She seemed focussed on her destination."

Why was she on that bridge?

As if reading her thoughts, Inspector Harlow said, "It was late for a stroll. Didn't that strike you as odd?"

"Only in hindsight." Guilt twisted Ruth's stomach. She should have followed Winifred. "I wish I had found it strange. I might have alerted a staff member. But this is Winifred's home. She's free to move about as she pleases." Even as she spoke, a nagging doubt lingered. Something about Winifred's demeanour, the late hour . . .

Inspector Harlow's attention moved to Greg. "What about you, young man?" she asked, her tone softening.

Greg looked up and gripped his knees.

Ruth gave him a reassuring glance. She shouldn't have asked him to help in the search.

Inspector Harlow kept her focus on Greg. "Can you add anything to your grandmother's statement that might help our investigation?"

Greg shook his head. "Sorry. I didn't see anything. Well—" He swallowed hard and mumbled, "Apart from the . . . body."

Ruth put a comforting hand on his arm. "There is one thing that springs to mind, now that I come to think of it." She sat forward and refocussed on the police officers. "Yesterday, earlier in the day, I was returning to my room after speaking with Blanche in the kitchen, when I overheard— *saw* an argument. Or rather, raised voices." She frowned, searching for the right words. "A heated discussion." Perhaps Winifred had been more upset than she let on.

Inspector Harlow's eyebrows arched. "And the participants?"

"Winifred Marsh and her grandson Ray. They were in her office." Through the window behind the officers, Ruth's gaze drifted to the courtyard beyond, the memory of that encounter playing in her mind: the grandson's frustrated tone, and Winifred's calm demeanour. "I'm not sure what upset him. It concerned his brother." She looked back at Inspector Harlow, and hesitated, careful not to misrepresent what she'd heard. "Something about money, perhaps? The younger brother, Orlando, had lost some inheritance, I think." She didn't want to paint an inaccurate picture, but any detail, however insignificant, could prove helpful.

Sergeant Pierce flipped through his notepad. "Orlando Marsh. You're right: Winifred Marsh's youngest grandson. She kept her maiden name when she married. So that makes the other man Ray Marsh." He looked up, his expression serious. "Can you describe his appearance? Would you recognise him again?"

Ruth tried to recall her fleeting glimpse of Ray. "I should be able to, yes. Dark hair. Slim build." She paused. "Like I say, he seemed agitated." She had initially considered omitting the presence of the other eavesdroppers. But determined to be truthful, she explained about Liam and the auburn-haired woman.

The inspector nodded, her face impassive. "Thank you. We'll look into it. That's all for now. Please remain at the hotel until we give the all-clear. It shouldn't be too long."

Ruth stood. "If we recall anything else, we'll let you know."

Greg rose too.

"One more thing." Inspector Harlow's gaze fixed on Ruth. "How much longer were you planning on staying at Hadfield Hall?"

"We were due to leave at six this evening." Ruth glanced around the quiet kitchen, a wave of sadness washing over her. It felt wrong to think about leaving, especially now, but the kitchen was in capable hands.

After all, most of the staff had been questioned and sent home.

Ruth would leave the annotated binder for Blanche, along with a message passing on her condolences.

Back in her suite, Ruth zipped her suitcase and checked on Merlin. He lay curled on the sofa in the sitting area, his soft snores a comforting counterpoint to the turmoil.

"We're off again," Ruth murmured, bending to retrieve his food and water bowls. As she did, a folded piece of paper slid under the door.

"What's this?" Ruth hurried over and snatched it up. After unfolding the note, she read the single chilling sentence scrawled across the paper.

Winifred was murdered.

Heart hammering, Ruth flung open the door, and sighed in relief when she found Greg standing there.

"What's wrong?" His brow furrowed.

Ruth peered up and down the hallway. "How long have you been here?"

Greg pointed to his bedroom door, which was only a few strides away from her own. "Like two seconds."

"So you didn't see anyone else?"

"No." Greg's expression shifted from concern to confusion as he looked left and right.

"They must have run off." Ruth pulled him into the room and closed the door.

"Run off? What's going on?"

She handed Greg the note.

His face paled as he read it, and then he groaned. "Please don't get involved. You promised. Let's just leave. The police are—"

They both jumped at a knock on the door.

Taking a deep breath to steady herself, Ruth opened it again.

This time, it was Mike, the porter, his face ashen. "Master Marsh requests a moment of your time," he said, his voice subdued and formal.

"Clarence Marsh?" Ruth's eyebrows shot up in surprise. "Me? Why?" She couldn't imagine what Winifred's brother would want with her at a time like this. He was ill. Surely, he wouldn't be concerned with the kitchen now.

"Don't go," Greg murmured, his voice tight with apprehension. "Let's get out of here."

However, Ruth's curiosity was piqued, so she took the note from Greg and stuffed it into her pocket. "We should see what he wants. It could be important." Ignoring her grandson's protests, she stepped into the hall and beckoned him to follow. "I thought Clarence had pneumonia."

"Master Marsh has made an exception to see you, given the tragic circumstances." Mike's gaze lingered on Ruth for a beat, an unreadable flicker in his eyes, before he led the way along the hallway, through a door, and to a spiral staircase.

Ruth shot a bemused glance at Greg as they climbed, twisting higher and higher. The seemingly endless staircase brought to mind an incident in Newcastle, thirty-six years prior. Her husband, John, had accepted a job from the Earl of Shaftesbury, and she had accompanied him on a hunt for a stolen artifact.

Their investigation had led them to the castle, and a potential hiding place at the top of a stone spiral staircase very much like this one.

Ruth, stupidly, had gone first, and had climbed two-thirds of the way when a knight's helmet came tumbling down the stairs and almost brained her. This was quickly followed by the armour's upper torso, along with its wooden stand.

John, upon catching up with their assailant, had been angrier than Ruth had ever seen him. It was the one and only time he swore in her presence.

Back in the present, after climbing what felt like four floors, Ruth's legs burned, and her breath came in ragged gasps. Finally, the staircase deposited them into a small dimly lit vestibule with a heavy wooden door.

Mike indicated two plush armchairs against the wall. "Wait here, please. The master will summon you when he's ready." He descended the spiral staircase, leaving them alone.

Ruth sank into one armchair while Greg slumped into

the other. The room, devoid of windows, offered nothing to hold the eye but plain brick walls.

"That porter reminds me of my cousin." Ruth smoothed the wrinkles in her skirt. "Same eyes."

Greg's brows rose. "Bernard? The one we'll visit soon?"

"That's him." Ruth smiled at the memory of her eccentric cousin. "He lives in Leighton Village, a couple of hours from here. I'm looking forward to seeing Bernard again. Betty too. It's been too long." A vivid memory surfaced: Bernard, young and carefree, regaling her with tales of his latest manuscript find, his eyes twinkling. "He's led an interesting life." She snapped out of it and looked back at Greg. "You two would get along. He's a walking encyclopaedia of British history. Bernard was our go-to guy for any puzzling artifacts your grandfather unearthed. He's a bit of a hoarder, too. He and Betty own a delightful antiques shop next door to their B&B."

Greg nodded. "I'm looking forward to meeting him."

"Leighton Village is charming. Your grandfather wanted us to buy a house and retire there."

Greg gaped at her. "You and Grandad were going to leave Morgan Manor?"

"That was the plan. We could have done it, too. Your mother has the business well in hand."

The truth was, without Sara, the entire cat breeding, boarding, and supply empire would have crumbled after John's death, and taken Morgan Manor with it.

Ruth's food consultancy work provided a decent income, but it wasn't enough to keep John's legacy alive. It was only through Sara's business acumen and dedication that the estate remained in the family.

Ruth glanced at her phone; almost ten minutes had passed. "I wonder what's taking so long." She was about to knock when a loud, raspy voice boomed from seemingly nowhere, making her jump.

"You may enter."

Ruth looked around for the source, assuming a hidden speaker or two, but found none.

Taking a deep breath, she rose and gestured for Greg to follow. Ruth opened the door, and they stepped into a vast, double-height sitting room. The exposed ceiling was a network of wooden beams and trusses. They were in one of Hadfield Hall's glorious towers, that much was clear.

Thick curtains blocked the windows, and the lights were dimmed. As Ruth's eyes adjusted to the gloom, she made out display cabinets filled with magic tricks, props, and paraphernalia under mini spotlights, each item lovingly presented and labelled.

Her gaze darted from one object to the next, taking in the sheer volume and variety of the collection. A set of handcuffs once owned by Houdini, the most famous escapologist of all time. A fanned deck of cards, with a plaque indicating they once belonged to David Blaine. Chris Angel's leather hat and shirt draped over one shelf. Cups, balls, coins, and strange, unidentifiable gizmos belonging to the likes of Penn and Teller, Paul Daniels, and Jeff McBride.

Vintage magic-act posters plastered the remaining wall space, adding to the surreal, almost overwhelming atmosphere.

Greg shook his head. "Incredible."

As if that weren't enough, magical tomes filled several bookcases flanking an ornate table where a gramophone played scratchy classical music.

With so much to draw the eye, it took Ruth a moment to locate the elusive Clarence Marsh. He sat in a high-backed armchair by the unlit fireplace, his presence almost swallowed by the dimness and the sheer volume of objects in the room.

Bundled in blankets from head to toe, he made no effort to acknowledge their arrival, his gaze fixed on some unseen point on the floor. A bushy white beard obscured most of his face, save for the remaining pallid skin, and piercing dark eyes.

Ruth took a step toward him, but he raised a shaky hand, halting her approach. He then gestured to two chairs on the far side of the room, near a closed door Ruth assumed led to Clarence's bedroom.

Of course, if he was recovering from pneumonia, his immune system would be practically nonexistent. Ruth couldn't fault him for wanting them to keep their distance.

Greg cast her an uneasy glance as they sat.

"It's a pleasure to meet you, Mrs Morgan," Clarence said at last, his voice raspy and weak, as if speaking was a monumental effort. He remained motionless, like a waxwork, or worse, a corpse. "A shame it's under such circumstances, but even so . . ." He trailed off, coughing into a handkerchief. "Margaret has told us much about you over the years," he wheezed. "Always speaks highly of her clever sister."

Ruth stifled a snort but managed a smile at the compliment. "Call me Ruth. And this is my grandson, Greg." Her expression turned solemn. "I'm so very sorry about your sister."

Clarence nodded slowly, the movement stiff and measured. "It's a profound tragedy. Even though I foresaw it, I was powerless to stop the worst from happening."

His words hung in the air.

Ruth stared back at him, unsure how to respond. "You foresaw her death?" she asked, her mind racing.

What does *he mean? Does Clarence know something? If so,*

he needed to speak to the police. *Or is it simply the grief talking?*

When he didn't elaborate, Ruth glanced around the room. "Quite a collection you have here," she remarked, hoping to steer the conversation to safer territory.

Clarence raised his handkerchief and sniffed. "A lifelong fascination. It's why it's locked away up here—wouldn't want word to get out that I'm a crazy hoarder." He chuckled without mirth.

"Thank you for inviting us," Ruth said. "Is there anything we can do for you? Before—" She swallowed, the memory of Winifred's body too fresh. "Yesterday, I helped a little in the kitchen. Blanche is doing a fantastic job. We were about to be on our way."

"My sister's death . . ." Clarence's voice caught. He paused, and took a deep, rattling breath. "She drowned."

Ruth, having discovered her body, already knew this. "Yes," she said softly. "I'm sorry."

"My sources tell me the authorities have already deemed the reason for her presence by the river as undetermined," Clarence continued, his voice laced with bitterness. "They seem disinclined to investigate properly."

Ruth frowned. It had only been a few hours since they discovered Winifred's body. Surely the police were still gathering information. They'd questioned Ruth and Greg and, no doubt, members of staff as well. All the statements would need filing, examining, and cross-referencing. She glanced uneasily at Greg.

Clarence adjusted a cushion at his back. "My dear sister was ever so fond of Hadfield Hall."

Ruth's throat constricted. His grief settled over the room like a heavy weight. It was a feeling she knew well, a bone-deep ache that lingered long after the initial shock. And with that grief came a wave of sympathy, a desire to help, to ease his pain even a little.

"Yes. Well"—Ruth licked her dry lips—"it's a lovely house," she said, and meant it. "You've both done a remarkable job converting it into a themed hotel. A clever idea." She'd tried to convince John to turn Morgan Manor into a hotel, but he hadn't been keen on inviting strangers into his ancestral home. "You must be proud of what you've achieved."

"We're fully booked for years," Clarence said, a hint of pride creeping into his voice. "The waiting list grows longer by the day. Halloween is particularly popular. We make a point of being open all year, except for this weekend." He coughed again, a deep rattle. "This weekend is the only exception."

"Winifred mentioned an event for the shareholders?"

"My sister and I inherited the estate from our parents," Clarence continued, as though he hadn't heard her. "We were only in our twenties. Hadfield Hall has been in the family for generations, so selling was out of the question. It wouldn't have felt right." He cleared his throat. "Instead, we divided the house into east and west wings and continued to live here. Together. I wanted to build a theme park— another lifelong fascination. But it was Winifred's idea to turn the house into a haunted hotel experience. I thought she'd lost her mind, but, as usual, she was right." He went into a coughing fit, hunching forward in his chair.

Ruth started to rise, but he waved her down.

She eyed a jug of water and a glass on a nearby table. "Would you like some water?"

Clarence wiped his mouth with his handkerchief. "I confess I'm dazed. It doesn't feel real, and yet I know it must be." He looked forlorn, despite his shadowed face. "You found her in the river that runs through the Marsh estate?" Clarence closed his eyes. "My sister couldn't swim. She had a fear of water since childhood."

Greg shifted uncomfortably in his chair, his gaze darting between Ruth and Clarence.

Clarence opened his eyes but remained focussed on the floor. "Last night was the first and last time Winifred went anywhere near that bridge. She always refused to cross it. Insisted we walk the long way round." He shook his head. "I don't know what came over her." Clarence gripped the handkerchief, twisting it between his fingers. "I promised myself that if anything happened to Winifred, I would do everything I could to keep the hotel running the way she wanted." He composed himself, and then Clarence said in a low voice, "Margaret told us you used to be a detective."

Ruth's heart sank. This was it. The moment Greg had been dreading. She ignored her grandson's low groan. Her gaze stayed on Clarence. "I started the training. Never finished."

"But you investigated your husband's death?" Clarence pressed, hope in his voice.

"I attempted to." Ruth tried to sound casual, even as Greg's eyes bored into her. "I was sacked for my trouble. Learned my lesson."

Silence descended, punctuated only by the soft strains of music from the gramophone.

Clarence adjusted his position. "I would like you to solve a murder."

And there it was.

Ruth continued to avoid Greg's glare. After all, it wasn't her fault. "I'm afraid that's a job for the police." Even so, the familiar tug of curiosity warred with her agreement to stay out of other people's business. "I'm a food consultant. Nothing more."

"No, Mrs Morgan." Clarence locked his dark brown eyes with hers. "You misunderstand. I'm not asking you to solve only my sister's murder."

Confusion swept through Ruth. "Who else's?"

"Mine."

5

I n Clarence Marsh's tower sitting room, stunned into silence, and a little confused, Ruth looked over at her grandson, certain she'd misheard. However, Greg's mouth hung open, mirroring her own bewildered expression.

Ruth's gaze shifted back to Clarence. She unstuck her tongue. "I—I'm sorry." She leaned forward, as if it would help her understand. "What did you say?"

Clarence kept her fixed with an unreadable stare. "I want you to solve my murder." His dark brown eyes bored into hers. "As well as my sister's."

"But—But you're alive," Greg whispered.

Ruth had to agree with her grandson's assessment. The lad was astute because Clarence did indeed appear very much alive. *Unwell?* Absolutely. *Ill?* Undoubtedly. But Clarence was breathing and talking, two things the dead rarely managed.

"Someone will murder me this weekend." Clarence shifted in his chair. "I guarantee it. Winifred was first. I'm next."

Madness, Ruth thought. Raw grief had pushed the man over the edge. *Delusional.*

"How do you know you're next?" Greg's scepticism mirrored her own. "Or that someone even murdered her?"

Clarence kept his focus on Ruth. "I sent you that note. Had my assistant slip it under your door when no one was looking."

She frowned. "Okay. Thanks. But why?"

"To get your attention." He coughed, a dry rattle that shook his whole body. "And . . ." Clarence adjusted his position in the chair. "To prove a point."

Ruth inclined her head, fighting the urge to flee the madness of Hadfield Hall and never look back. "What point?"

"I received a similar note." Clarence paused, as if allowing himself a moment of composure. "Winifred's killer said I'm next."

A shiver snaked down Ruth's spine.

He's serious. But why would a killer send a warning?

"Where is it?" she asked. "The note?"

Clarence held up a shaking hand, his face a canvas of fear and grim acceptance. "I need you to find out who's doing this, to see them brought to justice." He studied her, as if searching for something in her expression. "I thought they were bluffing, but what they did to Winifred has changed my mind."

Ruth leaned back and struggled to keep her face neutral. After all, it wasn't every day someone asked her to investigate a murder that hadn't yet taken place.

As far as she could tell, Clarence appeared sincere. But just because he believed something, it didn't automatically make it so.

She sighed, got to her feet, and sauntered around the

room, regarding all the magic paraphernalia. Smoke and mirrors. *Is that all this is? A trick? Or could he really be under threat?*

Ruth stopped in front of a cabinet, her reflection staring back from the glass. *Has he lost his mind? Delirious from the pneumonia and the grief?*

She pondered these questions as the gramophone scratched out a haunting melody, amplifying the room's strange atmosphere.

Ruth examined a stack of trick coins, opting to play along. For now. "Can I ask why you think someone is out to get you?" Ruth glanced at Clarence and made sure her voice was carefully neutral. "Besides the note, that is."

After all, Winifred's death had occurred only this morning. Determining whether it was an accident, or something more sinister, could take the police days, even weeks.

Clarence's gaze dropped to the floor. "They will call it an unfortunate mishap, I have no doubt. But they'll be wrong." He shook his head. "I refuse to believe it." He clenched his fists, tightening the blanket across his legs. "Someone murdered my beloved sister, and they're coming for me next. I know it with every fibre of my being."

That unshakeable conviction again.

Ruth thought of her late husband, John, and her own determination to solve his murder, a pursuit that had cost her a career. She empathised with Clarence's need for answers. Rushing into investigations while emotions ran high was not wise. Ruth knew that trap well. It was a mistake she wouldn't repeat, and she tried not to jump to assumptions.

Ruth sauntered to another cabinet and peered at a box adorned with Chinese writing and several secret compartments open.

His fascination with this stuff was certainly unique.

Clarence drew a rattling breath. "My sister and I grew up here, on the Marsh estate." He fussed with the blanket, his voice cracking. "W-When we were children, Winifred and I went out onto the frozen lake." His eyes misted over. "We were having such fun, but then Winifred fell through." Clarence shook his head, his face etched with pain. "Panic froze me to the spot. I couldn't move. I thought she would die. But then adrenaline surged through me. The next thing I knew, I smashed the ice, dove in, and dragged Winifred back to the surface." He slumped back, the memory clearly taking its toll. "It was a close call. We both spent a week in hospital with hypothermia. I lost hearing in one ear, and Winifred vowed never to go near water again."

Ruth understood that too. Cleithrophobia—her fear of being trapped—came and went with varying intensities, depending on the circumstance and her mood, but she avoided triggering situations whenever possible.

"Winifred kept her word," Clarence continued, his voice regaining strength. "She stayed away from the lake, the river, for the next seventy-five years . . . right up until this morning." His knuckles turned white against the dark fabric of the blanket. "I tell you, Mrs Morgan, Winifred wouldn't have gone near that bridge without a compelling reason. Something strong enough to overcome her phobia."

"And you think someone pushed her?" Ruth pictured the peacock brooch, the glint of gemstones, and the horrifying image of Winifred's body.

"For her to be on that bridge at all," Clarence said, his voice low and intense, "it had to be someone Winifred knew, someone she trusted. They lured her. There's no other explanation. And that's not all." He leaned forward. "Security cameras cover the grounds. The police reviewed the footage. That's how we know what time Winifred left for the bridge." He pulled a phone from his dressing gown pocket.

Seconds later, Ruth's own phone beeped with an email from him. Attached were several video files. She watched the CCTV images of Winifred leaving the rear of the house and following the garden path. It was as Ruth had seen from her window vantage point. No hesitation in Winifred's step, no sign of anyone else.

"Was Winifred married?" Ruth asked. "Anyone close, besides you and her grandsons?"

Most murders tended to be committed by the nearest and dearest. The "random stranger in the street" horror story was a headline-grabbing rarity. Thank goodness.

"That's precisely my point," Clarence said. "Whoever met Winifred on the bridge knew how to avoid the cameras." He coughed, wiped his mouth on a handkerchief, and sat back.

"Winifred's partner passed away when they were in their twenties. She returned to Hadfield Hall shortly after with their daughter, Janie. Thirty years later, tragedy struck again. Janie and her husband died in a car accident. Winifred raised their boys—Ray and Orlando, fourteen and twelve at the time—as her own. They never wanted for anything."

Ruth studied the vintage magic posters. Despite the gloomy interior, their bold fonts and images of prominent magicians were striking. A bygone era.

Ray was the man Ruth had overheard arguing with Winifred the day before. Her oldest grandson. And he'd mentioned his younger brother, Orlando.

Clarence shifted in his seat, and his gaze became distant. "They were unruly teenagers," he admitted, "Ray especially. But when they were old enough, the boys worked for the estate. It grounded them, forced them to grow up. Gave them purpose. Eventually, they became shareholders."

"And you suspect one of them killed Winifred?" Greg's tone was thick with disbelief.

Ruth turned from the posters and watched Clarence's reaction.

He huffed out a breath. "Ray, the elder, manages the park, whereas Orlando is the company accountant."

Ruth's stomach tightened. *Appointing a gambler to oversee the finances?* That was begging for trouble. She couldn't help but think it had been done on purpose. *But for what reason? To stir up arguments?* However, Ruth had the distinct impression Clarence didn't know about Orlando's weakness, and for some reason Winifred had kept it between herself and Ray. *Why? Fear? Embarrassment?*

Clarence kept his eyes lowered. "Including myself, five shareholders remain. Winifred was the sixth. Elias and Persephone, our longtime friends, are the others. When one of us dies, the remaining shareholders have the right to buy their stakes. We'll split Winifred's between us."

"Sorry to ask." Ruth circled the chairs and sat, her mind spinning. "But what happens if you should die too? Same deal?"

If murder was afoot, money was a powerful incentive to do bad things. And with someone threatening Clarence's life, it was a logical question.

"As with Winifred's shares, mine will be divided among the remaining shareholders." His expression hardened, a glint of steel in his eyes. "I hold the controlling stake, and therefore the final say in all matters. The others want to expand the park. Keep saying it won't survive without it, but Winifred and I refused. We like things as they are. Marsh

Park is fine the way it is. Things will pick up. They always do."

And there we have another possible motive, Ruth thought.

Greg cleared his throat. "Excuse me, but if you think one of them murdered Winifred and is coming after you next, you must have more proof." He glanced at Ruth. "Evidence, I mean."

"At that time, I didn't want to take my fears to the police and bring negative publicity to our business, so I hired a private investigator," Clarence said. "She came highly recommended. I suspected someone was blackmailing Winifred, although she denied it when I confronted her." He motioned to Greg, and then to a cabinet on the other side of the room. "Would you mind? Bottom cupboard."

Greg glanced uneasily at Ruth, then got to his feet and walked to the cabinet. He opened it to an empty interior.

Clarence let out a hoarse chuckle. "Charles's father designed that for me. We collaborated on many illusions, grand and small." He waved to Greg, a mischievous glint in his eye. "Close the door, twist the handle half a turn clockwise, then open it again."

Greg followed his instructions. This time, when he peered inside, something rested on the bottom shelf. He retrieved a folder and handed it to Ruth.

She placed it on her lap but didn't open it. *Don't rush this, Ruth. Something's not right.* Her instincts screamed at her to tread carefully, that Clarence was manipulating her. "Why do you want my help if you already have a private investigator?"

Clarence smoothed his beard. "Fiona called, asking to meet at the police station. She said she had definitive proof a shareholder was blackmailing Winifred." He paused, his face a mask of grief and anger. "However, Fiona never showed up." Clarence motioned to the folder. "Please."

Taking a deep breath, Ruth opened it. She pulled out a newspaper clipping, and her heart sank as she read the headline:

'*Local Woman Dies in Car Accident.*'

"They found Fiona's burnt-out BMW the next day." Clarence coughed, winced, and wiped his mouth with the handkerchief. "And her remains."

Greg cringed.

"Or so the police would have me believe," Clarence continued, his voice laced with bitterness. "I can't trust them, and I haven't slept properly since. Maybe I'm paranoid, but what if she's still out there, part of all this?" He shifted his weight. "Whatever proof Fiona had at the time was destroyed, supposedly. All that's left is what we'd uncovered before our meeting the previous month. It's become an obsession."

Ruth checked the folder. It was otherwise empty except for a poison pen letter on a single sheet of paper. It read:

I TOOK CARE OF WINIFRED
YOU ARE NEXT

"A little dramatic in its presentation," Clarence said. "But effective nonetheless."

Ruth swallowed. "Where's the rest of the evidence you gathered?"

"I told you Winifred knew her killer." Clarence's voice regained some steeliness. "And that Fiona narrowed down the blackmail suspects to shareholders and family. Someone my dear Winifred trusted. It was no accident."

"Did Fiona suspect someone was onto her?" Ruth asked.

"I tried to warn her I thought she was in danger, but she brushed it off." Clarence shook his head. "So did Winifred. Now someone is coming for me. This weekend is their best chance, with all the shareholders gathered. They're the only ones who'd benefit from Winifred's and my deaths."

Greg shot to his feet, chair scraping against the floor. "You want my grandmother to put herself in danger? Knowing there's a murderer here?" He glared at Clarence. "Tell the police. We're leaving."

Clarence remained calm. "As long as she keeps a low profile, she won't be in any danger," he said. "The shareholders only know Ruth as a food consultant. She's no threat. Which makes her the perfect choice." He gripped the arms of his chair. "And I've told you, I can't trust the police. They don't believe me anyway." His expression relaxed slightly. "Every year we invite a couple of outsiders to participate in our games. This year, that's you. They'll suspect nothing."

Ruth waved Greg down. "Games?" she asked Clarence, her curiosity elevated a notch.

Greg slumped back into his chair with a huff.

"Using the evidence Fiona and I gathered," Clarence said, "I designed this year's games to expose the guilty party." He tapped his temple. "All in here, Mrs Morgan. Meticulously planned. And now that blackmailer is also a murderer, it's even more vital."

Ruth looked down at the folder. "What evidence, though? There's nothing in here. Why won't you show me?"

"I'll expose their unique skill set, the skills they used to manipulate my sister." Clarence adjusted the blankets across his legs as he spoke. "You're free to join the games without raising suspicion. Blend in, observe, report back to me."

Greg looked unconvinced. "Tell. The. Police." He ground out each word. "They're downstairs. I can get them for you."

"I showed them the evidence I have," Clarence said with a dismissive flick of his wrist. "Weeks ago. Without a definitive suspect, they won't go beyond the bounds of their investigation." His steely gaze intensified. "If we prove someone blackmailed Winifred, bring them out into the open, the police will have a solid suspect, and can make the arrest. Right now, we don't have enough for them to consider." Clarence coughed, then seemed to weigh his next words carefully. "I'm prepared to pay ten times your standard food consultancy rate, Mrs Morgan, just to take part in the games. Triple that if you help me unmask the killer."

Ruth's eyebrows shot up. *Thirty times? That's ridiculous.* An absurd amount. Although money wasn't her priority, it was undeniably tempting, especially if she put it toward her grandson's tuition.

Greg leaned in to her and whispered, "This is way too dangerous, Grandma. We should leave."

"I hear you're off to study archaeology later this year." Clarence's gaze shifted to Greg, a knowing smile playing on his lips. "Oxford?"

Greg, his brow furrowed in confusion, nodded.

"And part of that course involves a year of fieldwork?"

Greg nodded again.

"Then you're familiar with Professor JT Wilson?" Clarence asked.

Greg's eyebrows lifted. "Of course. He's a genius. The most famous archaeologist in the world."

Now it was Clarence who nodded. "We go back decades.

In fact, JT is leading a fascinating dig here on the Marsh estate." He looked at Ruth. "If you help me, I'll put in a good word for your grandson. Guarantee JT takes him under his wing for that year of fieldwork." Clarence coughed. "If at any point during the games you feel you're in danger, you can walk away, and I'll still honour our deal. What do you say, Mrs Morgan?"

Ruth studied Greg's stunned expression. The conversation had started with murder and blackmail, and now sat firmly in the realms of bribery.

She glanced down at the empty folder on her lap. Something gnawed in the pit of her stomach, telling Ruth not to get involved, that Greg was right, and they should leave. But her insatiable curiosity, coupled with the promise of such an extraordinary opportunity for her grandson . . . it was hard to walk away from. "Why not show me the evidence now?"

"I want you to meet the shareholders without preconceptions," Clarence said. "Get to know them. Observe their behaviour during the games. Of course, you will also have to play, to not fall under their suspicion." He smiled, a genuine smile. "There are three games in all. At the conclusion of each, I'll share the corresponding evidence for you to evaluate."

"You want me to observe them first, then see the evidence?" Ruth blew out a breath, her mind already racing ahead.

"Precisely. Then you can decide for yourself who possesses the necessary skills to have lured and murdered my dearly beloved sister." Clarence dabbed his eyes with the handkerchief.

Greg murmured something unintelligible, but Ruth got the gist.

It took her a moment to gather her thoughts. "If nothing

else, we need to prevent your murder," she said, her voice firm despite her reservations.

Greg glared at her as if she'd lost her mind.

Clarence shook his head. "If we try to stop the killer, they'll know we're onto them and back off. We'll lose our chance to expose them." He met her gaze. "Please, Mrs Morgan."

"You want to stay in harm's way?" Ruth asked, incredulous.

"Whoever's responsible will deny everything, simply try again later. Or worse, they'll get away with Winifred's murder." His expression hardened. "I can't live with that. I've made my peace. I have seen this coming for months. The games are the only way to solve my sister's murder. After today's tragedy, I'm modifying them." He gestured to a notepad on a nearby table, covered in scribbles and diagrams. "My assistant is already making the necessary changes to the first game. I'll finish the others in time." He stared at her, his stare gaining in intensity. "The killer must remain oblivious, free to continue with their plan."

Ruth refused to believe it was hopeless.

"Hire bodyguards," Greg suggested.

Clarence let out a wheezy chuckle. "For the rest of my days? Twenty-four seven?"

"Sure. Why not? You're rich. You can afford it."

He had a valid point.

Nevertheless, it was clear there was no getting through to Clarence. "That'll scare off the killer."

"You're convinced someone murdered Winifred," Ruth mumbled, thinking aloud, "that it's one of the shareholders, and that they're coming for you next . . ."

"Grandma," Greg said through clenched teeth.

"And you're certain these games you designed will

expose them?" Ruth stared intently at Clarence, trying to judge whether Greg was right, and he was crazy. "All I have to do is play, observe, and report?"

Clarence gave a weary nod. "I have the evidence. I know the how, not the who. Help me tie them together, leaving no room for doubt."

"When are the shareholders arriving?"

"They're already here," Clarence said. "The games begin after dinner. The first is tonight. Game two tomorrow morning, which gives me time to modify it. Then game three in the afternoon." He coughed, wiped his mouth. "Sunday is reserved for congratulations . . . or condolences."

Ruth sighed.

What she should do is walk away from the lunacy. Instead, she said, her voice firm despite her reservations, "I will observe them, but I can't promise anything." She stood and strode to the door, Greg trailing her, muttering objections.

"Liam will assist you," Clarence said. "He's the only one I trust."

Ruth paused at the door, nodded to him, and then left the room with a heady mix of excitement and trepidation.

6

G reg closed the heavy oak door to Clarence's rooms, shutting out the faint strains of gramophone music. "You can't believe any of that," he whispered, his tone incredulous. "He's completely off his rocker."

Ruth stared at the door, her lips pursed, snippets of their conversation with Clarence replaying in her mind. "You know what?" She shrugged. "I think I do. Some of it, at least."

Clarence concealed a lot more than he told them. That much was certain. Especially when it came to informing the police. However, all that only fuelled Ruth's curiosity further.

"Find the who, not the how," she murmured. "Link the skills to the evidence." Ruth shrugged. "So strange. I love it."

"I don't mean to be nasty, but he's seriously lost his mind," Greg said. "As mad as that man on the road to Bonmouth. Remember? The lunatic in the builder's hardhat with parrot feathers and tinsel stuck all over it."

Ruth chuckled. "I thought he looked fantastic." Besides, helping Clarence, in whatever way she could, was her priority right now. The promise of a once-in-a-lifetime opportunity for Greg was a sweet bonus, of course—a fat cherry on the cake. And then there was that nagging sense of duty, that instinctive need to right wrongs, a need that had been a thorn in her side for as long as she could remember.

Anyway, they wouldn't be in real danger, only observing the guests and reporting back to Clarence. Nothing more.

Easy-peasy, Morgan-squeezy.

Greg glowered at her. "You're a weird magnet."

Ruth raised an eyebrow. "A what?"

"A weird magnet." He motioned wildly. "You attract weird things and weirder people, from all over the place." Greg crossed his arms. "You can't help yourself. Always getting into trouble."

"Look." Ruth rested a hand on his shoulder, and kept her voice lowered. "Even if Clarence is only partly right, we can't ignore him. What do you want us to do? Turn our backs? Leave? After what we've heard?"

Greg slumped against the vestibule wall, his earlier frustration replaced by grudging acceptance.

Despite herself, a voice whispered in the back of Ruth's mind—*But what if Greg's right? What if this is a big mistake, and I'm leading us into trouble? Am I a weird magnet? A danger magnet?*

But then an image of Winifred filled her mind's eye.

If there was the slightest chance someone had murdered that nice lady, and the police overlooked the possibility, surely it was Ruth's duty to see this through. She'd never forgive herself otherwise.

She adjusted her blouse and forced half a smile onto her face. "You know our day isn't complete without a little danger thrown into the mix." With that, Ruth headed down the spiral staircase, strong unease tinged with an unhealthy, some would say reckless, dash of excitement.

Back on the upper landing, one of the bedroom doors stood open, revealing Nadia the chambermaid meticulously cleaning windows. The young woman stiffened and avoided their gaze, a flicker of fear flashing across her features.

Ruth glanced at Greg. *Did I imagine it?* She opened her mouth to ask whether Nadia had accepted Mike's proposal, but heavy footfalls drew her attention to the man in question.

Mike the porter, burdened with bags and suitcases, waddled along the landing, a deep scowl cleaving his forehead.

Definitely not the time to bring it up, Ruth thought.

Later that evening, after changing her mind for the millionth time—about whether Greg was right and they shouldn't get involved with the hunt for a possible murderer —Ruth decided she couldn't ignore a cry for help, no matter how outlandish.

She wasn't one to shy away from a challenge, and this, Ruth had to admit, was shaping up to be a unique experience.

As for Clarence's certainty he was next on the killer's hit list, Ruth thought back to the incident that solidified her resolve never to dismiss anyone's fears, no matter how bizarre they seemed.

Some forty years prior, as an on-duty police constable, she'd made a similar mistake, and refused to do so again. Ruth had received an urgent call to a crime scene. Expecting the worst, the apprehensive young officer had arrived at an address in Hackney to find an irate woman in her eighties—floral-patterned nightdress, hair in curlers, oversized fluffy slippers—fuming about a missing plant.

Bertha, her prized begonia, hadn't wilted away, been abducted by aliens, or consumed by ravenous slugs, but had nonetheless vanished from the sitting room, pot and all. Now all that remained was a brass stand.

After a thorough examination of the window—it was locked—and the surrounding area—clean and undisturbed—plus both front and back doors—secure—Ruth had surmised the poor lady may be a little loopy.

And that was her youthful mistake.

As it turned out, Bertha, thoroughbred of the potted plant world, reappeared—as if by horticultural magic—at the Chelsea Flower Show. Stolen by a "friend," and displayed as her own.

Oh, the horror.

Not exactly the crime of the century, but Ruth had learned a valuable lesson that day—never dismiss someone as loopy, and never underestimate the depths people would sink to for a rosette.

The same went for Clarence Marsh. His claims might seem outlandish, but there was a ring of truth to them, a palpable fear that resonated with Ruth's sleuthing instincts.

So, she made sure Merlin had everything he needed and his fur-highness had settled in for the evening, then headed downstairs with Greg.

They found Vlad the Impaler—AKA Liam, Clarence's right-hand man—behind the reception desk, looking decidedly less intimidating without his vampire makeup, though a few stubborn smudges of white lingered around his ears.

No longer affecting his spooky accent, and speaking with a Northern twang, he escorted them to the dining room.

The vast space, fifty feet long by twenty wide, boasted a tall ceiling, crystal chandeliers, numerous oil paintings, and a giant stone fireplace at the far end.

As they entered, the lights flickered and the portraits shifted positions, their eyes following them with unsettling intensity, while a draught whipped through the drapes, creating a ghostly atmosphere.

A long, imposing dining table dominated the space, laid with gleaming silver cutlery, bone china, and a giant floral arrangement in the middle, resembling a peacock's impressive plumage.

Ruth admired the spectral ambience.

"Look at this bloke." Greg peered into a mock ancient Egyptian coffin that stood against the wall, his attention captured by the tattered remains of a mummy within, its arms folded across its chest. "Who do you think it is? Ramesses the Great?"

"Looks more like Roger the Mediocre." Ruth smirked. "The tragic victim of a pyramid scheme. So sad. This guy, however . . ." She walked up to a waxwork of a man in a green pinstripe suit, trousers tucked into knee-high socks, and a bowler hat.

He sported a handlebar moustache, a monocle, and held a leather overnight bag with "Mr Apple" stencilled in gold letters.

"Hello, kind sir," Ruth said to him, adopting a theatrical whisper. "What's that?" She leaned an ear to Mr Apple's mouth. "One of you a day keeps the doctor away. Is that right? Fascinating."

"That's likely the most intelligent conversation you'll get out of anyone this weekend," a posh male voice declared from behind her.

Ruth turned from Mr Apple as a slender gentleman with

black hair approached. Of course, she recognised him from Winifred's office the day before.

Ray Marsh wore a dinner jacket. Dark circles underscored his eyes, likely from long hours as park manager, and a waxy, dull pallor clung to his skin—more hallmarks of a workaholic.

Ruth had expected him to be tanned from his time spent outside in the theme park, but quickly reminded herself this was England.

Ray smiled, but it didn't reach his eyes, and as he extended a hand, Ruth couldn't shake the feeling something was off about his demeanour. He seemed overly confident.

"You must be Mrs Morgan." Their hands met in a firm shake. "My name is Ray Marsh." He spoke with accuracy and efficiency. "It's a pleasure to meet you." Tension coiled tightly beneath the older brother's polished facade.

"Likewise. Please, call me Ruth." She motioned to Greg, who was now inspecting a suit of armour. "My grandson, Gregory."

"Call me Greg. This looks real."

"It is." Ray stepped aside as a woman entered the room. "May I introduce my wife, Helena."

Ruth did her best to hide her surprise. The lady with auburn hair—the one who'd berated Liam for eavesdropping on Winifred and Ray's heated discussion—glided forward.

Helena Marsh, in a maroon dress with silver sparkles woven within the sheer fabric, looked in her thirties, a decade younger than her husband. She was the definition of elegance: poised, refined . . . Well, up until the moment she spotted Ruth. Then, her step faltered, and embarrassment flickered across her features.

Ruth bowed her head. "Pleased to meet you." She

thought of apologising about the previous day's eavesdropping incident, but now wasn't the time to bring it up.

"Hello," Helena said in stiff reply, her gaze already shifting away from Ruth.

Not dwelling on Helena's frosty demeanour, Ruth returned her focus to Ray. "We're very sorry for your loss."

His face was now solemn. "A total shock, of course. Grandmama was larger than life. We were only talking yesterday. I can't believe she's gone."

His grief felt performative. His eyes darted around the room, as if checking for an audience. Underneath that layer, resentment simmered, and frustration. It was subtle, but Ruth had learned to trust her instincts, and something about Ray Marsh's carefully constructed persona didn't sit right.

"Yes, it's terrible." Helena checked her watch. "Where are the others?"

"Right behind you." A man in his forties with black hair —Ray's younger brother, Orlando Marsh, Ruth assumed— also wearing a dinner jacket, strode into the dining room, his right arm interlinked with a pretty blonde woman in her early thirties.

She wore a black and white dress, diamond earrings, and a radiant smile that counteracted the gloomy, spooky dining room. "Hello," she said to Ruth. "Who are you?"

Ruth bowed her head. "Ruth Morgan at your service."

"The food consultant lady? You came to help the kitchen, right?"

"That's me."

"I'm Isabella, but everyone calls me Belle," she said with a twinkle in her eye and an infectious smile.

"Not Bella?" Ruth asked.

"Oh goodness, no. How ghastly." She gave a fake shudder, but the smile remained. "We'll get on splendidly. You must tell me everything you know. I simply love to cook. Don't I, darling?" She looked up at Orlando, her voice taking on a syrupy sweetness.

Orlando shuffled from foot to foot and avoided eye contact with anyone other than her. His face was pale and drawn, as though he rarely saw daylight. However, unlike his confident brother, Orlando appeared meek, shoulders slumped.

Helena scowled at Belle. "Perhaps Mrs Morgan can cater for Winifred's wake."

Belle gasped. "That's a terrible thing to say."

Ray frowned at his wife. "Indeed."

"What was she doing down by the river?" A new voice, sharp and accusing, cut through the air. "Everyone knows Winifred was terrified of the water. Couldn't swim to save her life."

Cringing, Belle stepped aside.

A lady in her late seventies, silver hair styled in an elaborate updo, wearing a deep green dress, and a gentleman, also in his seventies, thinning white hair swept back, wearing a dinner jacket, entered the dining room.

Their arms were linked, but the woman held herself stiffly, her chin raised, while the man's expression was unreadable.

Ruth looked from the man in the dinner jacket to the woman in the designer outfit and murmured to Greg, "Feel underdressed?"

Greg shrugged, clearly more concerned with when they would eat.

"Not entirely true," Ray said to the woman. "Grandmama would take strolls along the riverbank on occasion."

She regarded him. "With you, darling? Or alone?"

Orlando, staring at a spot on the floor, murmured, "Can we not discuss this now?"

The woman extended a limp hand to Ruth. "Persephone."

Ruth gave her fingers an odd wiggle. "Ruth Morgan, and my grandson, Greg."

Persephone retracted her hand. "Charmed." Although, she sounded far from it.

The man fist-bumped Ruth and Greg. "Elias."

"We're so glad to have you with us," Belle said to Ruth. "Even under such horrendous circumstances." Her smile faded as she surveyed the room. "Isn't it odd how quickly things can change? One minute you're sharing tea and biscuits, the next . . ." She trailed off, her gaze drifting to the empty chairs at each end of the table.

Meanwhile, Ruth studied the older couple. These must be the other two board members. Counting Ray and his younger brother, Orlando, that made up the four shareholders, with Clarence the majority shareholder with overarching control.

Ruth scanned the gathered family and friends.

Clarence thinks one of these people is Winifred's blackmailer and murderer, and they're out to get him next?

Ray nodded to Persephone and Elias. "We're so glad you both could still make it." He didn't sound particularly glad.

Persephone looked dubious. "Then tell your face." She sniffed. "What happened to Winifred is so deeply shocking to us all. What a tragic . . . accident." Her tone, however, suggested she wasn't entirely convinced it was an accident.

Heads bowed, and murmurs rippled around the room.

Elias's gaze shifted to Ruth and Greg. "So you're this year's extras, I suppose? Invited at the last minute?" He had a deep voice with a hint of a German accent. Elias didn't wait for an answer, though; instead he rubbed his hands together. "When do we eat? I'm starved."

"Me too." Greg rubbed his stomach.

"My grandson could eat for England," Ruth said. "In fact, it wasn't long ago I petitioned the Olympic Committee to make it an official sport." She nudged Greg. "Guaranteed gold medallist."

Belle giggled, and everyone else smiled politely, other than Helena, who kept glancing at the door as if expecting another visitor.

Orlando shifted from foot to foot. "Where's the staff?"

"All but one or two have gone for the weekend." Ray gestured to the dining table. "Shall we? Just like last year, Cook prepared our meals in advance, and Liam only has to warm them up."

"Fantastic," Helena said, her voice laced with sarcasm. "Reheated leftovers."

7

Ruth, Greg, the family and friends gathered around the dining table. Belle, with a mischievous grin, shifted her place setting next to Ruth's.

She plonked herself down, looking eager to converse. "I'm so glad Clarence chose you as this year's extras. You sound absolutely fascinating. You travel the country?" Her eyes sparkled with curiosity. "That's what Winifred told us in the email. Said you were coming to advise the kitchen, and that you're well regarded in your field. Mentioned you've advised hundreds of restaurants all over the country."

Ruth nodded. She couldn't place her accent. It sounded Northern, but with an Irish twang.

Ray pulled out a chair for Helena, who sat opposite, gaze fixed somewhere above Ruth's left shoulder. "Travel?" She sounded confused. "You stay in hotels?" The concept of lodging anywhere but a five-star establishment seemed beyond her comprehension.

"Mrs Morgan has a motorhome," Elias said. "That thing

parked outside." He shook his head. "Must be a nightmare to park."

Greg opened his mouth, no doubt to launch into his usual witty commentary about her driving skills, but Ruth silenced him with a sharp poke to the ribs. She knew her grandson was about to regale them with the theme park incident.

"Ow." He rubbed his side, but he seemed to get the message.

"A motorhome? Really?" Belle's face lit up. "Like Americans have? You live in it? They look so much fun. Can I see it?"

"You'll have to forgive Belle," Persephone said, her tone haughty as she sat several chairs away. Her disapproval of Belle's enthusiasm was evident. "She's forever fascinated by everything."

"Winifred's passing means nothing to her," Helena added.

Belle gasped. "That's not true. Why would you say such a horrible thing? I loved Winifred."

Orlando leaned over and rested a hand on her knee. "We all did, darling." He shot a furtive look at Helena, then lowered his gaze.

Belle, thankfully, didn't dwell on her dig. She leaned toward Ruth, whispering, "Grief is the price we pay for love."

Ruth recognised the painful truth in her words all too well. "Where did you and Orlando meet?"

"At a charity auction." Belle sighed. "A chance encounter. Winifred was there to donate a portrait, and I worked as an assistant to the auctioneer. Orlando was fetching the portrait from the car when he bumped into me. Literally." She chuckled. "He almost dropped it. Didn't you, darling?" Belle gazed affectionately at him. "Love at first sight." She looked back at Ruth. "Winifred didn't approve of us at first, but learned to adore me in the end."

"She was the only one," Helena murmured.

"Will you show me tomorrow?" Belle asked Ruth. "Your amazing motorhome?" Her eyebrows knitted. "I've seen inside a caravan." She glanced at her husband. "Remember, Orlando? That one they used as a first aid station at the summer fete? When you cut your finger." She shuddered theatrically, then turned back to Ruth, her eyes wistful. "Motorhomes seem so grand and exciting."

"I'd be delighted to give you a tour." Ruth glanced at Greg, who wore a bemused expression. He clearly didn't share Belle's enthusiasm, nor find the motorhome at all exhilarating.

As Belle launched into a detailed description of her dream trek across Europe and Asia, Orlando fidgeted in his seat. His gaze darted between the empty chairs at each end of the vast table, and he repeatedly checked his watch. Upon noticing Ruth observing him, Orlando placed his hands on his lap and stared at the table.

Clearly Winifred's death affected him deeply, and a pang of sympathy hit Ruth. Grief was the worst, especially when it came unexpectedly. She'd seen enough in her lifetime, and Orlando, unlike some of the others present, wasn't putting on a show.

Liam served smoked salmon starters, followed by a main of lamb shank, with sides of asparagus and mashed potato.

Helena watched him the entire time, and they exchanged brief looks—his, a mild yearning; hers an odd combination somewhere between apprehension and curiosity, but it was quickly gone when Liam left the room.

If the food was indeed reheated, he had done an excellent job masking it. The lamb was tender, the asparagus perfectly cooked, and the mashed potatoes creamy.

Helena, however, requested mayonnaise and slathered it over everything, acting as though she were being served a dry, tasteless mess.

"Are we really still playing the games?" Elias asked as they tucked in. "Even after what happened to Winifred? It seems a tad inappropriate."

"She'd want us to carry on, though, wouldn't she?" Belle asked as she picked at a parsley leaf. "Would not want us to mope about the place." She then winced and squeezed her husband's arm. "Sorry, darling. I didn't mean—"

Orlando forced a tremulous smile, but his grip tightened on his fork.

"You're right, Belle," Ray said. "Grandmama wouldn't want us moping." He shot a look at his brother and muttered, "Happy to see the business falter, but mope? Heavens no." Ray then said to Ruth, "We have the games every year. Clarence insists. It's tradition." He glanced around the table. "You know how he gets when we deviate from the routine. I say we carry on as normally as possible, given the . . . tragedy."

Elias cocked an eyebrow. "You've spoken to the old man?"

Ray sighed and shook his head. "He's still unwell. Sent a message instructing us to start the games without him."

Persephone set down her knife and fork. "My dearest friend has only been dead a few hours, and we're supposed to pretend nothing's happened?" Her gaze lingered on each of them in turn. "Does that seem right?"

"If it's what Clarence wants." Ray shrugged. "We must play."

Orlando's shoulders slumped further.

Ruth studied the brothers. Tension crackled between them, and Ray made no effort to hide it. *But what is the source of their animosity? Is it simply sibling rivalry, or is there something more at play? Orlando's early inheritance? His gambling?*

"Of course, Clarence wants us to continue as though nothing happened," Helena said, her voice laced with bitterness. "Why would he take our feelings into account? He's obsessed with our continued misery."

"I say." Elias glared at her. "That's going too far."

Helena tutted and looked away.

Ruth studied the others, but none seemed to want to contradict her.

"The games are so much fun." Belle's cheerfulness broke the tension. She bounced in her seat, eyes sparkling. "I can't wait. They can be really challenging puzzles. You'll love them, I know it."

"I'm sure I will." Though truth be told, games and puzzles weren't Ruth's cup of tea. She much preferred a long reading session with Mrs Beeton, or a brisk walk, rather than taxing her brain with riddles and codes.

Greg, predictably, seemed unfazed by the prospect of the games. He helped himself to more vegetables and a generous mound of mashed potatoes, drenching the lot in mayonnaise.

Helena nodded in approval.

Ruth had given up long ago trying to calculate the lad's daily calorie intake. Some things were best left as scientific oddities.

"Last year's games were easy," Elias said in a matter-of-fact tone. "Childish even." He looked at Persephone. "I do hope Clarence put more effort into them this year."

"Does he usually participate?" Ruth asked.

"Only as host and observer." Ray sipped his red wine. "Clarence knows all the answers. Wouldn't be fair if he played."

Helena chuckled without mirth. "He's played us all for years."

Ray glared at her. "Can you go one day without making snide remarks?"

She stared back at him, defiance in her eyes.

"Winifred used to play the games, though," Belle said in a small voice.

Ruth inclined her head at Helena, curiosity getting the better of her. "What do you mean? Played you how?"

Helena hesitated, her gaze flickering toward Ray, then back to Ruth. She opened her mouth to answer, then seemed to think better of it. Finally, she muttered, "Forget I said anything," and took a gulp of wine.

Belle, however, leaned in to Ruth and whispered, "Some of us think Clarence rigs the games to ensure a different person wins each year."

Persephone flicked her wrist. "That's nonsense."

Orlando abandoned his half-eaten meal, his appetite clearly gone, and he stared at the table.

"What kind of games are they?" Greg asked, now slathering butter on a bread roll.

"They're mysteries for the most part." Now it was Elias who shot Persephone a strange look.

Ruth couldn't quite place it. *Guilt? Or something else entirely?*

Persephone, as if sensing his scrutiny, turned to Ruth. "Mysteries combined with puzzles."

"The first game is often a treasure hunt," Helena added. "Well, a sort of treasure hunt. We follow clues to hiding spots."

"Second is a puzzle or logic game," Ray said.

Helena rolled her eyes. "I'm hopeless at those."

"And the third?" Ruth asked.

"Could be anything," Persephone said. "Clarence likes to surprise us. Keep us all on our toes."

Helena drained her wineglass and reached for the bottle.

"Allow me, dearest." Ray poured her a drink, eyes narrowed, jaw clenched.

"Each game is like an escape room," Belle said, seemingly oblivious to the tension, or perhaps accustomed to it. "Well, we only have a certain amount of time to solve them. Last year, we almost lost." She motioned around the table. "Luckily, Orlando came to the rescue at the last minute. Didn't you, darling?" Belle beamed at him. "You were brilliant. So clever. You won all the games. Had the most points."

He waved the compliment away, a flicker of enthusiasm momentarily breaking through his grief. But then his face turned solemn again.

As they ate, Ruth studied each guest in turn. They made almost polite conversation, but a seething resentment rippled beneath their words. Still, none of them seemed the murdering type. Aside from Helena, who clearly harboured some anger toward Clarence, they were all pleasant enough, and, surprisingly, interested in hearing about Ruth's travels and Greg's plans to study history and archaeology at Oxford University.

"I went to Oxford," Helena said to him. "I was supposed to become a lawyer. Those were the days"—her expression darkened—"before I was saddled with . . ." Helena's gaze shifted to Ray.

He hoisted a wineglass. "I appreciate your sacrifice."

"Do you?" Helena looked back at Greg. "If we have a moment after the games, I'll see what I can remember." She tapped her right temple. "There must be something useful still rattling around up there."

Persephone leaned toward Elias. "I was just reminiscing about Winifred, and all the fun we had together. That restaurant we started? The three of us?" She rolled her eyes. "What a disaster. If it wasn't for Winifred's kindness, you and I would not have joined the Marsh empire."

Elias nodded. "And we certainly would've never imagined being board members."

Persephone's eyes glazed over. "Do you remember that time she—"

However, whatever anecdote Persephone was about to share was cut short as Orlando pushed back his chair.

"If you'll excuse me," he muttered, his face pale and drawn. Without another word, he hurried from the room.

Ray sighed and tossed his napkin onto the table. "I'll go after him." He followed Orlando out, leaving the rest in an awkward silence.

After a minute, Belle finally said, "Winifred's death has hit him very hard."

"It's hit us all hard." Helena knocked back her wine, and poured herself another.

"Well, yes." Belle's brow furrowed. "We all loved Winifred, of course. I just think out of everyone here, Orlando was the closest. He'll be lost without her."

"What are we? Chopped liver?" Elias gestured between Persephone and himself. "We've known Winifred and Clarence for fifty years."

"I didn't mean—" Belle swallowed and turned to Greg. "Have you been on any exciting expeditions? Archaeology sounds fascinating." Her eyes widened. "Have you found any bones?" She gasped. "Human skulls?"

As Greg launched into a detailed description of a Saxon pit he'd helped excavate in Surrey the previous year, muffled raised voices drifted from behind a closed door.

Ruth leaned back in her chair. It sounded like a man and a woman arguing, their words indistinct. A few seconds later, the argument ceased as abruptly as it had started.

Ruth glanced around the table. *Have the others even noticed?* Greg, predictably, remained oblivious, his attention consumed by a large slice of chocolate cake.

Five minutes later, Ray and Orlando returned, both brothers looking forlorn. Ray's face was flushed, his jaw clenched tight, while Orlando trailed behind, his gaze fixed on the floor, shoulders slumped. Whatever they'd discussed, it was clearly far from resolved.

After two rounds of strong coffee, Elias clapped his hands. "When do we start the first game?"

"Right now, sir." Liam strode into the dining room and plucked an envelope from the middle of the table, where it lay hidden amid the floral arrangement. "Master Marsh left specific instructions regarding the games." His eyes flickered to Helena, and then he slid out a card and read aloud. "'Welcome, one and all. Please accept my humble apologies for not being with you in person this year, but as you know, I am rather under the weather. Therefore, I have entrusted my hosting duties to Liam. Please treat him as you would me.'"

"The old man won't be here?" Elias said.

"He must be truly unwell to miss this." Belle squeezed Orlando's hand, her face etched with concern. "Such a shame. This is Clarence's favourite event of the year."

Persephone's eyes darkened. "And no mention of Winifred?"

"Wait." Belle looked up at Liam. "Do it in his voice." She smiled at Ruth. "He does a marvellous impression of Clarence. It's so funny." Belle chortled and looked back at him. "Please?"

However, Liam, his face unreadable, continued in what Ruth assumed was his natural cadence and tone—a far cry from the faux Transylvanian accent he'd greeted them with. "'This year, I have outdone myself. You're in for a stimulating time.'"

Elias leaned forward, fingers interlaced, an intense look on his face. "About time he challenged us."

"'And now we come to the part you're no doubt itching to hear . . .'" Liam glanced around at them all. "'This year's prize.'"

Even Greg seemed intrigued. He polished off a biscotto, brushed crumbs from his shirt, and focussed on their host.

Liam continued to read. "'I, Clarence Theodore Marsh, will hereby resign from the board and sign over all of my Marsh estate shares to whoever has the most points after all three games.'"

A collective gasp echoed around the table.

Ruth scanned the gathered faces, taking in their reactions. Ray's shock seemed genuine, and his cheeks drained of colour. Elias, on the other hand, rubbed his hands together, a predatory gleam in his eye. Persephone sat ramrod straight, her lips pressed into a thin line, as if calculating the implications of this unexpected turn of events. And Helena . . . Helena seemed almost nonplussed, her expression unreadable, but something—*triumph? satisfaction?*—crossed her features.

"He can't be serious," Orlando whispered, his voice barely audible.

"What about these two?" Elias gestured between Ruth and Greg. "Surely Clarence doesn't intend to offer them the same prize."

Liam read from the card. "It only says that if they should win, they will receive a handsome reward."

Ray jumped to his feet, his face pale, his hands clenching and unclenching at his sides. He looked toward the door. "I need to speak to Clarence."

Liam set the card on the table, opened the door behind Ruth, and froze at the threshold. "No. No, it can't be." He stumbled back, knocking over a silver tray with a crash.

Belle spun in her seat, and her face contorted. "What is that?" Then she clapped a hand over her mouth and let out a muffled scream.

8

B elle and Liam's agitation rippled through the dinner guests, propelling them from the dining table toward the drawing-room door. A dimly lit space awaited, furnished with plush chairs, a Persian rug, and a well-stocked drinks cabinet, its grandfather clock ticking away in the corner.

Yet, none of these captured their attention. Instead, all eyes were drawn to the crumpled body sprawled at the foot of the fireplace.

"Nadia?" Persephone gaped. "Is that Nadia?"

As they stared into the drawing room at her motionless form, Greg, his face etched in disbelief, leaned in to Ruth and whispered, "This part of the game, right?"

The young maid lay facedown, her head tilted to the side with her cheek pressed against the exposed parquet floor, eyes closed. Her hair fanned out around her head, strands matted with blood, and a fire poker lay discarded nearby.

"It's not a game." Liam pushed past, his face pale and drawn. He knelt beside Nadia and pressed two fingers to her neck.

Silence descended, broken only by the ticking clock, and then Ray's sharp intake of breath. "Well?" He gripped the doorframe.

Finally, Liam straightened, his voice trembling. "She— She's alive."

"Thank goodness." Belle collapsed into a chair and sobbed. "It's awful. Who did that to her? What happened?"

Orlando, his gaze vacant, mechanically rubbed her back.

Liam, shock replaced by urgency, rushed past. "I'll call an ambulance."

"What about Mike?" Ruth called after him. "Is he here?"

Liam's step faltered, but he kept going.

"Call the police too," Ruth added, walking into the drawing room. Her eyes scanned every inch, lingering on the area around Nadia.

Blood soaked the back of the girl's head, but the flow seemed to have stopped. *A small mercy,* Ruth thought, unless there was a skull fracture.

Crouching, Ruth beckoned Greg. "Help me roll Nadia onto her side. Carefully."

Together, they manoeuvred the unconscious girl into the recovery position, mindful not to worsen her injuries or twist Nadia's neck in any way. Ruth propped her head with a cushion and checked her airway.

"Who could do this?" Elias's voice was tight with barely suppressed fury. He looked around at the assembled group, eyes narrowed. "What monster would do such a thing?"

Persephone scowled. "Don't tell me you suspect one of us?"

Helena stared at Nadia but remained silent.

Ray's gaze swept over each of them in turn. "The staff have gone home. That only leaves one other member here, besides Liam."

"That porter guy, Mike." Greg stepped closer to Ruth, his eyes darting suspiciously between the brothers.

So he noticed their absence at the time of the muffled argument?

Ruth glanced down at Nadia. *How long has the girl been lying there?* By the way the blood hadn't yet congealed, she estimated under thirty minutes, maybe less than fifteen, so the timeline matched.

Belle's voice, small and desperate, broke the silence. "This is a joke, right? It can't be real. Tell me it's a sick prank."

Another door at the far end of the drawing room stood ajar. Ruth edged her way over, and opened the door further with her foot. She peered into a narrow hallway. "Where does this lead?"

"The kitchen and pantry," Helena said.

Ruth glanced back at Nadia, her mind racing.

Did the attacker flee that way?

Ray exploded, his face flushed. "This is preposterous. I've had enough. The old man has lost his mind." He stormed across the dining room.

"We should stay together," Orlando called after him. "Where are you going?"

"To speak to that old fool. This has gone too far."

Helena hurried after him. "Slow down. You know what Clarence is like."

Seizing the opportunity, Ruth nudged Greg. "Go after them."

"What? Why?"

"Just go, please." Ruth needed eyes on every family member, especially during a crisis.

Greg hesitated, glanced down at Nadia, then took off after Ray and Helena, disappearing through the door.

Elias sank into a dining chair, his already gaunt face growing paler by the minute. "First Winifred, now this."

Belle, clutching Orlando's hand, peered up at him, her eyes wide with fear. He, however, kept his lips pressed together, gaze fixed on some unseen point on the wall.

Ruth used the opportunity to walk a slow circle around the drawing room. Her gaze swept over every detail, committing them to memory. The discarded poker and the open door, the blood—these were the only clues. No signs of a struggle suggested Nadia knew her attacker well enough to turn her back on them. Or she was taken by surprise. Given the overheard argument, Ruth doubted the latter.

She moved to the windows. Not only were they bolted, but someone had also latched them from the inside, requiring keys to open. The assailant could only have entered and left through the door.

Ruth cursed her earlier inaction. She should've investigated the raised voices.

Kneeling beside Nadia, she gently took the girl's wrist. "Can you hear me?"

Nadia's pulse was steady, but she showed no other signs of consciousness.

"I—I don't think you sh-should keep t-touching her," Belle stammered.

Ray, Helena, and Greg returned, their faces grim.

"Clarence has locked himself in the tower," Ray announced, exasperated. "Refuses to answer. Stubborn old fool."

"He's unwell," Orlando said. "Probably asleep. Leave him be. He's had enough shocks for one day. Any more might finish him off."

"Would that be such a bad thing?" Helena muttered.

Persephone and Belle shot her venomous glares.

"He's not asleep." Ray folded his arms and leaned against the doorframe. "I can picture him up there right now, smirking. Clarence knows exactly what he's doing, the chaos he's causing."

"You can't seriously believe he had anything to do with this." Elias jabbed a finger in Nadia's direction. "What? He came down here, bashed the girl over the head, and then went back to his rooms for a brandy?"

Liam reappeared, pale and strained. "The ambulance is on its way. Police too." He motioned toward the door at the far end of the dining room. "They ask that you all wait in the study. I'll stay with Nadia until they arrive."

"Do you have a key to Clarence's tower?" Ray asked.

Liam shook his head.

"What about Mike? Where is he?"

Liam shrugged. "Probably went home. But I'll check when the police get here."

Ruth observed the exchange. Liam seemed wary of Ray, avoiding his gaze, maintaining his distance. *Is it simply the stress of the situation, or does Liam suspect more than he's letting on? What would cause such a fear?*

The group hesitated, each lost in their own thoughts, their faces a mixture of shock and suspicion. Finally, they began to file out of the dining room.

"Would you like us to stay?" Ruth asked Liam. She gestured to herself and Greg.

He shook his head again, more forcefully this time. "The police were specific." His eyes darted between Ruth and the door, a sheen of sweat forming on his forehead.

Ruth understood the police would want everyone together, away from the crime scene. "Perhaps we should find Mike." She pressed. "He could be hurt too."

A flicker of a frown crossed Liam's face. "The police will deal with everything. Please do as they say and wait in the study," he insisted. "They'll be here soon."

Ruth cast one last look around the drawing room, then followed Greg and the others, down a corridor next to the reception desk, and deeper into the house. They rounded a corner and entered a large, imposing study through a set of open double doors.

Like much of Hadfield Hall, this room was a testament to wealth and power. Thirty feet square, it boasted a well-stocked bar, a massive oak desk, chairs, a sofa, a coffee table, and enough leather-bound books to rival a small library.

Greg was immediately captivated by a Satsuma vase with a lid, gilded dogs as handles, and hand-painted panels depicting various repeating patterns and Japanese faces.

"Who could have hurt her?" Belle's voice, tight with anxiety, drew Ruth's attention. She perched on the edge of a high-backed chair, her hands twisting in her lap. "If Clarence is ill, he couldn't have done it. Could he?"

"Clarence didn't do it." Persephone rolled her eyes. "It was that porter fellow. Mike. Who else could it be? We were all at dinner. It had to be him. There's no other explanation."

"Actually," Elias interjected, "I thought I saw someone lurking near the drawing room door earlier. Couldn't quite make out who it was, though."

"Male or female?" Ruth asked.

A deep furrow appeared between his brows. "Couldn't say. Only got a glimpse."

Ruth glanced over her shoulder, mentally retracing their steps from the dining room, mapping out Hadfield Hall's layout. If Mike was the guilty party, he could have easily slipped out and be long gone by now.

Given the limited evidence, Ruth had to concede Persephone had a point. However, she reminded herself to keep an open mind because there were still those unaccounted-for minutes during dinner when both Ray and Orlando were away from the table.

"Do you think she turned down his proposal?" Greg murmured in her ear. "Mike?"

Ruth recalled a particular incident during her time on the force. A seemingly open-and-shut case, where a couple had owned a restaurant in Hammersmith—a riverside district in West London. The woman—Sonia—had been away on a business trip, sourcing new suppliers, while her significant other—Nathaniel—ran the restaurant and kitchen.

During their brief time apart, Sonia had bought a ring, and then headed home early to propose to her man, only to discover Nathaniel having an affair with a fetching brunette.

Later that night, that same brunette had wound up dead, murdered on her own doorstep.

Everyone in the entire world had pointed fingers at Sonia, but it turned out she had a solid alibi in the form of CCTV footage from the restaurant.

After discovering Nathaniel and the brunette in flagrante, she'd gone to the restaurant after-hours and worked on the accounts. Sonia had explained she used the quiet time to clear her head and calm down.

All accusations had shifted to Nathaniel, and he'd spent a lot of time in police custody, answering difficult questions, being the last person to see the victim alive, and without a solid alibi.

Ruth sighed.

Nothing was ever as it seemed, and she needed to keep an open mind to the day's strange events.

At the bar in Hadfield Hall's opulent study, Ray filled tumblers with whisky. "Don't be so sure Clarence didn't put the porter up to it."

"How can you even suggest that?" Orlando, perched on the arm of Belle's chair, sounded genuinely shocked. "The old man might be losing it, but actually having someone hurt? He's not that far gone."

Helena snorted and took a tumbler from Ray.

Belle looked up, her eyes wide. "So, this isn't part of the games?"

Elias shook his head. "Definitely not."

Ruth wasn't sure what to believe. She couldn't imagine how Clarence would gain any insight into his guests by having a maid injured in such a brutal way.

However, if it is true, what am I supposed to observe? Their reactions to a crime? Their capacity for suspicion and deceit?

Orlando cleared his throat. "You know, Clarence hired a private detective. I told Grandmama about it."

Persephone, about to take a sip of her whisky, paused, her eyebrows shooting up in surprise. "What on earth for?"

"Don't know," Orlando mumbled, avoiding her gaze.

Although, something about his expression, the way he wouldn't meet her eyes, told Ruth he knew more than he was letting on. If she could get him alone, she might be able to pry it out of him.

"How do you know he hired a private investigator?" Helena asked.

"Recognised the woman from the newspaper." He paused, met their puzzled expressions, and elaborated. "She came to the hotel one afternoon to meet Clarence. Didn't know who she was at the time, but I never forget a face. Only recognised her later, in the newspaper."

Ray, having worked his way down the line, offered Ruth and then Greg a tumbler of whisky.

Ruth held up a hand. "No thank you."

When Greg also declined, Ray downed their drinks and poured himself another.

Persephone fixed her gaze on Orlando. "Let me get this straight. You saw some unknown woman visit Clarence, and then later recognised her in the newspaper?"

"Yes. Couple of months after. Saying how she'd died in a terrible car crash."

Belle shuddered. "That's awful."

"Well, aren't we just surrounded by death lately?" Persephone downed her drink.

Ruth recalled the article in the folder, with the image of the investigator next to a black-and-white picture of the car wreck.

"See?" Ray slammed his glass down, sloshing whisky onto the bar. "Clarence is obsessed with conspiracies. He so desperately wants to believe someone is plotting to oust him from the board, he'll hire any Tom, Dick, or Harry to investigate us." His eyes lingered on Ruth for a beat before he waved a dismissive hand. "Thinks we're all out to get him." He shook his head, cheeks flushed. "The old fool sees conspiracy theories everywhere."

"Can you blame him? Look at what happened today." Elias took a large gulp of his whisky and grimaced. "What was Winifred doing near that river?"

"Lest we forget, Winifred hasn't been herself recently either." Persephone's gaze shifted to Ray, her eyes narrowed. "You were the one constantly reminding us she was no longer fit for the board, that she should step back."

Ray straightened, his jaw tightening. "She wasn't. Didn't mean I wanted anything bad to happen." His eyes glazed over. "I loved her dearly." He then glanced at his brother and away again.

"Why not?" Ruth asked before she could stop herself. When everyone's gaze moved to her, she added, "Sorry, I mean why wasn't she fit for the board?" Ruth should keep her head down, play the role of the harmless guest, observe, not interfere, especially under the grim circumstances, but her need to understand got the better of her. She forced a small apologetic smile. "I don't mean to pry. Only trying to make sense of things."

Greg shot her a look that clearly said, *"So much for staying beneath their radar."*

Helena glared at her. "I fail to see how it's any of your concern." She folded her arms. "In fact, why are you still—"

"Leave her be, Helena." Ray leaned against the bar. "It's no secret." He took a breath. "I was frustrated, Mrs Morgan. Frustrated that both Clarence and Winifred kept rejecting our park expansion ideas." He tugged at his earlobe. "Despite the years of careful planning, the conservative financial projections, they wouldn't listen. Neither of them."

"He's right," Persephone interjected. "The business needs to change to survive. It's struggling. We can secure investment, but that won't hold forever. Besides, the park guests are crying out for expansion. So I also fail to see why they rejected the proposals."

"Because they're shortsighted and blinkered," Elias said. "Quite the combination." He adjusted the cushion at his back. "We'd all benefit from the expansion. Every one of us. That's why we worked so hard at all the planning and investment nonsense. For what?" He drained his glass.

Helena gritted her teeth. "If only they'd cared to know how much we sacrificed for their park."

"Our personal lives have nothing to do with it," Ray muttered.

Helena's expression darkened. "And yet, here we are."

Orlando, still hovering by Belle, seemed oblivious to the tension crackling between them. He was more intent on murmuring soothing words in his distraught wife's ear.

Belle clung to his arm, her eyes wide and unfocussed, the whisky in her glass untouched.

"I bet that private investigator took one look at this place and realised what a cash cow it would be," Persephone said, her voice laced with cynicism. "Probably made up a load of rubbish to keep Clarence on the hook."

Frustration surged through Ruth as she watched the interplay. They were all quick to point fingers, to assign blame. The bickering and infighting . . . *But which one of them is truly hiding something? Which one has blood on their hands?*

9

After an uncomfortable silence that seemed to stretch on for an hour in the study, Ray said, "We have a choice to make. We either call it quits here and now or we play along, solve the games, and get those shares." He looked around the room. "Then we'll be free to expand the park as we see fit. No resistance."

"Unless Clarence is bluffing," Persephone murmured. "He might not have any intention of following through with his offer."

"He's not bluffing," Elias stated, a glint in his eye. "Clarence is manipulative, but his word is his bond."

Greed and anxiety etched lines on Ray, Helena, and Persephone's faces. Helena, her steely gaze fixed on her husband, seemed the most determined of the three, ambition radiating off her in waves.

Orlando remained passive, which made Ruth suspicious of him. *Could his gambling issues have pushed him to murder?*

Belle appeared in a constant state of shock and bewilderment, and seemed the least likely to commit such a terrible act.

Then there was Elias, fluctuating between detached and intensely focussed. Ruth struggled to get a read on him. At one moment he seemed not to care about what was happening around him, and the next completely engaged.

As if sensing Ruth's scrutiny, Helena said, "What's with these two?" She gestured dismissively toward Ruth and Greg. "Are they part of Clarence's games?"

Ruth raised her hands. "I was hired to evaluate the kitchen, that's all." She indicated Greg, and opted to leave a few details out. "We were leaving when Clarence invited us to participate."

Persephone's eyes narrowed. "And you agreed? Right after Winifred's murder?" Suspicion dripped from her words.

Annoyance prickled Ruth, though she couldn't deny the suspicion was somewhat justified.

"No—No one is saying she was m-murdered," Belle countered, her voice trembling. "It was an accident. A tragic, horrible accident." She squeezed Orlando's hand tighter.

Ruth observed the couple. Belle, with her delicate features and anxious eyes, seemed genuinely distressed. But Orlando, though pale, kept averting his gaze, as if hiding something. *Guilt?*

"And the maid?" Helena asked Belle, sarcasm lacing her tone. "Where does that fit into your accident theory? She slipped and bashed her head repeatedly on a fire poker?"

Belle screwed up her face in disgust.

Liam appeared in the doorway. "Paramedics have stabilised Nadia and are taking her to the hospital. She needs a brain scan, but they believe the head wound is superficial. A glancing blow across her scalp. She should recover." His eyes flicked to Helena, then Ray, a flash of something unreadable passing between them. The moment vanished as quickly as it appeared, leaving Ruth questioning if she'd imagined it.

Belle released a shaky breath. "Thank goodness Nadia will be okay."

"What about the police?" Greg asked.

"They'll want to interview us, I assume," Helena said.

"No need, madam." Liam tugged at his cuffs. "Mike confessed. They've arrested him."

This resulted in another round of stunned silence.

The gazebo, the roses, the fairy lights, the outline of a ring box in Mike's pocket all went through Ruth's mind. "Did he say why he hurt her?" It made little sense.

"The police haven't shared that information with me." Liam's gaze darted again to Ray and then Helena. Neither seemed to notice this time.

"Perhaps I should speak with them," Ray offered.

"Unnecessary, sir." Liam said. "The police will call once they've interviewed Mike and will update us on Nadia's condition. I've taken the liberty of providing them with my number."

"Poor Nadia," Belle said. "And to think she was talking about leaving after that awful—"

"Well done, Liam," Elias interrupted. "Everything seems under control."

Ruth narrowed her eyes. *What awful business is Belle referring to? And is everything truly under control?* Mike didn't strike her as violent; perhaps he'd been coerced into a false confession. It wasn't as though the family were short of a pound or two.

During her time on the force, Ruth had known plenty of fabricated confessions. They weren't uncommon.

"She'll be all right." Belle's shoulders relaxed. "It's over." However, the tremor in her voice lingered.

"My deepest apologies for bringing this up." Liam adjusted his tie, addressing a point on the wall. "But do you intend to continue with the games? The first is about to start."

As the gathered looked between themselves, Ruth studied their reactions.

Ray seemed in no doubt as to what he wanted. Orlando, his face pale and drawn, appeared to be wrestling with a difficult decision. Helena, her ambition likely battling with the gravity of the situation, pressed her lips together and stared intently at her husband. Belle murmured something unintelligible under her breath, whereas Elias and Persephone appeared impatient to get on with it.

"We've wasted enough time," Ray said, his voice strained. "There's no need to delay now we know Nadia is all right, and Mike is in custody."

Helena sighed. "You're right. We must press on."

Orlando hesitated, and then nodded in agreement.

Helena then turned to Persephone, a challenging glint in her eye. "And heaven knows you could use the money."

Persephone's face soured. "How dare—"

"Where does the first game start?" Elias interrupted, rising from the sofa and smoothing his jacket.

Liam consulted a card. "The library, sir." He checked his watch. "We must hurry."

Ray's eyebrows lifted. "The old man put timers on the doors again?"

"Like last year?" Belle groaned. "Timed games?"

Orlando sighed and muttered, "Clarence is always controlling us, no matter where we are." He squeezed Belle's shoulder. "We'll get through this. Together." He addressed the others. "Let's forget about points and work as a team. We will divide the shares between us. Concentrate on winning."

After a few reluctant murmurs of agreement, the group filed out.

Ruth was about to follow Greg when Persephone blocked her path. She leaned in close, her lavender perfume a cloying cloud settling around them. "Do you know something we don't, Mrs Morgan?"

Ruth kept her face impassive, refusing to give the woman the satisfaction of seeing her squirm. "Such as?"

Persephone sniffed. "I find it odd that Clarence insisted you and your grandson take part in these *private* games. He usually invites people connected to the business—suppliers, investors—so why you this year? What's changed?"

Ruth chose her next words carefully. Revealing her true purpose would jeopardise Clarence's plan, but she also couldn't evade the question entirely, so she opted for a truthful deflection. "Like I said, up until this morning, I was here to take a look at the kitchen." She shrugged. "Perhaps Clarence had other people in mind, but they backed out at the last minute?"

Persephone stared, her eyes cold and assessing, then she spun on her heel and marched away.

Greg matched Ruth's stride as they headed down the hallway. "What do you think of that business with Mike?" he whispered.

She pursed her lips. "Not sure."

Mike's confession didn't sit well with her. It was too convenient.

"It's weird he admitted to it so quickly, don't you think?" Greg echoed her thoughts.

Ruth stopped and faced him. "Wow."

He frowned. "What?"

Ruth studied her grandson for a few seconds. "You didn't

want me to investigate or get involved, but now you're playing detective?"

He hesitated, and then his face dropped. "Forget it." Greg strode away, his long, gangly limbs eating up the distance.

Ruth jogged to keep pace. "No, I like this new Greg."

"There's no new Greg," he grumbled. "Not a new anything. Same old Greg with just an observation. Sorry. Won't happen again."

"So I can investigate?" Hope tinged Ruth's voice.

"Absolutely not."

They rounded a corner and continued down another hallway lined with dusty, cobweb-laden portraits. They finally reached a set of double doors. A lock spanned them, connected to a glowing keypad.

Liam punched in a code, and the lock sprang apart.

"I'll do the honours." Ray announced, grabbing the handles. "Here we go. For better or worse." He took a deep breath and pushed the doors open.

Ruth, Greg, the four shareholders, Liam, Helena, and Belle stepped into a vast library. Thirty feet wide by seventy long, it stretched three floors high. Balconies circled the edges, with stairs at either end.

A hand-painted ceiling depicted a fierce naval battle. Galleons fired cannons amid plumes of smoke. Ships splintered, decks ablaze.

As for the library itself, tens of thousands of antique books filled every shelf, each section labelled with a brass plaque.

On the balconies stood ghost pirates, eight in all, realistic dummies dressed in coats, lace-up vests, shirts, baggy trousers, sashes, boots, and linen bandanas, along with swords, daggers, and flintlock guns tucked into their belts and scabbards.

Adding to the atmosphere, tattered drapes billowed in an unseen breeze, while light shimmered, creating water effects for an authentic nautical ambience.

Props completed the scene: barrels of rum, crates and chests of looted booty, telescopes, and even a mechanical parrot perched on a balustrade, its head swivelling, wings twitching.

Greg breathed, "This. Is. Amazing."

Ruth, momentarily speechless, merely bobbed her head in agreement. She wasn't sure what she'd expected, but this was a thousand times more striking than anything she could've imagined. It was like stepping into an interactive museum exhibit.

She glanced at the others, but they all seemed to take the impressive scene in their stride, as though it were perfectly normal to have a pirate adventure amid the mansion's vast library, which alone was remarkable enough.

"Here we go." Orlando gestured toward a reading nook in the far corner of the room. "This way."

How he'd spotted it amid the chaos was a mystery.

Surrounded by stacks of books, next to a tall window overlooking the garden, sat a lifeless pirate captain in a high-backed chair.

The nine of them gathered round, and Ruth sighed in relief, for this victim was made of nothing more than wax, plaster, and plastic.

He sported a large black beard, wore the customary eye patch, and a tricorn hat. The pirate captain slumped to one side, as if passed out blind drunk. However, a trickle of blood ran from the corner of his mouth and down the front of his shirt, staining it a deep crimson.

"Murder mystery," Greg whispered to Ruth. "Should be a breeze for you."

"I'm not allowed to investigate," she hissed back. Besides, her role wasn't to solve the games, but to observe the players.

Adding to the effect, an ethereal, ghostly version of the captain drifted high above their heads, projected onto the sheer curtains. He scowled down at them, as if urging the players to avenge his untimely demise.

Greg pointed to a hidden projector behind a stack of books, aimed at the curtains.

Ruth focussed on the victim. His right arm draped over the chair arm, a bejewelled hand dangling. On the floor beneath his limp fingers lay an overturned tankard.

"Poisoned," Helena said with conviction. "Clarence loves it so. Every year someone is poisoned." She eyed the pirates on the balconies above. "One of them no doubt did the deed. Our suspects."

"Mutiny," Elias said, a glint of amusement in his eyes. "That can't be a coincidence either."

Though it did appear the captain was poisoned, Ruth knew better than to jump to conclusions. Years on the force had taught her that appearances could be deceiving. What looked like poison could be a distraction.

She reminded herself to remain silent, a passive observer, for now.

"Look." Belle stepped to a pirate's chest, a few feet on each side, secured with an iron padlock. "It's the only one locked. We need the key."

"Simple enough," Orlando said. "Solve the murder, find the key, open the chest."

"Is it ever simple with Clarence?" Persephone examined the lock. "Why assume the killer has the key?"

"Or knows where it is," Belle added.

Helena smirked. "Shall we ask them, Bells?" She gestured to the inanimate pirates.

"Persephone's right." Ray shifted his attention between the chest and the captain. "Clarence's games are never straightforward, but the first is usually the easiest." He looked at his brother. "Year before last, we were done in five minutes. Remember?"

"That was a lucky guess." Orlando leaned over the treasure chest and pulled a curtain aside to reveal a screen. "Knew it. Same as before." He stepped aside.

Green numbers on a black background counted down on the monitor: *1,171 . . . 1,170 . . . 1,169 . . .*

"One a second," Elias said, a hint of urgency in his voice. "We have a little under twenty minutes."

Helena frowned. "That's all? We usually get an hour. That maid business delayed us." She shot a look at Liam, who stood apart from the group and met her gaze with a concerned expression.

Below the countdown timer:

Two attempts remaining.

Belle stared. "Attempts?"

Orlando pointed at the lock. "Two tries to open it. Must be more than one key, and they'll probably look alike."

"Clarence feeling generous?" Elias chuckled. "Giving us two bites of the apple? That's unlike him. He really must be ill."

Persephone gestured to the pirate captain. "Let's solve his murder first." Her cold gaze settled on Ruth. "Why don't you do the honours? Examine the corpse for clues." Her tone was thick with sarcasm and abruptness.

Irritation flared within Ruth, but she wouldn't rise to the bait.

Belle glared at Persephone. "Mrs Morgan is our guest. Be welcoming."

Ruth chose not to take offence. They were under pressure, believing they could win the controlling shares of the Marsh empire.

Helena lifted her chin. "We appreciate any help you can offer, Mrs Morgan."

Ruth glanced at Greg, and he gave a small shake of his head. He was right. Getting too involved was a bad idea.

Ray's brow furrowed. "Is there a problem? You're here to play, aren't you?"

Persephone crossed her arms. "Given her reaction, we can assume she's here for more nefarious reasons. Clarence is up to something."

"Like what?" Belle asked.

"I—" Ruth swallowed, looking at Greg again for guidance, but his blank expression was no help.

She was caught between a rock and a hard place. Refusing to aid them would confirm Persephone's suspicions. But by helping too much with the games, she may inadvertently take away the impact of their ability to unmask Winifred's blackmailer and possible killer.

On the other hand, Clarence had expressed no concern over that. In fact, he'd encouraged Ruth and Greg to get involved to avoid suspicion.

Her grandson now gave her a look as if to say, "*I told you not to get caught up in this nonsense. Now look at what you've got us into.*"

Ruth took a deep breath. She'd tread carefully. "I'll help where I can. We're a team, aren't we?" She stepped closer to the captain, trying to clear her mind.

Despite the fact his head was made of hard wax, someone had taken the time to paint realistic flesh tones, dirt, and add a prominent scar across his cheek. The captain's beard was suitably grizzled, greasy, and even had bits of what looked like his last meal caught in the wiry hairs.

Greg grimaced. "Gross."

"Thank you for that." She leaned closer. "Need more light."

Greg switched on a nearby lantern, angling it toward the captain.

"Clarence really has outdone himself this year," Elias said as he rounded the chair, his gaze sweeping over the scene.

Ray rolled his eyes. "He's always been ever so fond these over-the-top spectacles."

Orlando nodded. "Remember that Father Christmas mannequin he made when we were kids?"

"How could I forget?" Ray's voice was tight. "Clarence's early foray into animatronics. The thing spoke in a creepy voice, its lips moving . . . out of sync. Like a badly dubbed . . . horror film."

Orlando shuddered. "I still have nightmares."

Their banter, though lighthearted, did little to alleviate the tension.

Helena lowered her voice, addressing Persephone. "Do you think Clarence will actually hand over the shares? It seems like there's more to it. Is he hiding something?"

Persephone shrugged. "Clarence has always been eccentric, but ever since that argument with Winifred, he's been distant. Almost like he blames us for something."

Ray scoffed. "Ridiculous."

Ruth looked at them. "Argument?" Clarence had painted

a picture of a loving relationship with his sister. She supposed it had something to do with the blackmail.

"We don't know what it was about," Ray said. "Clarence and Grandmama have never got on particularly well. They always tolerated one another. Nothing more."

Confusion washed over Ruth. This contradicted what Clarence had told her. He'd painted a picture of closeness between himself and Winifred.

Why would he lie?

"I know what their last fight was about."

Ruth's gaze snapped to Orlando.

He gripped the back of the captain's chair. "Grandmama hit the roof when she found out he'd hired a PI for some reason. Clarence said it was to protect the family, but she wouldn't hear of it. Told him to stop."

"And did he?" Persephone asked.

"I think so," Orlando said. "I never saw the PI lady again. Not until that newspaper article."

"You think it's connected to her accident?" Belle asked.

"None of us pushed Winifred into that river," Helena said. "We all know she wasn't happy." She looked to Liam. "Isn't that right?"

Seemingly caught off guard by the question, he nodded.

"But Clarence hired an investigator. Something happened and—" Ray's eyes widened. "He thinks one of us killed Winifred."

"Don't be ridiculous." Persephone shook her head. "Clarence hired her months ago. That can't have anything to do with what happened to Winifred."

Elias leaned against a nearby chair. "Who's to say one of us didn't do in the old girl? Is it such a stretch?"

Belle flinched. "Don't say that. Winifred was lovely. We all liked her. None of us would—"

"Can we focus? We're running out of time." Helena nodded to Ruth.

She returned her attention to the captain, while processing the new pieces of information.

Winifred and Clarence didn't get along?

In that case, what is he hiding?

10

In the hushed atmosphere of the library, Ruth examined the pirate captain's face, furrowing her brow in concentration.

His scar ran across his left cheek, but it looked like an old wound, depicted as a raised, flesh-coloured mark, rather than an open cut, or something recently stitched together in the heat of battle.

Even so, Ruth made a mental note his attacker had been right-handed.

She lifted the captain's tricorn hat to reveal dark hair matted to his head, tied in a messy ponytail at the back, held together with a worn leather strip. The wig was so convincing Ruth expected lice to crawl up her fingers at any moment.

However, not finding anything out of the ordinary among his greasy locks—nothing a good soak in a bath wouldn't solve—she replaced the hat and moved down to the collars of the captain's shirt and coat.

Ruth ran her fingers around and under each, noting the weave. They appeared clean, crisp, not frayed. As though they were new, or he'd taken care of them. Oversized brass buttons adorned the coat—nine down the front, four on the cuffs, each stamped with a crossed-swords emblem.

"Does anyone recognise this symbol?" Ruth asked the group.

Several people shook their heads.

Orlando sucked in a breath. "Wait. I do." He rushed across the library and jogged up the stairs to one of the upper balconies.

Ruth, meanwhile, had discovered something unsettling. The crimson stain that bloomed across the captain's chest wasn't the result of the blood dripping from his mouth. Another wound hid beneath his shirt.

She was about to ask for a pair of disposable gloves but quickly reminded herself again this wasn't a real dead body, so between thumb and forefinger, Ruth lifted the left-hand side of the captain's coat.

There, exposed beneath the fabric, was a clean puncture wound that went through the captain's shirt and penetrated his chest.

Ruth's pulse quickened. "Someone stabbed him in the heart." Her gaze moved around the other pirates on the balconies. "And they all seem to have daggers."

"One of them must have snatched the key from the captain," Helena said.

Elias scratched his chin. "But which one?"

"We'll need to check each of their weapons for dried blood," Ray suggested.

Ruth had a strong feeling it wouldn't be so easy.

She eyed Liam, who stood apart from the group, hands in his pockets.

Clearly, he wasn't prepared to give out any hints.

Does he know the hidden intent behind this game?

So far, Ruth was at a loss.

Before she could dwell on it further, Orlando returned with a triumphant grin on his face. He held aloft a leather-bound book, its title immediately recognisable.

"*Treasure Island*," Greg said. "I like that story."

"Me too," Ray said. "Grandmama must have read it a million times to us as kids. The original title was *The Sea Cook*."

Orlando flipped the cover to reveal the title page, and then he turned it so they could all get a clear look. An illustration of a pair of crossed swords matched the exact design on the captain's buttons.

"Let me see." Persephone took the leather-bound novel from Orlando and riffled through its pages. "I don't get it. What's the clue? There's nothing obvious."

"Could be a coincidence," Belle said. "The symbols matching, I mean."

"Highly unlikely," Elias said. "Clarence has always been methodical with these games. He engineers every last detail."

Ruth agreed. Her working assumption was everything on the captain was a potential clue pointing to his attacker, and ergo the key to unlock the chest.

"We need to speed this up." Ray indicated the countdown on the screen. "Under fifteen minutes remaining."

Elias looked over at Liam. "Come on, old fellow. Help us out. You don't even like Clarence. Why are you on his side?"

"I do like him," Liam said. "Master Clarence explained, and I forgave him. Why else would I stay working here?"

"To pick a good time to exact your revenge," Persephone said. "And that time could be now."

Liam looked away.

"Oh, leave him alone," Helena said. "None of this is his fault."

"Why are you always jumping to his defence?" Ray asked.

"I don't like bullies," she shot back.

"Can we stop arguing?" Persephone said. "We're wasting time."

Ruth straightened. "Everyone please stand by a pirate suspect. I'll call out clues as I find them." Her insides squirmed at the prospect of the timer running out before they completed the task.

What then? We all go home? The killer gets off scot-free?

Greg, Ray, Orlando, Helena, Persephone, and Elias hurried across the library and up the steps, but Ruth grabbed Belle's arm, stopping her.

She whispered, "What's the deal with Clarence and Liam? What happened between them?"

Belle glanced over at Liam, clearly making sure he wasn't within earshot, and murmured, "A couple of years ago, Liam got an amazing job offer at Westworth House, working as Lord Montague's personal assistant." She took a breath. "However, Clarence told Lord Montague that Liam stole jewellery from Winifred, and he retracted the offer. Liam missed out on the opportunity to earn many times his current salary. He was absolutely devastated. Poor guy."

Ruth gaped at her. "Why would Clarence do that?"

Belle shrugged. "He can be very manipulative." She glanced over at Liam. "Helena said Winifred was in on it too, but I'm not sure I believe her." Belle half smiled. "That's all I know." She raced off to join the others on their respective balconies with the pirates.

Ray leaned over the railing and called down to Liam. "Will you help or not?"

Liam didn't budge from his spot. "I'm only allowed to observe, sir." His gaze lingered on a female pirate with a red sash for a beat too long, a flicker of something unreadable in his eyes, before he smoothly masked his expression.

"We've got twelve minutes left," Elias chimed in from above. "Get up here."

"Please, Liam?" Belle said in a sickly sweet voice. "We're not asking for clues, only an extra pair of eyes."

Ruth agreed. The quicker they got through these games, the faster she could find the killer among them.

Liam, seemingly resigning himself to the inevitable, trudged up the stairs and took his place beside the remaining female pirate.

Ruth, her stomach twisting with anxiety, glanced at the timer, and did a quick mental calculation: eleven minutes, thirty-eight seconds.

Come on. Focus.

As she checked the captain's pockets, she called up to the others, "Remember to look at their daggers. Any blood?"

Greg, Liam, Orlando, Helena, Belle, and Elias replied they did indeed find blood on all theirs.

"That's reduced the suspects from eight to six," Ruth called back as she pulled a piece of parchment from the captain's inside coat pocket. "Persephone and Ray, join the others and help them."

Ruth squinted as she held the parchment up to the light. The ink had faded and was hard to make out, but it appeared to be a portion of a treasure map—a crudely drawn island fringed with palm trees, an *X* marking a spot near the middle.

Setting the map aside, Ruth continued her meticulous search. On the captain's left pantaloon, she discovered a long straw-coloured hair, a stark contrast to the captain's own dark locks. "Mousy blonde hair," Ruth called up to the group. "Long. At least shoulder length." With her heart hammering, she continued her examination.

"Four suspects left," Greg's voice echoed from above.

Her grandson now stationed himself beside Liam and the female pirate with the red sash, while Ray and Orlando remained by another; Helena and Belle checked out the third; while Elias and Persephone stood next to the fourth pirate.

"Hold on." Belle's voice rang out. "This one has a leather pouch." As she untied it from the pirate's belt, it jangled. "It might be keys." She loosened the drawstrings and peered inside. Belle's shoulders slumped. "No. It's only coins."

Nine minutes remaining.

Ruth pulled in a juddering breath and continued down the captain's legs to his feet. "Do any of your pirates have mud on their boots?" she asked, scanning the floor for footprints, but finding none.

Perhaps the pirate captain and his assailant argued earlier, somewhere outside, and their confrontation spilled over into the library.

"No mud here," Greg called down.

"None on this one."

"Nor here."

"Nope, all clean."

Ruth swore under her breath. "What am I missing?"

Eight minutes.

Her gaze fell on the overturned tumbler lying near the captain's chair. Ruth got down on all fours and sniffed the spilled liquid. "Rum." She wrinkled her nose. "Cheap rum." She looked up to the balconies. "Smell them."

Ray frowned down at her. "What?"

"Smell their clothes." Ruth pointed to the captain. "If

someone stabbed him, it means they were close and they fought. He might have spilled his drink on them."

"This one does." Greg motioned to the female pirate.

"This too." Orlando indicated a short male pirate.

Both remaining pirate suspects also had long mousy blonde hair and bloodstained daggers.

Progress.

Ruth searched the captain once more but could find no further clues. Then an idea struck her. Her attention shifted to the display monitor.

Two attempts remaining.

It was then that it struck her.

Two suspects, two keys, two tries." She didn't need to reduce the suspects any further.

Ruth leapt to her feet. "Keep looking for keys."

Eight minutes left.

The group split up, one half focussing on the female pirate, the other on the male.

After a minute of frantic searching, Greg called down, "Nothing here, Grandma. No key."

"We're coming up empty too," Ray confirmed.

Ruth's stomach plummeted. "There has to be. Look again."

Persephone helped remove their coats, and searched pockets, while Belle even looked inside their boots.

Finally, Belle shouted, "We've found it," and extracted a key with a triumphant smile.

Everyone roared with relief as she raced from the balcony, and down the stairs.

"Well done, Bells," Elias called after her. "With only six minutes to spare. Brilliant."

She beamed, inserted the key into the treasure chest's lock, and turned it.

There came a two-second pause, then a loud claxon, followed by the screen flashing red.

ONE ATTEMPT REMAINING.

Everyone gaped, stunned into silence.

With her heart hammering in her chest, Ruth spun to face the pirate captain once more. "What am I missing? I've overlooked something." Her eyes flitted over every inch of his clothes, hunting for any small thing that stood out.

"Five minutes, thirty seconds." Elias slumped against the railing. "Looks like we'll fail. That'll be a first. Clarence has beaten us."

"We have had a stressful day," Belle said.

Ruth balled her fists. No way she'd allow that to happen. She scanned the captain's body several more times, and then she finally spotted something unusual. His right arm hung limp over the side of the chair, while his left hand was wedged between his leg and the upholstery.

With effort, pulling his leg to one side and gripping his coat cuff with her free hand, Ruth managed to unleash his clenched left fist.

Inside she found a silver ring on a broken leather cord.

"Yes." With excitement coursing through her veins, Ruth jogged across the library and up the stairs, with Belle shadowing her.

"What have you discovered?" Ray asked as the others grouped round.

Ruth held up the ring and then examined the male pirate suspect from top to toe. Finding nothing unusual, she raced around the balcony to Greg. The others followed but kept out of the way as she checked the female pirate's hands. Sure enough—no ring, but that meant little in this case.

Ruth then scanned the woman from top to toe, and her eyes came to rest on the red mark at her neck. "Huh. He tore it off."

"What do you mean?" Orlando asked. "It's a necklace?"

Ruth indicated the mark and spoke in a rush. "She stabbed the pirate captain, and in the tussle, he tore it from her neck." She held up the corded necklace with the ring. "During their fight, she killed him." Sure enough, tucked into the pirate lady's sash was a bloody dagger, its blade the right size and shape to match the stab wound. "My bet is the captain was blind drunk and she saw the opportunity to take the key from him." Ruth stared into her lifeless eyes, wishing she were a real person she could interrogate.

A swift confession would come in handy right about now.

"But she doesn't have a key," Greg said. "We checked." Even so, he patted the pirate's clothes again to make sure. "Nothing."

Helena peered over the balcony. "A little over four minutes left. This is hopeless."

Belle wrung her hands, her brow creased.

"I say, old boy," Elias called down as Liam descended the stairs, his voice laced with barely concealed desperation. "Could you possibly see your way to extending the count-down? A few more minutes should do it. We lost valuable time with that whole dreadful maid business."

Liam shook his head, his expression apologetic. "I'm sorry, sir, but Master Clarence was quite specific with his instructions."

"For goodness' sake, man," Elias exploded, throwing his hands up in exasperation. "The old fellow isn't even here. How would he know?" When Liam didn't answer, Elias let out a slow breath, and said through gritted teeth, "Could you at least tell us if we're on the right track? Clarence would give us a few pointers along the way."

Liam backed across the room. "I really don't know anything about all this, sir. I'm sorry, but the master did not share his plans. I didn't help him set up the games this year."

Ruth, however, detected a tremor in his voice, a subtle tell that betrayed the lie. A whopper. Besides, Clarence had explicitly stated that Liam had helped modify the games. Which meant he must have sworn Liam to secrecy, and forbidden him from interfering.

Given the circumstances, the extreme nature of Clarence's accusations, Ruth understood the rationale.

"Fat lot of use he is," Elias muttered to the others.

"Leave him alone," Helena snapped, her voice sharp. "It's not his fault."

Ray, his jaw tightening, opened his mouth to retort, no doubt about to chastise his wife for her tone, but she folded her arms and looked away.

Ruth examined the ring in her hand. "There's something etched inside." She squinted at an inscription. "Looks like . . . Latin?"

"May I see?" Orlando gently took the ring from her and held it up to the light. "Amor Vincit Omnia," he read aloud. "That means—"

"Love conquers all," Ray finished.

Helena, Persephone, and Elias bobbed their heads in agreement, while Belle continued to look perplexed.

"This pirate knows Latin?" Orlando faced the shelves and rubbed the back of his neck. "We're in the Latin section of the library."

"That can't be a coincidence, can it?" Greg glanced at Ruth. "She's hidden the key somewhere."

Now they all scanned the shelves.

"There's a few thousand books in just this one section of the library," Helena said in an exasperated tone. "How are we supposed to find it?"

"What are we looking for precisely?" Persephone asked Ruth. "Something the key's hidden inside?"

Ruth's stomach twisted into a tight knot.

The truth was, she had absolutely no idea.

11

If Ruth had participated in Clarence's unusual Marsh games in previous years, maybe she would have understood how his mind worked. She might even have applied that thinking to this situation. As it stood, though, most of the others seemed as baffled as she was.

Orlando, his face a mask of concentration, stepped around his wife and selected a book from the shelf. "Look at this."

Its title, embossed in faded gold lettering, read,

Insula Thesavraria.

"*Treasure Island.*" Orlando flipped over the cover, revealing the familiar crossed swords symbol on the title page. He riffled through the other pages and stopped. A smile spread across his face.

"What is it? The key?" Persephone peered over his shoulder. "Oh. Someone's written on a sticky note."

"What does it say?" Belle asked.

Orlando peeled the note from the page, and his brow

furrowed as he read. "Acta Non Verba." A spark of recognition lit up his eyes. "I think I know where this is leading us." His voice took on a new certainty, a confidence he'd lacked until this moment. "Winifred loved word games. It means 'Deeds, not Words.'"

Helena, her patience clearly wearing thin, threw her hands up. "How does that help us?"

Persephone scanned the shelves. "Could it point to another book? Something Winifred enjoyed, with a title or inscription related to actions rather than words."

They all turned back to the shelves, their gazes sweeping over the rows of leather-bound spines.

"Two minutes, thirty seconds," Liam called from below.

Ruth had attended a school that stuck to the main subjects. Latin might as well have been Chinese to her. She looked at Greg, hoping his historical knowledge might offer a clue, but his mouth hung open, eyes vacant.

Brilliant.

Ray ran his finger over several spines, then stopped abruptly. "What about this?" He lifted a book titled *Vox Populi, Facta Legionis* and flipped through the pages. "This was another one of Grandmama's most cherished. Ah-ha. A note." Ray peeled it off and read aloud, "Fortune favours the brave." He glanced at the others. "Anyone remember Winifred ever mentioning anything about bravery? A book, a saying..."

Belle screwed up her face in concentration. "Why has Clarence made this game all about Winifred?"

"Ask him when we're done," Persephone snapped. "Here." She lifted a book from a nearby shelf. "*Fortuna Audcacibus Arridet.*" She flipped through the pages, and chuckled, a low, humourless sound. "Typical Clarence." She peeled the note out and held it up. "Seize the day. He's still toying with us."

"Carpe Diem," Greg said. "Everyone knows that one."

Elias plucked a book from the shelf. "*Iter ignotumque*. Or an uncharted journey."

Ray's face brightened. "You're right." He turned to Belle, who still looked utterly lost. "This is all related to Winifred's favourite books. She loved stories about adventure and exploration." He glanced at his brother. "Another one she read to us as kids." Ray gestured to the book in Persephone's hand. "This story follows explorers who embark on a dangerous expedition. 'Carpe diem' becomes their motto as they face unknown dangers and seize the opportunity for adventure."

"Yes, yes." Helena peered over the railing. "Can we hurry up, please?"

Elias riffled through the pages and found the note inside. "Sequere pecuniam," he snorted. "Follow the money."

They scanned the shelves, their eyes darting over the titles in a frantic search, hunting for any mention of money, wealth, or fortune.

"One minute remaining," Liam called, his voice strained. Ruth imagined him downstairs, his gaze glued to the timer.

"Follow the money." Orlando paced back and forth. "Follow the money." He glanced at Belle.

"Don't look at me." Her cheeks flushed pink. "I wouldn't know Latin from Sanskrit."

Helena, her movements brisk and efficient, lifted a book. "*Pecunia Obscura*. This?" She flipped through the pages. Her face fell. "No." Helena huffed out a breath and replaced the book.

Ray reached for the uppermost shelf and removed a

book titled *Aurum et Potestas*. "Gold and Power. This has to be the one. I remember it." He flipped open the cover and grinned, a triumphant glint in his eye. "Yes." Ray handed the book to Ruth. "You were right, Mrs Morgan."

Someone had carved out the pages inside, creating a recess. Within lay a brass key.

"Twenty seconds left," Liam called.

"Grandma." Greg extended a hand.

She gave him the key, and he raced down the stairs, across the library, and inserted it into the chest.

Ruth held her breath as Greg turned the key, then sighed in relief as the lock sprang open.

The timer on the display froze at six seconds.

Everyone clapped, cheered, hugged, and high-fived. Their relief was palpable, a welcome break from the bickering.

"Take that, Clarence." Ray smiled at Ruth. "Well done, Mrs Morgan."

"Yes, indeed." Elias's eyes gleamed with an almost manic intensity. "We would have been lost without you."

As they headed downstairs to join Greg, Ruth wasn't so sure about that. She worried that helping them play Clarence's game might hinder his grand plan to reveal the blackmailer.

"Well." Ray rubbed his hands together, his expression a mixture of anticipation and greed. "You can do the honours, Greg." He motioned to the treasure chest. "Open it. Let's see what we have."

Greg's eyebrows lifted. "Me?" After an encouraging nod from his grandmother, he swung the lid up. "What the—?"

Ruth stepped beside him and peered into the treasure chest. Lying inside, nestled on a bed of red velvet, was a music box. She lifted it out. The box was eight by six, walnut, with inlaid filigree in the lid, depicting an exquisitely crafted peacock with its feathers fanned.

The others gathered round for a better look.

Ruth noticed something else: etched into the base of the music box was another Latin phrase: "In Vino Veritas." This one needed no translation. *In wine, there is truth.*

"Open it," Ray said, his voice laced with impatience.

"This should be interesting," Elias murmured, and took a step back.

Greg looked between them. "It won't explode, will it?"

Ray chuckled. "Clarence isn't that twisted." His face then turned serious, and his eyes flicked to each of them in turn. "At least, I hope he isn't. He's not been himself lately."

Greg blinked at him, his anxiety clearly not assuaged. "That's reassuring."

Deciding a bomb was unlikely, Ruth held her breath, her fingers trembling slightly, and opened the music box.

Instead of a ballerina, a wooden puppet painted in purple and silver popped up and rotated while music played. The delicate craftsmanship of the box juxtaposed jarringly with the puppet's eerie movements.

"Funeral March of a Marionette." Orlando groaned and looked at his brother. "Remember how Winifred made us play it at every one of her birthdays when we were kids?"

Ray nodded, his face solemn. "We took turns. Must have played it a million times." He grimaced. "I heard it in my sleep for weeks afterward."

"I still do." Orlando leaned over, flicked a switch inside the music box, muting it, and sighed. "Much better."

They chuckled; the first hint of warmth exchanged between them. For that moment, they were simply brothers, united by a shared childhood memory, not adversaries vying for control of an empire.

"Well?" Belle asked. "What does it mean?"

"We're going to the music room," Ray said.

Ruth examined the ornate box inside and out, but found no clues or obvious additions of note, other than the creepy dancing marionette. She closed the lid and set it back inside the chest.

As the group filed out of the library, Ruth leaned toward Greg and whispered, "Stay close to me from now on. Understood? No running off on your own. Nothing reckless."

"You're the reckless one." He tensed and gave her a sidelong glance. "Hold on. Are you expecting trouble?"

Ruth darkened her eyes. "I always anticipate trouble, Gregory. It's in my nature."

"And yet you still blunder into it." He rolled his eyes. "Why don't we leave?" He stopped at the door and faced her, his expression earnest. "Seriously, Grandma. If one of them is a killer, why are we getting involved?"

"You just answered your own question," Ruth said.

"Stop and think about it." Greg glanced over his shoulder. "Do you really believe one of these people murdered Winifred? Clarence could be making it all up. They seem pretty harmless to me."

Ruth shrugged. "Murderers don't march about carrying signs declaring their guilt and intent to do more harm." She sighed at her grandson's look of exasperation. "We can't leave. What if Clarence is right? What if one of them killed her? What if they really will murder him next?"

Greg's brow furrowed. "You know how unhinged that sounds, though, right?"

Ruth grinned. "Of course."

"I say he's playing you." Greg waved a hand in the direction of the hallway. "They all think Clarence is losing his marbles. They all say he's not a nice guy. What if he's wrong about them? What if Winifred fell into the river, and no one is coming after him next? It's all a grand delusion."

"Then we've lost nothing but time." Ruth rested a hand on Greg's shoulder, her voice firm but gentle. "We must stay neutral and keep an open mind until we know for sure either way. Clarence believes someone murdered his sister. We must look into it. We'd never forgive ourselves if we turned our backs now."

"I'd forgive myself quite easily," Greg muttered, though he didn't say it with any real conviction.

"Are you two coming?" Persephone called from the hallway.

Ruth winked at Greg. "You never know, Greg, the next game might reveal a hidden chocolate and burger factory with a free lifetime supply."

Greg snorted. "Fat chance."

The group marched down another hallway lined with portraits whose eyes followed them as they passed.

One oil painting depicted a creepy child with a hollow smile. He wore a tattered sailor's outfit, his sunken skin revealing the cheek and jawbones beneath.

Ruth shuddered and averted her gaze as she gave the delightful painting a wide berth.

The group rounded another corner and stopped at a set of double doors. An electronic lock with a keypad spanned the gap between them.

"What's the code?" Helena asked.

Ray pressed several keys, each emitting a separate note. "Funeral March of a Marionette." He pointed at the display. "Won't let us in yet anyway." The timer showed it wouldn't open until 9 a.m. the next day. "I was hoping to get a head start tonight."

Elias yawned and traipsed off down the hallway, back the way they'd come.

"Where are you going?" Persephone called after him.

"To see if Clarence will talk to me," Elias said over his shoulder. "I want to make sure he's of sound mind if he is about to hand over the keys to the kingdom. Don't want to go through all this to have some darned lawyer renege on the deal. I'll see you in the morning." He rounded the corner and disappeared.

"Bed sounds like a good idea. See you all tomorrow." Persephone hurried after him.

"Next, they'll want a doctor and a psychologist to check Clarence over," Ray murmured.

"Would that be so bad?" Belle said. "We don't want to take advantage."

Ray smirked. "Speak for yourself."

Belle frowned.

He held up his hands. "A joke, Bells."

"A bad one." Helena looked at Liam, her expression impatient. "Can we open this door sooner?"

"Sorry, but no. Clarence was very specific about the timing."

Orlando yawned. "Well, I've had enough for one day." He threw an arm around his wife and headed back down the hallway.

Helena's gaze lingered on their retreating figures for a moment. "I'm going to bed." She shot her husband a look and marched off, her heels clicking against the hardwood floor.

"Thank you for your help today, Mrs Morgan." Ray turned his charming smile up to eleven. "If there's anything you need, please don't hesitate to ask. We'll see you in the morning." He bowed his head, and then left, followed by Liam keeping a wary distance.

Greg started to leave too, but Ruth grabbed his arm. "Seeing as we have time to spare, I want to look at something." She led him in the opposite direction, ignoring his groans of protest.

After a few turns, they headed down a narrow hallway, their footsteps echoing. "Here we are." At the end, Ruth opened a door and stepped outside into a small courtyard with a low wall, fountain, and potted trees. She took a deep breath, enjoying the fresh air after the closeness of the house.

Greg looked around. "Why are we here?"

Ruth removed her phone and navigated to Clarence's email with the video files. "These CCTV recordings show Winifred heading toward the bridge last night."

Lanterns lit the grounds and paths, casting long shadows across the manicured lawns and hedgerows.

Greg studied the images, then gestured at two security cameras mounted high above them, facing each way. "I think if someone stayed close to the wall . . ." He stepped to the side and mimed the action. "Someone could leave the house and reach the bridge unseen."

Ruth looked from the CCTV images to Greg, up at the cameras, and back again. "I think you're right." She studied the videos, working out their line of sight, and then followed the path behind Greg, staying close to the left-hand wall.

"They show Winifred on CCTV but no one else, right?" Greg said. "But even if the killer avoided the cameras, it doesn't mean they came from the house." He opened a gate, and they slipped through. Beyond lay a vast expanse of manicured lawn with trees at the far end.

Ruth checked the videos and images again, watching the

path Winifred took, and where they needed to walk to remain hidden. "It definitely seems possible, though."

They continued to follow a gravel path next to raised flower beds, their shadows stretching before them in the dim light.

At the corner of the building, Ruth held up a hand and stopped. She studied the corresponding video closely, noting the bushes and positions of the trees. "To stay hidden but follow Winifred, it looks like we cut across there."

She indicated a raised area with an ornamental pond.

They circled it, staying close to the hedgerows, walked on through the trees, and then followed the riverbank.

"None of the CCTV cameras can see out this far." Ruth pocketed the phone. A minute later, they stepped onto the familiar bridge.

Halfway across, she stopped and turned on the spot. "This is where we found Winifred's brooch."

Greg leaned over the railing. "They say she fell over this?" It reached halfway between his chest and belly. "No way she did that accidentally."

"And if you received a message to meet someone on this bridge, where would you wait?" Ruth asked.

"In the middle." Greg pointed at the boards. "Right here."

Ruth let out a slow breath. "Well, this part of Clarence's suspicions checks out. Someone could have come here and returned to the house unseen. It's plausible." Though, as Greg had pointed out, they couldn't rule out the killer approaching from any other direction. "Come on." Ruth yawned. "Let's go back. It's been a long day." And she had the distinct feeling it would only get worse.

12

Ruth and Greg traipsed across the grounds of Hadfield Hall, following the path through the trees, and were within feet of the walled garden when Ruth froze midstride.

Greg almost bumped into her. "What are you doing?"

She rocked back onto her heel, then forward, then back again.

"Cool dance." Greg watched her with mild amusement. "Did you invent that all on your own?"

Ruth shuffled forward until the glint of light she'd spotted through the trees became more apparent. "Hmm." She pointed to a spot beneath a weeping willow. "What do you suppose that is?" Ruth squinted to identify the shape.

Greg stepped behind her and peered at the spot. The light expanded suddenly, six feet tall, three wide, and a silhouette of a figure moved in front. No sooner had they appeared than the light vanished.

Ruth blinked away the ghostly afterimage. "A door."

"I think they're heading to the house." Greg whispered. "Gardener's tool shed?"

"With such a bright light inside?" Ruth gave him a

dubious look. It had to be running on electric, not battery, which made it more likely a permanent building. "And what are they doing at this time of night? Nocturnal horticulture? Moonlighting?"

"Perhaps it's Count Pruner." Greg smirked. "Dark lord of the carnivorous shrubberies."

Ruth stared at him.

"Count Pruner," Greg repeated. "You know, like—"

"Yes, I get it." Ruth sighed. "I suggest you leave the jokes to me." She cleared her throat. "You're a bright lad, but spontaneous humour isn't exactly your forte."

Greg frowned. "Thanks."

Ruth switched on her phone's torch function, aimed it at the ground a few feet ahead, and beckoned her comedy-impaired grandson to follow. She jogged through the trees, careful of her footing. A twisted ankle was the last thing she needed.

Greg kept pace, his face pale in the phone's reflected light. "Maybe we should just go back," he said, his voice tight.

"Did you see if it was a man or a woman?" Ruth had only glimpsed a fleeting figure. The trees had obscured most of her view.

"Couldn't tell," Greg said. "Too far away. By the way . . ." He clambered over a fallen log while Ruth skirted it. "Whenever something creepy or dangerous happens, why are we always the ones rushing toward it?"

"As far as I know, everyone should be in the house." Ruth ducked under low-hanging branches and pushed onward.

"Must be a member of staff." Greg stumbled over tree roots, swore, and then activated the torch on his own phone.

"The police arrested Mike the porter," Ruth said. "Nadia

is in hospital, and Liam told us they were the only remaining staff. He sent everyone else home." She reached a clearing dominated by a stone structure the size of a potting shed. It had a single door, no windows, and a slate roof.

The door, unlike the moss-covered stonework, was metal with visible rivets, and freshly painted a deep green. It looked jarringly out of place.

Ruth reached for the handle.

Greg gripped her arm, and whispered, "Can we be careful, please?" He checked his phone for a signal. "Winifred's killer could be hiding in there."

"Yes, you're right," Ruth said. "Brilliant idea."

"What idea?"

"Volunteering to go first." Ruth stepped back and gestured to the door. "If someone tries to axe you to death, I'll make a run for it while you fight them off with your karate."

Greg's brow furrowed. "I had one lesson."

"Should be plenty."

"When I was seven."

Ruth nodded. "Like riding a bike—you never forget." She mimicked chopping.

Greg's frown deepened. "Ten minutes into the lesson, I tripped over a gym bag and broke a finger. Mum took me to casualty. I never went back." He hesitated, his gaze darting between his grandmother and the door. And then he rolled his eyes. "Fine. But if I die, you can explain to Mum how it was all your fault." He grabbed the handle.

Ruth flinched, imagining the difficult conversation with her daughter. Sara would never forgive her. It would be a fate worse than death. "On the other hand, perhaps I should go first."

Greg nudged her aside. "Too late, General Haig."

Ruth inclined her head.

"Doesn't matter." Greg held his breath and threw open the door, his body tensed for whatever lurked within.

They both squinted under the bright light.

However, instead of a garden shed filled with lawn-mowers and dangerously sharp horticultural implements, where Ruth's grandson could swiftly become *Greg the Impaled,* a set of metal stairs led down.

He groaned and went to close the door, but Ruth stopped him. "Please don't make us go down there, Grandma."

"Stop moaning." Ruth cleared her throat, trying to ignore the prickle of unease crawling up her spine. "At least it's well lit."

Greg folded his arms. "Which only means we'll have a few extra seconds to see the axe murderer coming for us."

"Stay here, then." Ruth squeezed past him and headed down the stairs, her hand trailing along the stone wall. "Wait in the dark forest for me to return," she hissed over her shoulder. "I'm sure you'll be fine. And if something bad happens to me, you can explain to your mum how you left your dear old grandmother to fend for herself."

Although, knowing Sara, she'd blame Ruth no matter what. Golden boy Greg could do no wrong in her eyes.

Teenage footfalls and mutterings followed Ruth down.

She smiled to herself.

Good lad.

At the bottom of the stairs, they entered a long corridor that stretched into the distance, broken by the occasional archway. The first of which was thirty feet away.

Ruth marched toward it.

"This tunnel is heading away from the house, not toward

it," Greg said, his voice echoing. "What do you think it's for?"

"Only one way to find out." Ruth reached the archway and peered into a room twenty feet wide by sixty long, filled with racks of costumes. She stepped to the nearest one; it held a penguin outfit, a bright yellow bird with a comically oversized beak, and a creature that resembled a raccoon crossed with a badger.

She looked up at the ceiling to get her bearings. "We must be under the theme park."

Greg picked up the head of a crocodile and examined the straps used to fix it to the nearby costume. "That person we saw leaving must be a park employee."

Ruth walked along the racks, checking out the huge variety of costumes. There were even several space suits, complete with fishbowl helmets, backpacks, and oversized moon boots. "It's late, and I doubt there will be many staff about. Well, apart from cleaners and security guards." Ruth's hunch told her someone from the house had come down here for a reason and then returned to Hadfield Hall. She paused at a bunny rabbit costume.

Only questions are who, and for what reason?

Ruth marched from the vast costume department and headed to the next archway along the hallway—this time on the left-hand side. This room was a similar size, but filled with racks of clothes. Normal, human-style outfits, all neatly labelled and organised by size.

She examined the rack nearest the door. Thirty princess costumes hung in various sizes, along with princes', villagers', and town criers' outfits of red and gold.

Greg pulled out a set of wizard's robes, complete with a hat and long white beard. "This must get incredibly hot in the summer." He wrinkled his nose. "Smells like it too."

Ruth stepped in front of a row of vanities, each mirror lined with bare bulbs. "A circus clown's paradise." She was about to leave when a reflection caught her eye. Ruth gasped and spun.

A blood-stained maid's outfit hung on a wire hanger.

Greg stared at it too. "Is that Nadia's?"

Ruth nodded slowly, while the implications slammed into her.

"Wait." Greg frowned. "She faked her assault?"

Ruth continued to nod, and then her brain went into overdrive, thinking through the events, and she tried to fit the pieces together. "It was staged." She gaped at her grandson. "We didn't see the paramedics, the ambulance, the police, or—"

"Her boyfriend, Mike, being arrested."

Ruth slapped her forehead. "I'm such an idiot." Then, a knot of worry tightened in her stomach. The cold, calculated cruelty to it all sent chills down her spine.

Greg pointed to the next rack, where a porter's outfit hung. "Why would they fake the assault? Clarence set up the games to flush out Winifred's killer. I thought he was trying to be subtle. A fake attempted murder and arrest aren't exactly keeping things low-key. And why have it happen outside the games?"

"All good questions." Ruth pursed her lips. "I'm not sure." She faced the nearest makeup table, where stood several bottles of fake blood.

It had certainly been convincing enough to fool her, and she cursed herself for not seeing through the charade.

"I still don't get it." Greg glanced over his shoulder at the corridor. "Liam could have just said they'd both gone home, like the rest of the staff. Why make such a show of it?"

Ruth peered around at all the theme park costumes. The

truth was, she had no idea why they'd faked the incident, and why Clarence hadn't warned her.

"What's that?" Greg's gaze flicked to the door and the hallway beyond, then he lurched back. "Someone's coming."

Sure enough, footsteps echoed, growing louder, approaching from the direction of the house.

Ruth grabbed Greg's arm, shoved him behind the nearest clothes rack, and joined him. Then, with her heart pounding in her ears, she waited.

The footsteps grew louder, then faded as whoever it was continued down the corridor, moving away from them.

Ruth put a finger to her lips, motioned for her grandson to stay put, then slipped out from behind the rack and tiptoed to the archway. She held her breath and peered out.

A woman in jeans and a baggy shirt marched along the corridor, heading toward the theme park. She reached a door farther down, opened it, and as she turned, Ruth recognised her profile—Nadia.

"Who is it?" Greg whispered.

Ruth jumped and spun to face her grandson. "I told you to wait back there."

"You didn't say anything." Greg peered around her into the corridor and whispered, "So?"

"Nadia."

Greg's eyes narrowed. "It's true, then—she's not injured."

"Not injured," Ruth repeated. She hesitated, weighing their options, then curiosity got the better of her, and she slipped into the corridor. "Stay. Please."

"Where are you going?"

"To see what she's up to."

"Are you insane?"

Ruth arched an eyebrow. "You need to ask?"

Greg sighed. "What if she catches us? Nadia could be the murderer."

"That seems very unlikely." Although Ruth couldn't rule anything out, she had a feeling Nadia was a pawn in a much bigger game. "I'll be back in a minute." Ruth crept along the hallway, senses on high alert, eyes locked on the door ahead.

She only wanted a peek at what Nadia was doing. If she could get an idea of Clarence's plan and how these latest events fitted into his grand scheme, Ruth could—

A scrape from behind made her almost jump out of her skin. She wheeled around, fists raised.

Greg's brow furrowed. "What?"

Ruth clutched her chest, breathing hard, feeling as though she might faint. "I told you to stay put."

Greg shrugged. "We shouldn't split up."

He had a point.

After a few more deep breaths, Ruth spun back around, crept up to the door, and turned an ear to it. Hearing nothing from the other side, she motioned for Greg to stand clear, grabbed the handle and opened the door an inch.

Beyond was a basement storeroom filled with crates and boxes. Opposite, a set of stairs led up to another door that stood open.

Ruth hurried across the basement and up the stairs, Greg shadowing her. They emerged into a gift shop, complete with all manner of Marsh Park–branded souvenirs and tat—everything from mugs and key rings to stuffed animals and clothing, packed from floor to ceiling.

Ruth pointed to the shop's front door. It stood open.

"We're in the theme park's main street," Greg whispered.

Ruth put a finger to her lips, tiptoed to the door, and peered out. Sure enough, beyond lay a brick-paved street lined with more shops, cafés, and amusement arcades, all fronted with faux facades of Georgian, Victorian, and Edwardian designs washed in an array of pastels.

A little farther down the street, between *Ye Olde Sweet Shoppe* and *Maisie's Gift Emporium*—because you could never have enough souvenir shops—stood a giant fake oak tree with a trunk twenty feet across. Among its enormous roots was an archway, ten feet tall and seven wide, with a sign above that read:

ALICE'S WONDERLAND

To drive the point home, in case anyone had missed it, a golden hand with a pointing finger aimed at the door, under another sign that read:

THIS WAY!

Nadia hurried inside.

Ruth looked around to make sure they were alone, then went to dart after her, but Greg followed. She stopped and held up a hand. "Wait here. I mean it this time. If I'm not back in ten minutes, call the police."

Greg frowned. "What about the coroner?"

"Sure, him too." Ruth cleared her throat. "Anyone but your mother."

"We should stick together."

Ruth set her jaw. "There's more chance of getting caught." And a greater risk she'd put Greg in harm's way. Ruth forced herself to appear relaxed, and she offered him a reassuring smile. "I'll be fine."

Before he could argue further, Ruth ushered him across the shop to a door marked, "Personnel Only," and opened it to reveal a store cupboard. "Wait in here."

"You can't be serious."

Ruth shoved him in. "Deadly."

Greg checked his phone. "Ten minutes. No more."

"Agreed." Before he could change his mind, Ruth pushed the door closed, raced across the shop, and slipped outside.

She jogged along Main Street, scanning her surroundings, but it was eerily quiet. A little too quiet. It set her nerves on edge. She had expected security officers and cleaners hard at work.

Ruth stopped at the entrance to Alice's Wonderland, her heart hammering against her rib cage.

An animatronic white rabbit tapped his foot and checked a pocket watch. "Don't be late. Don't be late."

Hearing nothing through the arch, Ruth jogged along a wood-lined hallway lit by faux gas lamps hanging every few feet, down a ramp, and around a corner.

13

Furniture clung to the ceiling of the Alice in Wonderland walkthrough ride: a dining table and chairs, a grandfather clock, a fireplace, bookshelves, even a vase of flowers hung upside down on a table beside an armchair.

Ruth followed the path along another hallway with a chequered floor, the walls closing in, forcing her to duck as she reached a door at the far end, barely four feet tall.

She turned an ear to it.

Muffled footfalls sounded from the other side, so she eased the door open a crack.

A vast, fantastical forest teemed with all manner of cartoon-style creatures. Deer, badgers, and foxes mingled with hedgehogs, squirrels, and a robin redbreast, all chirping, snuffling, and moving with uncanny realism.

An elephant, its long trunk sweeping the grass for peanuts, peeked over a bush.

"A common sight in the British countryside," Ruth murmured, and then reminded herself she was in an underground forest straight out of a fantasy novel, so anything was possible.

Movement caught Ruth's eye. Nadia, her baggy shirt and jeans a blur against the vibrant greenery, disappeared into a thatched cottage with leaded windows. Ruth ducked behind a low stone wall and waited, heart in her mouth, ears straining.

Two minutes crawled by. Then three.

Ruth pictured Nadia, face pale in the cottage's gloom.

What is she doing?

Finally, Nadia emerged, a picnic basket tucked under her arm. Her expression unreadable, she marched past Ruth and back the way they'd come.

Ruth sighed. She'd come all this way and learned nothing. Cursing under her breath, she straightened, about to leave, but hesitated. *What if Nadia left something behind? A clue?*

It was a long shot, but irresistible.

She darted into the cottage. A half-scale sitting room greeted her, complete with a comfy armchair and a fireplace. One door of a floor-to-ceiling cupboard hung ajar. Ruth nudged it open.

Rows of stick puppets lined the shelves: soldiers, parrots, a creature that could be a monkey or a bear, a gingerbread man, and five green boggle-eyed aliens. Gaps punctuated each shelf, and an entire bottom row sat empty.

Ruth estimated, if the cupboard had been full to start with, twenty puppets were missing. "Why would Nadia need those?" she muttered, her mind awhirl with possibilities. "Something to do with the games?" It had to be.

Anxious to return to Greg, she backed out of the cottage.

Ruth hurried through the forest, ears straining for any

sound, along the hallways, and emerged onto the high street.

Ahead, Nadia entered the gift shop. As soon as she disappeared inside, Ruth followed, and threw open the storage cupboard door.

Greg frowned and held up his phone. "Fifteen seconds late." He shoved it back into his pocket. "I was about to call MI5."

"Very helpful," Ruth said. "Come on. Let's go."

On their return journey, Ruth explained about the missing puppets, and her theory they must have something to do with the games.

"But why fake her injuries? And Mike getting arrested?" Greg asked. "What difference does it make if we know they're helping Clarence behind the scenes?"

To that, Ruth had no answer.

They stepped through Hadfield Hall's back door, and Liam rushed up, face flushed, tie askew.

"There you are." He glanced over his shoulder. "Clarence wants you to see this before the next game tomorrow. Nine o'clock. Breakfast at eight." He thrust a red envelope into Ruth's hand and then scampered off, his rapid footfalls echoing down the hallway.

Greg stared after him, then turned to Ruth. "Not a thank-you card, I'm guessing."

"I have a feeling you could be right." She tore open the envelope, slid out a sheet of folded notepaper, and opened it. "As I suspected."

"Suspected?" Greg craned his neck to see.

"What the last game was trying to prove."

Scrawled across the paper in a messy hand were the words:

Winifred's killer knows Latin.

   I have left proof and an explanation in her room.

   Tell no one.

   CM

Below his monogram was a crudely drawn diagram pinpointing Winifred's bedroom within the vastness of Hadfield Hall.

Greg groaned. "Now?" He checked his phone. "It's gone eleven."

He was right. It had been a long day, and Ruth felt the first tingle of a migraine. She must take time to process the events, to try and make sense of everything.

Although eager to check out Winifred's room, they needed to call it a day.

"Come on. Bed." As she headed down the hallway, Ruth said over her shoulder, "Oh, and Greg?"

"Yeah?"

"You're sleeping on my sofa tonight."

The next morning, after a restless night thanks to Greg's incessant snoring, Ruth navigated them through Hadfield Hall's labyrinthine corridors using the crude map.

Winifred's rooms, in the east tower, stood in stark contrast to Clarence's in the west. Where his were dark and crammed with display cabinets, hers were light, clean, and expansive.

Modern minimalist furniture upholstered in white and accented with beige filled the space. A sofa and two chairs faced French doors that led to a veranda, offering commanding views of the theme park.

Stylish steel flood lamps ensured there was plenty of light in the evenings, and potted plants added a touch of life to the contemporary rooms.

A six-foot bookcase, crammed with romance novels, stood to the right of the main door. A metal peacock, twelve inches high, perched on the top shelf, stained glass gleaming at the end of each feather.

The impressive apartment was also a stark contrast to the rest of the ghost-themed Hadfield Hall.

Greg whistled. "I like this place." He turned in a circle. "Could definitely live somewhere like this."

Ruth raised an eyebrow. "And what exactly is wrong with the motorhome?"

Greg snorted.

Ruth put her hands on her hips. "Even after the recent improvements to our standard of living?" When her grandson smirked, she added, "You know full well since I glued and taped down the skylights the roof hasn't leaked once. Okay . . . twice. If that's not an improvement over water pouring in day and night, I don't know what is."

"Right. Shall we mention the TV?"

"What about it?"

"Since we *lost* the aerial . . ." Greg put a huge and unnecessary emphasis on the word "lost," knowing the fragile antenna had met an untimely demise back in Edinburgh. ". . . we have no channels."

"We didn't have any to start with," Ruth said, defensive. "The stupid aerial never worked properly."

Even when it was attached to the roof of the motorhome it still had a poor signal. However, Greg somehow managed to watch the Formula One, despite it looking like they were constantly driving through a blizzard.

"Besides, Gregory, you haven't used the TV for ages." Ruth wiggled her fingers through the air. "You stream."

He chuckled. "Don't mention streams. The bathroom taps are a disaster. Your motorhome has been dreaming of becoming a submarine ever since the Vanmoor River incident."

Ruth huffed. "Can we focus, please?"

Winifred's bedroom, connected to the sitting room by folding doors, continued with the same décor: a low bed, steel bedside tables, and a wool rug on wooden flooring.

Ruth walked to a sideboard in the sitting room. Framed photographs lined its surface. Ray and Orlando, no older than three and five, beamed alongside a handsome young couple Ruth assumed were Winifred's daughter and son-in-law.

And so, the photos continued, chronicling their lives: Ray at scout camp in his uniform; Orlando navigating a winding river in a canoe with friends; both at a picnic with family; each at their graduations, proud in their robes and caps.

Ray, the serious one; Orlando, shying away from the camera—they appeared a happy family. On the surface, at least.

One picture showed Ray in a yellow hardhat, examining blueprints while heavy machinery broke ground at the edge of the theme park.

"Perhaps this is where he got his first taste of empire building."

Several more photos documented the brothers' weddings. Orlando and Belle radiated happiness, while even Ray looked proud. Helena's smile, however, seemed strained.

"Have the cracks always been there?" Ruth wondered as

she traced a finger along the silver frame. *An undercurrent of resentment simmering beneath the surface?*

The last photo showed Orlando on a veranda, gazing across the park. He looked serious, haunted, his eyes shadowed. Ruth felt a pang of sympathy. Whatever demons plagued him, they weighed heavily on his mind.

Her gaze darted to the French doors. "He stood right there." She picked up a gold-framed photograph from the back: a portrait of Winifred's daughter, a beautiful woman with dark hair and bright green eyes.

"She reminds me of your sister. Same cheeky smile."

"Grandma, look at this." Greg's hushed voice came from the far end of the room. He knelt by a compact fireplace, back to her.

Ruth set the photograph down and joined him. A sealed clear plastic bag lay on the hearth alongside an envelope addressed to her in messy cursive.

Greg handed it to Ruth.

Inside, a card typed in bold red font read:

On Winifred's birthday six months ago, I came here to give her a present. While waiting, I recovered this from her fireplace.

She never came to me before, or afterward, or explained what it could be in reference to, but I'm certain it's connected to what happened.

CM

Ruth held up the bag containing charred paper. "Why would Winifred burn this? And why would Clarence connect it to her death?" Latin covered the fragment of a page inside. "Well, well. It seems our Latin theme wasn't just for show. Clarence has his evidence, and he expects us to link it to one of them."

At least five of the six players knew Latin—Ray, Orlando, Helena, Persephone, and Elias. Belle had seemed genuinely mystified. *Unless it was an act.*

"Do me a favour." She handed the evidence to Greg. "Search those words on your phone. I'd like to know what book it's from."

Greg settled into a nearby chair. As he worked, Ruth walked slowly around the sparsely furnished room, hands clasped behind her back, head bowed.

She considered each suspect. Ray, the elder brother: nice enough but clearly harboured resentment about the business and possibly some underlying jealousy toward Orlando and his perceived favoured treatment.

Has it festered over the years, turning into something darker, more dangerous?

Orlando, though, was different. Meek and reserved, he seemed more intelligent than he let on.

Still waters run deep, but do those depths conceal something more sinister than a gambling habit?

Ruth found Belle sweet and well-meaning enough, if a little annoying on occasion, and prone to overreacting.

But is there more to her than meets the eye? Is her ditzy persona a facade?

Helena was brash and standoffish. Ruth sensed a sadness in her eyes, a vulnerability she tried hard to conceal. It was apparent there were problems in their marriage.

And lastly, Persephone and Elias, the seasoned shareholders who'd no doubt weathered countless Marsh dramas. Like watchful hawks.

Do they have hidden agendas?
Undoubtedly.

"Any one of them could be guilty," Ruth murmured.

"Got it." Greg held up his phone. "This piece of burnt page is from the Vulgate."

Ruth crossed the room to stand beside him.

"A Latin Bible," Greg added.

"I know of it," Ruth said. "Someone gifted a version to your grandfather before he died. What part is it from?"

"The Parable of the Prodigal Son," Greg said, clearly pleased with himself. "The tale of two brothers."

Ruth arched her eyebrows. "Two brothers? Interesting. Go on."

Greg scanned an article on the phone's display. "So, there were these two sons." He glanced at Ruth. "You'll love this story." He cleared his throat and continued. "The younger one asked for his share of their father's inheritance, which his dad granted. However, the younger son's careless-ness and indulgence led him to squander the wealth. In no time, it left him destitute." Greg looked up at Ruth. "What do you think? It must be a reference to Orlando, but they're all rich, aren't they?"

Ruth pursed her lips and motioned for him to continue.

"The younger son, having spent all his inheritance and now poor, returned home. He begged his father to accept him back, which he did." Greg tapped the phone screen. "Warmly, and celebrated his return." He took a breath. "Meanwhile, the older son, consumed with envy, refused to participate in the welcome home festivities. When confronted, the father said to him, 'You are ever with me, and all that I have is yours, but your younger brother was lost and now he is found.'" Greg's brow furrowed, and he looked up at his grandmother again. "What do you think that means? I don't get it. Why did Winifred burn this?"

Ruth let out a breath. "Best guess, someone gave it to her

as a message. She likely took it the way it was intended." She nodded to the fireplace. "Blackmail be gone."

"So it is about Ray and Orlando?" Greg asked. "Ray is jealous of his brother? Orlando lost a load of money? One of those people we've met threatened to expose what Orlando did to the others?"

Ruth shrugged. "All speculation right now." It did, however, fit with the argument she'd overheard. She checked her phone—8:22 a.m. Liam's words echoed. The game—and whatever confrontation it might bring—loomed. "We'd better get to breakfast." She took a step toward the door but stopped, a subtle shift in the air across her face giving her pause. Turning back, Ruth held up her hands.

Greg pocketed his phone. "What's wrong?"

Ruth rotated on her heels, feeling the air. "Now I come to think of it, this room is different."

"Different to what?" Greg asked, looking around.

Ruth lowered her hands. "The towers are identical, so even allowing for Clarence's display cabinets . . ." Ruth stepped to the door, pressed her back against it, and looked about. "It's a lot smaller in here. And missing a window." She faced the bookcase. "Here." Ruth examined the left-hand side, where the edge of the shelves met the wall. "Must be behind this."

Greg peered at the bookcase too. "What are you—" He stiffened as Ruth gripped the edge and pulled it away from the wall.

The bookcase slid easily on castors, revealing a short corridor, only a few feet long, ending in a closed door.

Ruth swallowed and gestured. "After you."

"What?" Greg's eyes widened. "Why me?"

"You're young. Agile. If there's a booby trap, you can leap out of the way before it gets you."

"I've got my whole life ahead of me." Greg smirked. "You're older, and therefore more expendable."

Ruth cocked her head. "Want your inheritance early?"

"I might squander it."

"Your sister definitely would."

"Fine." Greg took a deep breath and squared his shoulders, feigning bravery. "But if I get murdered to death, I'm telling Mum it was your fault."

"Noted." Ruth checked her phone again. "Hurry up."

14

Greg edged along the narrow hallway behind Winifred's bookcase, flinching with every creak of the floorboards. "Think there's one of these in Clarence's tower?" he whispered. "Maybe you misjudged the size with all those cabinets."

Ruth paused, mentally retracing the layout of the rooms in her mind's eye. "No. I don't think so. Winifred's sitting room is smaller, even accounting for the displays."

The open-plan design and wide double doors leading to the bedroom had initially fooled her. The illusion of grandeur belied the room's actual dimensions. It gave the impression it was much larger, when in fact the inverse was true. She should've realised sooner.

Greg hovered his hand over the door handle, apprehension flickering in his eyes as he glanced back at his grandmother. "You sure about this?"

Ruth hesitated, then grasped his arm. "Not entirely, but just be careful."

He rolled his eyes. "Thanks for the sage advice." A

playful smirk tugged at his lips. "Next time we stumble upon a hidden lair, you're going first."

"Absolutely," Ruth declared, with no intention of upholding that promise. Her gaze darted back to the bookcase, to be sure it wouldn't suddenly swing shut, trapping them, and sending her cleithrophobia into a raging tantrum. She shoved the uncomfortable thought down and focussed on the task at hand.

Greg took a deep breath, opened the door, and stepped through.

The room they entered was a cramped six feet by eight. Opposite the door sat an office chair and a desk with a laptop and printer. Shelves took up the wall to the right, crammed full of various items. Among them were several antique mantel clocks, faux plants in pots, statues, figurines, candlesticks . . .

Greg frowned at it all. "Was Winifred a hoarder?"

For a moment, Ruth wondered if Winifred had stashed everything in here to keep her main living spaces clutter-free, like her sister, Margaret. Then, something else caught her eye—a smoke alarm on one of the shelves. A quick inspection revealed a tiny camera lens concealed behind the mesh grille.

"Hmm," Ruth murmured, holding it out for Greg to see. "Seems Winifred was into covert surveillance."

"Is it any wonder, with this family?"

Ruth approached the computer desk and ran a finger across the laptop's trackpad. A password prompt flashed on the screen. Next to the laptop lay a memory card and an external card reader. "Think we can access this?" she asked.

Greg shook his head. "My tablet's back at the motorhome, and it doesn't have a standard USB. We'd need an unlocked computer."

Ruth hadn't seen any computers readily available within the main areas of Hadfield Hall. "There's probably one in the office behind reception. Hopefully, it's not password protected." She tucked the card into her pocket and unplugged the card reader.

Taking out her phone, Ruth snapped several pictures of the room, focussing on the hidden camera within the fake smoke detector. Satisfied, she said, "Come on, let's grab breakfast before they send out a search party."

"No arguments here."

They slipped back through the corridor and carefully manoeuvred the bookcase back into place, concealing the entrance. Their hurried steps echoed through the tower as they made their escape.

Reaching the reception hall, Ruth stopped short. "Go on without me. I'll be there in a few minutes."

"What should I tell them?" Greg's eyes darted toward the dining room entrance.

"I'm feeding Merlin." With a reassuring pat on his arm, she stepped around the reception desk and slipped into the office behind it.

It was a sparsely furnished room: with a desk, a chair, a filing cabinet, and a computer. Ruth sat and shook the mouse, her pulse quickening as the screen flickered to life.

No password required.

She plugged the card reader into the back of the computer, inserted the memory card, and navigated to the newly appeared drive. Two folders were visible, labelled "*E*" and "*P.*"

Ruth's gaze flicked toward the door, her hand hovering over the mouse. With a deep breath, she clicked on the first folder. It contained three files: two images and a document.

She opened the top image. It showed Elias in the dining

hall, engaged in conversation with Winifred. A timestamp in the corner indicated it was taken a few weeks prior, a little after four in the afternoon.

It seemed innocent enough but meant there was a hidden camera in the dining hall, placed by Winifred. Judging by the angle, it was somewhere high up, near the main entrance.

"The smoke detector."

The second image, taken minutes after the first, showed Elias handing a thick envelope to Winifred. Her face was contorted in anger, her entire posture radiating hostility.

"What were you up to?" Ruth murmured.

With time not on her side, she opened the document. It contained a list of dates, times, and locations, meticulously tracking Elias' movements both within Hadfield Hall and the theme park.

"She had you followed?"

Several entries had notes next to them. One, in particular, caught Ruth's eye:

Elias plans to force a vote for the park expansion and has conspired with Persephone and Ray.

This was more than sibling rivalry; this was a full-blown power struggle.

Unable to resist, Ruth clicked on the next folder, labelled "P." As expected, it contained similar files: images and a document. The first image showed Persephone in a heated discussion with Elias in the dining hall, mere minutes before Winifred's arrival. In the next image, Persephone stood with a tall man outside a ghost train ride, gesturing toward one of the distant towers.

The accompanying file also documented Persephone's

movements throughout the grounds, but again one note stood out:

Proof Persephone lied to us.

It was written beside the name and address of a restaurant within the theme park.

Ruth removed the card from the reader and was about to stand when Liam appeared at the doorway.

"Mrs Morgan." His gaze flicked from Ruth to the computer screen. "What are you doing in here?"

Her mind raced as she got to her feet, blocking his view of the card reader. "I'm so sorry, I tried to find you." With her hands behind her back, she surreptitiously unplugged the reader from the USB port. "The internet on my phone is playing up. I wanted to check my emails." She forced a smile.

Liam's gaze lingered on her face for a few seconds before he stepped aside and gestured to the door. "Please, enjoy your breakfast. The others eagerly await your arrival."

"Thank you." She squeezed past him, slipping the memory card into her pocket.

As Ruth entered the dining room, a wave of relief washed over her.

Everyone was already seated at the table, except for Greg, who loaded his plate at the breakfast buffet.

"There she is," Ray boomed, a wide grin on his face. "Glad you could join us. How's the feline companion?"

"He's fine, thanks," Ruth mumbled, avoiding his scrutiny as she headed to the teapot.

"The game starts in fifteen minutes," Persephone said, her voice haughty. "You're cutting it a bit fine, don't you think?"

"We're all a little on edge," Belle added.

Ruth poured herself a cup of tea before joining Greg at the buffet. As she loaded her plate with scrambled eggs and toast, Greg leaned closer.

"How'd it go?" he murmured through the corner of his mouth. "Find anything interesting on that card?"

Ruth glanced over her shoulder to make sure they weren't overheard. "Winifred had a hidden camera in the dining hall. She was spying on at least two of them. Having them followed, too."

"Who?"

Ruth mouthed, "Elias and Persephone." Now her black-mailer suspicions had shifted to them. After all, they both had a lot to gain from Winifred and Clarence's deaths, and Helena had made a dig at Persephone about money.

Liam appeared in the doorway, his gaze fixed on Ruth.

She offered him a small, tight smile before sitting at the table.

Greg dropped into the chair beside her and dug into his breakfast with gusto.

Ruth only picked at her food, her mind a whirl. *Should I update Clarence on what we've found?* But they needed more than suspicions. So far, nothing concrete linked any of them to blackmail, let alone murder.

Helena, her sharp gaze fixed on Ruth, suddenly stood, circled the table, and settled into the seat on her right. She leaned in close, her voice a low hiss. "You're not here as a guest, are you?"

Ruth's blood ran cold. *How does she know?* Her mind raced, searching for any missteps, any slipups that might have revealed her true purpose.

"I know exactly who you are," Helena continued, her voice laced with venom. "You're a private investigator. It all adds up. Clarence thinks one of us had something to do with Winifred's death, and you're here to prove him right."

"I arrived before Winifred died." Every muscle in Ruth's body tensed, but she kept her voice steady, her gaze fixed on her mug of tea. "I'm not here to prove anything."

Helena leaned back in her chair, eyes narrowed. "You can point an accusing finger all you want. I have nothing to hide. None of us do." Her expression darkened. "But if you don't play the next games to win, I'll know you're here just to spy on us, and I'll call you out for it." With that, she stood, her voice ringing with confidence. "Come on, let's get this over with. I'm tired of waiting."

Ruth's mind reeled, but she had a job to do—a murder to solve—and she wouldn't allow Helena or Persephone to throw her off.

From now on, she needed to tread more carefully. Ruth would play the games to the best of her ability, so as not to raise suspicions with the others too, but she must balance a fine line, and remain an observer.

She sighed.

Clarence had certainly not made any of this easy for her.

"Poor Helena," Belle said, watching her retreating back. "Stuck in a loveless marriage."

Ruth frowned and whispered, "If that's the case, why doesn't she divorce him?"

"Helena is used to the finer things in life. No way she'd give any of it up. She's trapped."

"And she signed a prenuptial agreement," Elias said from behind. "It all goes in Ray's favour."

"Prenups are not legally binding in the UK," Ruth said.

"No." Elias cleared his throat. "But if they're entered into freely, with full understanding, they are given a lot of weight by the courts. Helena would have to prove infidelity, or some heinous act, and Ray is unlikely to offer her such a get-out." He slipped past them and said over his shoulder, "Besides, Ray's confident they can repair their marriage," and strode down the corridor.

"I don't see him doing that," Belle said in Ruth's ear. "Ray's a workaholic, obsessed with money almost as much as Helena."

They rounded the corner, and stepped through a set of double doors, Liam having already unlocked them.

The music room at Hadfield Hall was a symphony of grandeur and opulence. A vaulted ceiling, adorned with a breathtaking fresco depicting a scene from ancient Rome, soared above them. Sunlight, filtered through stained glass windows, painted the parquet floor in a kaleidoscope of colours, which in turn reflected off the hundreds of crystals that adorned an immense chandelier.

Instruments of every shape and size lined the walls, some mounted on the stonework, others cradled in stands, all displayed like precious artifacts.

Greg, his eyes wide with awe, turned in a slow circle, taking it all in. "Insane."

Ruth couldn't help but agree with his sentiment. It was spectacular. She had rarely seen such a lavish display of wealth. The sheer magnificence of the room was breathtaking. And yet, there was also an underlying discordance.

Violins and cellos gleamed under soft spotlights in recessed alcoves, while trumpets, trombones, and saxophones stood proudly, their brass surfaces polished to a mirror sheen. Drums of various sizes, cymbals, flutes, clarinets, and even an electric theremin with its strange wire antennae completed the eclectic collection.

Scattered throughout the room, adding to the surreal atmosphere, were ten animatronic figures, each dressed in ghostly white, their lifeless eyes staring blankly ahead as they forever mimed playing the instruments.

Belle gasped. "There." Her voice, high-pitched and thin, cut through the eerie silence, drawing their attention to the middle of the room.

They gathered around a magnificent Steinway grand piano, elevated on a raised platform. Slumped over the keys was a lifeless form, dressed in a finely tailored dinner jacket, as though he'd been silenced midchord. His head tilted at an unnatural angle, and fake blood trickled from a bullet hole in his back.

Belle winced, and her hand flew to her mouth. "That's not nice."

"When is murder ever nice?" Helena said, her voice laced with indifference.

Ray pointed to a digital screen perched on a stand on top of the piano. A timer counted down from twenty-five minutes. Next to it sat a silver microphone, angled toward the player.

"Please tell me they don't expect you to sing," Greg whispered to Ruth, his tone light, but his eyes reflecting genuine concern.

She shot him a mock-scandalised look. "What's that supposed to mean?"

Greg's lips twitched.

"Another victim." Elias stepped to the body. "Game Two is usually a logic-based affair." His eyes darted around the room. There was a calculating glint to them, a ruthlessness that belied his laid-back demeanour.

"This time, it's a shooting," Ray said. "That has to mean something."

"Clarence hates guns." Orlando turned to his brother, his expression a mix of confusion and apprehension.

"He's never used a gun in one of these setups." Like Elias, Persephone's suspicious gaze swept the room. "What do you think it means?"

Ray shrugged, but Ruth wasn't fooled by his feigned indifference. There was a new sharpness in his eyes.

An uneasy silence descended.

Belle clutched at her throat, her face pale. Even Helena seemed unsettled, a dark flicker crossing her features.

Ruth leaned closer to the mannequin, examining the bullet wound in its back. She and Clarence had something in common, it seemed. She loathed guns too.

During her time with the Metropolitan Police Force, she'd come close to being on the receiving end of a bullet only once, as far as she knew. And it hadn't been while on call.

The event occurred during a taster course in handling guns, where Ruth was to decide whether to train as a firearms officer.

Most UK police officers didn't carry those types of weapon, but all forces had an armed response unit. At the time, Ruth had been working for London's Metropolitan Police, and the prospect of higher pay had been tempting. So, she'd signed up for the training, figuring it was an opportunity not to be missed.

However, a cocky young sergeant named Terry Stanford had played up during the entire morning briefings by interrupting the training officers about how he'd spent half his life game-hunting with his father, and how guns were second nature to him.

As it had turned out, they weren't.

No sooner had Terry stepped foot on the shooting range, ear defenders firmly in place, than he'd launched into an impromptu, and woefully unqualified, lecture in handling firearms, all while casually swinging the loaded gun around as he spoke.

Of course, it had gone off.

The bullet missed Ruth's head by a hair's breadth; the closest she'd come to death as an officer, and all thanks to a colleague with an inflated ego.

If she had been a cat, that would have used up at least six of her nine lives.

The memory still sent shivers down her spine. The sharp crack of the gunshot echoing in the enclosed space, acrid cordite stinging her nostrils, the look of sheer terror on Terry's face.

The chief instructor had promptly marched Terry off the premises, his face a mask of fury. Ruth never saw Terrible Terry again. She walked out of that training session and never looked back.

If she'd died that day, Ruth wouldn't have met her husband, had Sara, and gone on a thousand adventures.

Some things were best left well alone.

"Grandma?" Greg's voice, soft and insistent, broke through her memories.

Ruth blinked, startled. "Yeah?"

"Are you all right?" he asked, his brow furrowed with concern.

"I'm fine." She forced a smile.

Helena's sharp voice cut through the silence. "There are no suspects."

"Yes, there are." Greg indicated the ten ghostly mannequin musicians around the room.

"They're always here," Ray said. "Part of the décor. Not likely anything to do with the game. Mere set dressing."

"Everyone's a suspect until proven otherwise." Helena's

eyes narrowed at Ruth with a flicker of challenge. "Isn't that right, Mrs Morgan?"

Ruth chose to ignore the barb. Her attention returned to the bullet hole penetrating the pianist's back. She turned on the spot, picturing the bullet's trajectory. It had come from the nearest window. Ruth crossed the room, her footsteps echoing on the polished floor, and pulled back the heavy velvet curtains, revealing another mannequin.

The killer.

15

The mannequin behind the curtain depicted a woman with dark hair tied back into a sleek bun. She wore a long coat, purple blouse, black trousers, and high-heeled boots—a lady of action, or at least dressed for it.

Her right arm hung by her side, a revolver clutched in her hand. Its shiny metal glinted in the light.

Ruth squatted to examine the weapon. No bullets occupied the visible chambers, but it appeared real. She adjusted her position for a closer look. Perhaps a magician had used it—*something from Clarence's collection?*

She took the wrist and tried to move it, but the arm had little movement and seemed to be connected to something mechanical inside.

Ruth checked the rest of the figure but found no further clues: no telltale signs to explain a motive for murder, nothing in her pockets, no hidden messages from Clarence.

She straightened and faced the group. "We have our victim." Ruth motioned toward the body by the piano. "And our killer." She nodded at the gun-toting mannequin. "That leaves us searching for a motive."

Unless, of course, Clarence deliberately misled them.

"Maybe she wasn't fond of his playing." Ray leaned against the piano, posture relaxed, eyes alert as he watched Ruth.

Has Helena shared her suspicions with him?

Ruth examined the killer again, and then the victim, but nothing new stood out beyond the bullet hole. Her gaze swept the music room, absorbing every detail. "You all know this place well. Does anything stand out?"

Murmurs rippled through the group as they too examined the room, the animatronic ghost mannequins still performing their silent concert.

Elias stepped to a blackboard on a stand, peered behind it, and then pulled back, shaking his head. "Everything seems in order."

Ruth returned to the killer. "In that case, we must be missing—" Something to her left caught her eye, a detail she'd missed before: a glimmer of light reflecting off metal. Ruth grabbed the curtain and pulled it open, revealing not only the floor-to-ceiling windows in their full glory, but also a door with a gleaming brass handle. "Is this where she came from?" Ruth opened the door to a side room.

A circular, raised platform dominated the smaller space. It reminded Ruth of a child's playground roundabout, or the base of a merry-go-round.

Five-foot-tall partitions divided it like slices of a pie, with a chair in each, seven in total.

"Seven?" Greg whispered to Ruth, his brow furrowed.

"Six of them and one of us," she murmured, mind racing. "Unless Liam is supposed to play." Ruth glanced at him.

He remained distant, expression unreadable, quietly observing the group, with the odd furtive glance at Helena.

What is he thinking? What does he know?

In Clarence's eyes, Ruth and Greg weren't suspects, but for both of them to abstain would raise more suspicion, particularly from Persephone and Helena.

Ray strode past Ruth into the side room, his footsteps purposeful, determined. "What do we have here? Privacy shields? Are we taking exams?" Ray tapped a divider with a sardonic laugh. "Are these to prevent us from cheating?"

The others entered the room.

Persephone clucked her tongue, her disdain evident. "As if we'd stoop to such a thing." Her tone dripped with feigned innocence, but Ruth had no doubt Persephone was capable of doing anything to get what she wanted.

Same for Elias.

Belle frowned at Persephone. "What about a few years ago when you—"

Persephone silenced her with a sharp jab in the ribs with one of her long fingernails.

"Ow." Belle rubbed her side.

"I knew you two cheated," Orlando said with a mischievous smirk. "That's how you won the second game so easily. Never again should anyone let you team up."

Persephone sniffed and turned her back on him.

Ruth sauntered around the edge of the circular platform, which stood a few inches off the ground. She knelt and peered underneath. "It's like a turntable." Several wheels were spaced evenly around the edge.

Greg joined her. "You're right. There's an electric motor in the middle."

They both stood.

"It better not spin too fast." Belle clutched her stomach. "I get dizzy bad. Hated merry-go-rounds as a kid."

Ruth nudged Greg. "Guess I'll be taking the seventh seat."

He crossed his arms and nodded. "Probably wise."

Liam wheeled a black wooden box on castors across the room, and stopped with its open side facing the platform.

Belle screwed up her face. "What's that for?"

It stood five feet tall, five wide, three deep, and was divided down the middle.

Ruth pictured everyone seated on the circular platform as it rotated, with their respective pie sections gliding past each half of the box in turn.

The first half held a table. On it rested a couple of hundred white tiles, each around half an inch square, with numbers ranging from zero to nine printed on them. Racks clamped to the back edge of the table could hold the tiles in rows.

Ruth leaned into the box as far as she dared.

A mechanical device lurked behind the shelves, attached to them by a series of complicated pulleys and gears, but its purpose eluded her.

Perhaps something happens when someone places enough tiles?

Ruth picked up a tile and flipped it over. Four magnets were embedded in each corner. Another tile had three magnets clustered in the middle. In fact, each numbered tile had a unique arrangement. Finally, she selected two nines and compared them. Both had six tiny magnets arranged in two identical rows.

"Find something?" Elias peered over her shoulder.

"A strange contraption." She showed him the backs of the tiles. "Do you suppose the device reads the magnets and identifies the number placed?"

Elias leaned in to get a good look. "It's complex. Has electronics. I see wires and circuit boards."

"Seems like Clarence had one of the ride engineers build it," Ray said.

Ruth returned the tiles to the table. "Elaborate, to say the least."

"That's Clarence for you," Helena said, her tone annoyed. "He has all year to concoct this ridiculous stuff."

Ruth moved to the second half of the box, but a black curtain obscured its interior.

She fought the urge to peek.

Liam read from a card, mumbled something under his breath, and then gestured to the chairs. "Please, everyone playing take a seat."

"Clarence has outdone himself this year." Elias's voice held the merest hint of admiration as he stepped onto the turntable and sat down, facing outward. "Quite the setup."

With obvious reluctance, Persephone followed suit. Then Helena, her expression unreadable, eyes fixed on Liam.

Belle glanced nervously at Orlando.

He squeezed her hand. "It'll be fun. You'll see."

She exhaled, gave him a tremulous smile, and they both took their seats, each player obscured from one another by the partitions.

Orlando looked to either side of him. "Really is like we're taking an exam."

"Or voting," Elias said.

Ray stared at the open box, arms folded. "I don't like the look of this. What is it exactly? What does it do?"

"Sit down and find out," Orlando said.

Ray's gaze shifted to him. "You always blindly do whatever anyone says."

Orlando shrugged. "It's a game."

"With massive consequences," Ray countered.

"Even so," Elias interjected. "Looks like musical chairs. How hard can it be?"

"Come on, Ray." Persephone's voice took on a persuasive tone. "Us against Clarence, remember? We can win this if we work together. Looks like only one of us needs to complete it. Those shares are as good as ours."

Ruth forced a smile at Greg and sat down, facing outward like the others. It was easier to play along, at least for now.

"Oh, do hurry up, old boy," Elias said to Ray, his impatience evident. "We're on a time limit. The sooner we start, the sooner we beat this game and take Clarence's shares off his hands. Goodness knows I'd like to see him step aside and let us expand the park in peace."

Ray sighed and looked at Liam, who stared at the card in his hand, avoiding eye contact. "Fine."

No sooner had Ray dropped into the remaining seat than Liam spoke. "Everyone please stand."

Belle snickered, and even Helena seemed to stifle a smile.

With some muttering of annoyance, the rest of the group complied, and peered over the top of the dividers at one another.

Liam stepped beside the open box and read from the card. He indicated the left-hand side with the curtain. "As you face this device, it will show you a scene. Within the scene are sets of numbers. Memorise them in their groupings. Left to right."

"A memory game?" Belle groaned. "My memory is terrible."

Ruth had a feeling memorisation was only part of it.

This was Clarence's design, after all, and nothing so far was straightforward.

"The carousel will turn, letting you each look at the scene, one by one. Hold the numbers in your head until you complete a full rotation on the carousel." Liam indicated the right side of the box with the mechanical device. "Place the corresponding numbered tiles in their correct sequence on the shelves before your turn ends, and you'll be presented with the next scene."

Ruth murmured under her breath, "Look at the scene, memorise the numbers, hold then in your head until you can place the tiles on the shelves." *Then straight on to the next scene without time to gather myself?* She blew out a puff of air. This was going to be far from easy.

"How fast will this thing spin?" Ray asked.

"I don't know, sir," Liam mumbled, eyes still glued to the card.

Elias gave him a dubious look. "Haven't you had enough of this charade? You helped Clarence set this up. You always scheme together throughout the year." He waggled a finger at Liam. "Tell me the truth, old boy. What are we dealing with here?"

Liam shook his head. "The ride engineering team built this game, following the master's instructions."

"As I suspected," Ray muttered.

"I only know what's on this card," Liam added.

Ruth still found that hard to believe.

What hold does Clarence have over him?

"In that case, why don't we call them? The engineers." Orlando grinned. "Get the cheat codes."

"Right," Ray said. "Clarence doesn't need to know. We'd keep it strictly between us." He winked at Liam. "We would reward you handsomely. You'd never need to work another day in your life."

"Oh, leave him alone, for goodness' sake," Helena snapped. "Don't you think Clarence swore everyone involved to secrecy? Probably had them sign NDAs." She glanced between the brothers. "He knew you'd try something like that. You two are beyond predictable."

Persephone's lips curled into a humourless smile. "Remember the year he hired actors for that ridiculous horror skit?" She rolled her eyes. "During the break between games, Elias tried bribing one of them."

Elias gave a wheezy chuckle. "Almost worked."

Persephone glared at him. "She thought you were propositioning her. Poor girl. Threatened to call the police. Took us half the second game to calm her down. We almost lost because of your antics."

Elias looked away and mumbled, "Not my fault she misinterpreted my intentions."

"It was definitely your fault," Ray said.

"Can we get back to the game?" Helena nodded to Liam, her expression softening. "Please continue."

Liam reached beneath the turntable and held up a metal case attached to a cable. He opened it, revealing a giant red button inside. "Please, be seated. We'll begin."

"Up, down, up, down," Elias grumbled. "My back can't take this nonsense."

"Be careful," Greg mouthed to Ruth.

She gave him a thumbs-up, attempting to appear confident despite the unease churning in her stomach. They'd all be watching her closely now, waiting for her to slip up and confirm their suspicions. Ruth balled her fists. She would do everything in her power to win the game.

What is this about to entail, though? Another test of observation? Or something more sinister?

Liam held the button aloft. "Three, two, one." He pressed it.

Greg needn't have worried about the spinning platform making him feel ill. He would've been fine, as it inched round at a glacial pace, taking a couple of minutes to complete a single revolution.

The downside was Ruth had to hold sequences of numbers in her head for that time, without being distracted.

After the second rotation, Liam cleared his throat, the sharp sound slicing through the hushed anticipation. "We'll start with you, Belle, and Mrs Morgan will follow." He consulted the card. "No conferring allowed. Everyone, memorise the numbers you see within the scene."

"Oh, I think I understand what's about to happen." Ray's voice came from over the dividers. "Grandmama used to love these little shows Clarence put on for her when they were kids."

"Why are all these games about Winifred?" Belle asked. "It's almost as if Clarence knew she was about to be—"

"Once you return to the tiles side of the box," Liam continued, "remember to use them to recreate the number sequences in the order they were presented, from left to right, starting with the uppermost rack. There will be three rounds." His gaze swept over the players, lingering on each face for a beat. "Understood?"

"Not really." Belle's timid voice piped up from behind the divider to Ruth's left.

"Typical Belle," Helena said. "Always the first to admit confusion."

"Then you go first," Belle snapped in a rare sign of annoyance.

"Gladly."

"Ignore her, darling. You'll get the hang of it," Orlando said, his voice soothing despite the underlying tension.

Ruth still couldn't quite get to grips with Orlando. He seemed affable enough, but something beneath his meek demeanour bothered her.

"Of course, dear Orlando. Some of us will get the hang of it." Helena's voice dripped with sarcasm and a confidence that bordered on arrogance. "Besides, only one of us has to win, but the game does sound like it might be beyond some people."

"She'll be just fine, you'll see," Orlando said. "Care to wager on it, Helena?"

"Everyone focus, and stop bickering," Persephone said. "These seemingly simple tasks are what trip us up. Can I remind everyone we're on a time limit?"

"Do we work on the numbers sequences as a team?" Elias asked Liam. "Belle gives her best guess, and we see if we can improve on it."

Liam shook his head. "It resets for each person, and the players who fail are eliminated."

Ruth exchanged uneasy glances with Greg as Belle took her turn in front of the box, her anxious mutterings coming from the other side of the divider.

And then Ruth's slice of the platform glided past the first side of the open box housing the table, racks, and tiles. She took a deep breath as she swung in front of the second side.

The curtain had opened, revealing a miniature scene illuminated by carefully positioned spotlights.

A gilded frame of intricate filigree, painted in vibrant red and gold, surrounded a miniature stage with meticulously painted flats. The backdrop to the puppet theatre depicted a bustling jazz club, a silhouetted audience in the foreground.

The effect created a sense of forced perspective, like something out of a vintage cartoon. It was charming, in a slightly disconcerting way.

On the left, painted cardboard stick puppets of a saxophone player and a cellist sprang to life, their limbs jerking in time with silent music. A trumpeter popped up in the middle, followed by a singer.

Ruth pictured Nadia crouched beneath the stage, brow slick with sweat as she manipulated the stick puppets above her head.

Despite the odd situation, a wave of nostalgia washed over Ruth, reminding her of the Punch and Judy shows she'd watched as a child, and the puppet programs on TV.

However, acutely aware of the ticking clock, she forced her attention back to the task at hand. Ruth scanned the scene as the platform continued its slow rotation, her mind laser-focussed.

And then she spotted the first set of numbers neatly printed along the lower bout of the cello: 313.

Relief washed over her.

Now, where are the others?

It didn't take long to find the next set: 705, emblazoned across the top of the footlights. The final set proved more elusive, cleverly concealed down the length of the microphone stand: 912.

The numbers seemed random, meaningless.

Are they supposed to signify something? Is there a code to crack? Ruth's mind raced to find a pattern, a connection, but came up blank.

She fixated on each set of digits, muttering them under her breath. "Three-one-three, seven-zero-five, nine-one-two."

The puppet jazz club spun from view. Ruth squeezed her

eyes shut, the sequence imprinted on the insides of her eyelids. "Three-one-three, seven-zero-five, nine-one-two . . ." She only had to hold on to them for a couple of minutes. Easy. Or so you'd think . . . "Three-one-three, seven-zero-five, nine-one-two." *Wait. That's not the correct order from left to right.* "Seven-zero-five, three-one-three, nine-one-two."

Ignoring the mutterings and frustrated sighs emanating from the others as they took their turns, Ruth repeated the sequence like a mantra, willing the numbers to stick. And that's when a thought struck Ruth, sending a jolt of panic through her.

"Liam," she called out. "Do the numbers need to be in any particular order? The three sets, I mean?"

Liam, his tone devoid of inflection, replied, "Like I explained—they must appear in the order they were presented in the scene."

"What?" Belle's shrill voice cut through the air. "Are you serious? That's impossible." A few seconds later, a claxon blared, followed by a shriek. "I got it wrong. I'm so sorry." Belle sounded on the verge of tears.

Well, that's one down already, Ruth thought.

A wave of sympathy washed over her, but was quickly shoved aside by a surge of adrenaline.

Six players to go.

As Ruth reached the table with the numbered tiles, she sprang into action. Her fingers flew, arranging them in the correct order from left to right on the top rack: Seven, zero, five, three, one, three, nine, one, two.

Ruth's heart pounded in her chest.

The moment she slotted the last tile into place, a mechanical whirring filled the air. The shelf tipped back, swallowing the tiles, and a triumphant chime rang out, echoing in the tense silence.

Ruth released a long breath.

"Well done, Mrs Morgan," Orlando said, a hint of admiration in his voice.

Two more rounds.

Ruth mentally prepared herself for the challenge.

There was no time to rest on her laurels. The puppet theatre swung back into view, with the scene now transformed.

Gone was the smoky jazz club.

In its place raged a rock concert in full swing.

16

R uth's stomach lurched as her eyes darted over the miniature rock concert, frantically searching. "Where are the numbers?" Stick puppets, dressed in leather and sporting long hair, thrashed on a miniature stage. A flamboyant vocalist, a stoic bassist, an enthusiastic guitarist, and a keyboard player shrouded by synthesisers performed in silence. Brightly coloured stage lights flashed, and at the back, a drummer pounded on his kit.

Numbers, she reminded herself. *Find the numbers.*

Trying to maintain her focus, Ruth's gaze swept back and forth several times over the rock concert, noting the various instruments, lighting, and band mates. Finally, she spotted it; a series of four numbers printed on one of the stage amplifiers on the left: 8337.

Ruth continued her relentless search, and at last she located the next four digits emblazoned across the vocalist's chest: 1204.

As the platform continued its slow rotation, Ruth strained her neck for a glimpse of the final set of numbers.

Another claxon shattered the silence. This time, it was

Elias who swore. "For goodness' sake. How on earth was that wrong?"

"I'm sorry, sir," Liam said, his voice devoid of any real sympathy. "You're out."

Five players left.

With seconds remaining before the scene vanished, Ruth spotted it—the last number, cleverly concealed within the painted backdrop on the far right: 8902.

She squeezed her eyes shut, mentally reciting the sequence over and over. "Eight, three, three, seven. One, two, zero, four. Eight, nine, zero, two . . . Eight, three, three seven. One, two, zero, four. Eight, nine, zero, two."

A clear, melodious chime rang out.

"Thank heavens for that," Persephone said, a rare crack in her composure.

"Congratulations, Madam," Liam said. "You're doing well." His tone was flat, but a flicker of amusement danced in his eyes.

Ruth blocked out the symphony of chimes, claxons, sighs, and muttered curses. Her focus remained absolute. She had to keep the sequence fixed in her mind.

"Eight, three, three, seven . . . . One, two, zero, four . . . . Eight, nine, zero, two . . . . Eight, three, three, seven . . . One, two, four. Wait. No. Zero. One, two, zero, four . . . Eight, nine, zero, two." She furrowed her brow in concentration, repeating the sequence, her voice a low murmur. "Eight, three, three, seven . . . . One, two, zero, four . . . . Eight, nine, two, zero . . . . Was it?"

The box containing the numbered tiles swung into view.

Ruth wasted no time—her fingers flew across them, arranging the tiles in order on the second shelf.

Once done, she held her breath, every muscle taut with anticipation.

The mechanism whirred.

A second later, the chime sounded.

"Well done, Grandma."

Ruth allowed herself a small smile. "One more to go." Her attention was already on the final scene.

The stage had transformed, now depicting a lively folk festival. Trees, painted in shades of green and brown, flanked the stage. A roaring campfire crackled in the middle, flames casting flickering shadows. Above it all, colourful bunting fluttered.

As expected, a troupe of stick puppet dancers sprang to life. Long, flowing tassels and scarfs adorned their bright costumes. They whirled and swayed, accompanied by a lively guitarist, banjo player, and violinist.

It was cheerful, almost aggressively so, and Ruth couldn't help but feel it clashed with their odd situation.

Is it only Nadia under there? Or Mike too?

For a second, Ruth pictured them, hands full of puppet sticks, controlling each with fevered enthusiasm.

Her eyes darted across the scene, from left to right, searching for the elusive numbers.

On the first pass, she spotted seven, eight, three, two, and one, printed on a gnarled tree stump to the right. It was followed by six, two, seven, nine, five cleverly camouflaged among the flames of the campfire.

Ruth's gaze remained fixed on the left-hand side of the stage as it began to swing away. She knew the last set of numbers was hiding somewhere in that area.

Sure enough, at the very last second, as the scene was about to disappear, she found it: five, one, two, one, three, almost invisible against the painted backdrop.

Ruth squeezed her eyes shut, and whispered the sequence in order. "Five, one, two, one, three. Six, two, seven, nine, five. Seven, eight, three, two, one." Her eyes flew open, a flicker of doubt crossing her mind. *Three sets of five numbers? Did I miss any? No, that's all. I'm sure of it. Or am I?*

The table with the tiles glided into view. Ruth's hands trembled as she arranged them on the bottom rack.

Third and final task completed, she held her breath.

The shelf tipped back, and . . .

A claxon blared, its harsh sound echoing through the room like a death knell.

"I'm sorry, Mrs Morgan," Liam said. "That's not correct."

Ruth let out a disappointed breath. "That was hard," she muttered, more to herself than anyone else.

Fifteen seconds passed, punctuated by another claxon.

Someone else got it wrong. Who's left?

"I'm sorry, sir. That's not correct."

Moments later, a chime filled the air, its melody a stark contrast to the harsh claxons.

"Oh, well done," Belle exclaimed.

Another chime sounded. And again.

Ruth relaxed.

Three out of seven, she thought. *Kudos to them. That last round was a toughie.*

The wheel shuddered to a stop, and everyone disembarked the merry-go-round, their faces a mixture of triumph and disappointment.

"So, who are the champions?" Ruth asked as she joined Greg.

Helena's chin lifted a fraction. "I was successful, naturally."

Of course she was.

"Me too," Ray said, a smug grin plastered across his face. "Easy." He shot his brother a triumphant look.

"Failed," Orlando mumbled, his gaze fixed on his shoes.

"And you're the company accountant." Helena snorted. "Perhaps you should consider a different career."

"Who else got it right?" Belle looked between them.

Persephone raised a hand.

"This way, please." Liam led them back into the music room. Once they'd assembled, he picked up a piece of chalk and wrote the sequence of numbers on the blackboard in one long string.

"Thank goodness we don't have to recall them ourselves." Persephone rolled her eyes.

Liam stepped back, allowing them a clear view of his handiwork.

Belle's face fell. "The game isn't over?"

To Ruth, the numbers were a jumbled mess. She glanced at Greg, but he appeared equally perplexed.

"Care to shed some light on this enigma?" Persephone asked Liam.

He shook his head. "I'm afraid I'm unable to provide any further clues. I am merely a guide, following Master—"

"Master Marsh's instructions." Ray faked a yawn. "Sure you are, pal." He leaned against the piano, his arms crossed.

"I guarantee you, sir, I am unaware of the answers." Liam waved the card about. "As I say, I'm simply carrying out my designated tasks."

"Well, that's great." Elias looked around the room, his frustration evident. "We have a sequence of numbers. Now what? What are we supposed to do with them?" His eyes widened as they landed on the computer display on the piano next to Ray. "Nine minutes? That's all?"

"Perhaps the numbers add up to something." Belle rushed to the blackboard and began counting, using her fingers and muttering under her breath.

"Maybe it's a combination," Helena suggested. "A code.

Perhaps there's a hidden safe. A bonus of some kind." She looked around, her eyes gleaming.

Ruth's gaze swept over the numbers, but she still couldn't discern any pattern. The sequence was too long to be a simple combination.

Her attention shifted to the music room, lingering on the grand piano, the killer mannequin, and finally, the slumped figure of the pianist.

And then it hit her.

"Could the numbers represent musical notes?" Ruth turned to the others, a spark of hope igniting within her.

Ray frowned and straightened. "Musical notes? I suppose it's possible." He sounded dubious but intrigued.

"Let me see." Orlando hurried to the blackboard. "We could substitute one to four with notes C, D, E, and F. Which would give us . . ." He scribbled the letters beneath the corresponding numbers. "And then five, six, seven . . ."

"Eight could be a half rest," Ray suggested. "Nine a full rest?"

"We're assuming a standard four-four time signature?" Orlando looked around for confirmation, but received mostly blank stares in return. "I think it must be."

Ruth grabbed a blank sheet of music and a pencil, handing them to him.

"Thank you." Orlando meticulously transcribed the numbers, transforming the once seemingly random sequence into musical notation.

"Hurry." Belle wrung her hands. "Less than eight minutes remaining."

"We certainly like cutting it fine," Persephone said.

"Done." Orlando stepped back, staring at the sheet.

"Now what?" Belle asked.

"We play it, of course," Ray said.

"The pianist was playing something when she murdered him." Ruth pointed to the femme fatale mannequin.

"Perhaps our pianist friend was on the verge of uncovering something through his music. Something that got him killed."

Ray took the transcribed notes and set them on the piano stand. "Help me with this guy, would you?" he said to his brother.

Together, they manoeuvred the dead pianist out of the way.

"I'll play it." Orlando stepped forward, flexing his fingers.

Belle's eyes darted between her husband and the gun-wielding mannequin.

"Don't tempt fate, Orlando," Helena warned. "Knowing Clarence, anything is possible."

"He might be a bit . . . eccentric," Elias said, "but Clarence is not psychotic."

Greg muttered under his breath, "Famous last words." He took a large step back and gestured for Ruth to do the same.

She hesitated, torn between curiosity and a healthy dose of self-preservation. But Ruth couldn't help but agree with the lad, so joined him, and watched in tense silence.

Belle bit her lip. "It's just a game," she murmured. "Right?"

"Five minutes," Elias announced, his voice tense. "It's now or never."

Orlando spared his brother a quick glance, took a deep breath, and rested his fingers on the keys.

The music that filled the room was . . . strange, to say the least. To Ruth's ears, it sounded like a random collection of notes, devoid of any discernible melody or rhythm. But something about it sent a shiver down her spine. It was creepy. Unsettling.

She studied the reactions of the others, but none seemed to recognise the disjointed tune. They all looked as bewildered and disturbed as she felt.

Orlando reached the end of the short piece, his fingers lingering on the final note. "Anything happen?"

The others looked around and shook their heads.

To Ruth's relief, the mannequin remained motionless, its gun still lowered.

"We've got less than four minutes remaining." Ray placed a hand on his brother's shoulder. "Try it again."

Ruth's attention shifted to Liam. For a fleeting moment, a ghost of a smile played at the corners of his mouth. *He knows what's about to happen.* She was sure of it.

Orlando played the sequence again, but still, nothing changed. He sighed, his shoulders slumping. "It's not working. We're missing something."

"Maybe the killer removed part of the score," Ruth said, her mind racing. *Why else shoot the pianist midperformance?* There had to be a connection.

She hurried over to the slumped mannequin and checked his pockets and clothing. Finding nothing, Ruth crossed the room and stopped in front of the killer. "Why are you still here?"

"Perhaps this is a moment frozen in time," Helena suggested. "The precise second the pianist was shot?"

"Three minutes," Elias said.

Ruth's eyes narrowed. "The killer has lowered her gun, and the pianist has had time to collapse. This scene suggests some time has passed since the murder. It's not a snapshot of the exact moment of death."

"The killer is lingering for a reason?" Belle asked.

"Exactly." Ruth rubbed her chin. "If the pianist wasn't playing something important, why silence him?"

"She wanted to prevent him from finishing it," Orlando said.

"But how could he?" Persephone's brow furrowed in thought. "He has no sheet music. Was he playing from memory?"

Ruth widened her eyes. She looked over at the other mannequin musicians. Several of them now faced the killer. Had they heard the shot? No doubt. But had they also seen her take something from the pianist? It was as if the killer, once back behind the curtain, had turned to the room again, ready to shoot anyone who may challenge her.

Ruth checked under the mannequin's coat, and her fingers brushed something tucked into her waistband. She pulled out a folded sheet of paper. "Here we are." Opening it revealed a handwritten musical score. "The killer must have taken this from the pianist." She handed the sheet to Orlando, who placed it next to the one they'd already transcribed.

He studied the two sheets for a moment. "There's gaps in this one." He indicated several missing musical notes in the mannequin's score. "If I transpose the notes we uncovered across, filling those gaps . . ." He screwed up his face in concentration, glancing between the two sheets.

"Last try." Elias indicated the screen. "Less than two minutes."

Ruth attempted to pry the gun from the mannequin's fingers, but it was no use.

Greg, clearly understanding, rushed over. Together they tried to spin the mannequin around. But it wouldn't budge.

Greg grabbed its arm and heaved. "It's mechanical," he

said, his voice strained. "Made of steel." He let go. "Locked in position though. No way to move it."

Ruth ushered him back.

Ray, his face pale but determined, nudged his brother away from the piano. "I'll do it." Before anyone could protest, music flowed from Ray's fingertips, and this time, it was different. The notes, once a meaningless jumble, now formed a haunting, beautiful melody, filled with both sorrow and a strange sense of peace.

Orlando stared. "I recognise it. That's—"

The arm on the killer mannequin snapped up, and the gun fired.

17

Belle screamed, making Ruth's heart leap into her throat. For a moment, the room seemed to tilt. Then, she, Orlando, Persephone, and Elias rushed toward Ray.

He stood frozen, eyes wide, staring at the killer mannequin. "I'm all right." Ray held up a trembling hand. "I am fine. It's okay. Knew that would happen." Even so, he sucked in a breath, his gaze fixed on the smoking gun in the mannequin's hand. "Must— Must be a blank firer. Just as I thought. Nothing to worry about. All part of the game."

Elias, already at the piano, swept his sharp gaze over the polished wood and the wall behind it. "Or," he said, his voice low and heavy with suspicion, "the shot missed."

"The timer has stopped," Helena announced. "So it worked."

Ruth joined Elias, searching for any sign of a bullet hole. Nothing.

Thank goodness, she thought, relief washing over her. Ray was right. It had been a theatrical, albeit unsettling, part of Clarence's game.

Her attention darted across the room, settling on Greg.

He stood with his arms crossed, a deep scowl etched into his face. His scepticism mirrored her own. Clearly, he wasn't buying the *"it's all part of the game"* excuse any more than she was.

Belle clutched at her chest. "Clarence has gone too far," she said, her voice thin and reedy. "Way too far." She shot a nervous glance at Helena. "Last year was nothing like this. I think you're right: he's lost his mind." Her eyes lingered on the gun. "So dangerous. Even if it was a blank. It nearly gave me a heart attack."

"Maybe that's his plan." Helena shook her head. "The old fool wants to frighten us to death."

"Or make us give up." Persephone lifted her chin. "Scare us into submission. After all, there's the ultimate prize riding on this. Maybe he has no intention of handing the shares over. Wants us to walk away. Call it quits."

There was something odd in the way Persephone spoke that made her suspicious—almost as if she'd delivered lines. Deadpan. Emotionless.

Is it the shock?

And Elias appeared unimpressed by the events, watching everyone with passivity.

Ray, his colour returning, balled his fists. "We won't give him the satisfaction."

Ruth understood their determination to win the game, to claim the Marsh fortune, but she didn't think it was worth risking their lives.

Orlando put a comforting arm around Belle's shoulders. "You know what he's like, darling," he said, his voice soothing. "Thrives on other people's misery. It's a power thing. Don't let him get to you."

Helena nodded in agreement, but her eyes remained cold, her gaze fixed on the killer mannequin as if daring it to fire again. "It's all part of his nasty little game," she muttered.

Ray, seemingly recovered from his near-death experience, glanced around the room, his impatience evident. "Well, what exactly did I risk my life for?"

A low hum filled the air, and the ghostly mannequins sprang to life, their instruments emitting a sombre melody. Violinists swayed, cellists bowed, and the drummer's skeletal arms beat a haunting rhythm on the timpani, its head nothing more than a skull.

Even the piano, as if played by a phantom, filled the room with melancholic notes, while its pianist still slumped on the stool, head lolling to one side.

The sudden, eerie music sent a shiver down Ruth's spine. She spun on her heel, her eyes searching every corner, every shadow for anything out of place or unusual.

Well, more unusual than a room full of animatronic ghosts playing instruments. The spectral musicians and music set her teeth on edge.

Greg, however, grinned, seeming to enjoy the macabre show, his eyes bright with amusement. He stepped closer to Ruth and murmured in her ear, "This is pretty awesome, right?"

A minute later, the room fell back to silence.

Helena put her hands on her hips. "And what, pray tell, was the point of that?"

As if in answer, a curtain next to the killer mannequin pulled to one side. Ruth peered over the mannequin's shoulder. "What's this?"

Greg was instantly next to her. He followed her gaze, his eyebrows shooting up.

Outside, beyond the windows, a line of lights now

glowed orange in the late-morning gloom. They led to a workmen's tent adjacent to the house.

"They weren't lit up earlier," Ruth said. "I would've seen them." She pulled back the curtains, revealing a previously unnoticed door to the side. She turned to the others. "It seems Clarence would like us to go outside."

"I'll fetch coats." Liam, ever the efficient and silent host, marched out of the room.

Ruth looked back at the path, the tent, and the shadowy expanse of the gardens beyond. Everything seemed peaceful.

Unease knotted her stomach.

If Clarence is willing to go as far as scaring us with a gunshot, what else is he capable of?

Liam returned with identical dark green parkas.

With a mix of apprehension and curiosity, Ruth accepted the offered coat. She couldn't shake the feeling they were being herded into new danger.

Once the group were bundled up against the chill, she opened the door and stepped out. A biting wind whipped at Ruth's face, sending another shiver down her spine. She pulled the coat tighter and hurried along the path, the others close behind.

"Be careful, Grandma," Greg said as she reached the entrance of the tent.

Ruth hesitated, her hand hovering over the flap. "Would someone else care to go first?" she asked, her voice betraying a hint of nervousness.

Normally, she would gladly make calculated decisions, or what her daughter often lovingly referred to as "insane risks that will wind up getting you killed *one day,*" but Ruth wasn't keen on any more jump scares.

The others, however, seemed content to let her take the

lead. They exchanged nervous glances, their faces a mixture of apprehension, curiosity, and mild amusement.

Greg, obviously sensing his grandmother's rare hesitation, sighed and stepped forward. He was about to push past Ruth—Greg knew he was usually the canary in the coal mine when it came to these situations—but she ducked under the tent flap.

The interior was surprisingly bare. A single lantern hung from a middle pole, casting flickering shadows on the canvas walls.

On the left, a sturdy wooden door, set into the house's wall, stood ajar. A set of steps led down into darkness.

Ruth's eyes narrowed. "A basement?" she murmured. "A very creepy basement." She edged closer, her curiosity piqued, senses on high alert. The musty smell of damp earth hung in the air.

"There was a flood."

Ruth's heart leapt into her throat, and she spun.

Helena stood at the entrance to the tent, a smug smile on her face. "Sorry, Mrs Morgan," she said with faux regret. "I didn't mean to scare you."

"A burst water pipe." Ray ducked under the tent flap and joined his wife. "In the basement."

She stepped away from him.

One by one, a few of the others entered the tent; Greg, his face pale but resolute, stuck close to Ruth's side. Orlando looked around with apprehension. Liam, ever the picture of stoic calm, remained near the entrance, his gaze fixed on a point somewhere beyond the canvas walls.

"It's been quite the ordeal," Ray continued. "They've been working down there for months."

"Months?" Ruth frowned. "Must have caused a lot of damage." She glanced back at the door, her curiosity overcoming her apprehension. "Anyone been down there since? Other than tradespeople, I mean."

"Why ever would we?" Helena sniffed. "I like to keep my feet dry, thank you very much."

"I hate basements." Belle's voice came from outside the tent, small and wavering. "No way I'm going down there."

"We'll stay right here, dear," Persephone replied. "If there's a scream, we'll assume the worst and run in the opposite direction."

Greg smiled.

However, solving the game had led them inside this tent. Which meant it was also part of Clarence's grand plan.

Ruth stared at Liam. He stood there, impassive, unreadable. Surely he knew what awaited them below. He must be privy to the work being done, to the secrets hidden beneath the house. But his expression revealed nothing.

Resigning herself to the inevitable, Ruth turned back to the door. Someone had strung a series of LED bulbs along the walls of the stairwell, leading down into the subterranean rooms. They'd also mounted a temporary switch nearby—a recent addition.

Ruth flicked it on, and the LEDs bathed the steps in a bright, clinical light. It appeared too newly fitted, too deliberate, to be for the benefit of the workmen.

Clearly sensing impending danger, Greg leaned in to her ear. "Send someone else down first."

"I'd be happy to oblige." Ray stepped forward.

Orlando, his face pale, gripped his arm. "No, I'll do it. Let's see what Clarence has in store for us." He glanced at Liam, a quick, questioning look, but Liam remained impassive, his expression still unreadable.

With a resigned sigh, Orlando strode through the door

and started down the steps, disappearing into the darkness below.

Ruth followed close behind, her pulse quickening with each step. Greg stuck to her like a shadow, his hand hovering near his pocket where she knew he kept his phone with its built-in torch at the ready.

Ray, Helena, and Liam brought up the rear, Ray's face showing hints of curiosity, Helena's a mask of distrust.

At the bottom of the steps, they found themselves in a wide hallway. A stone archway, its edges worn smooth with time, loomed at the far end, beckoning them forward.

As with the stairs, the way ahead was well lit, leaving no danger of tripping on the uneven flagstones. This wasn't the dark, cobwebbed cellar Ruth had been expecting.

Greg marched past Ruth, his long legs making short work of the distance to the archway, and peered around the corner. A sharp intake of breath, and he stiffened. "What the —? No way."

Fearing the worst, Ruth joined Greg at the archway, and her eyes widened in astonishment as she took in the sight before them.

The vast room beyond—held up by immense rough-hewn stone pillars—was missing its floor. Workers had meticulously removed and stacked the flagstones, setting them neatly to one side.

But it wasn't the missing floor that stole Ruth's breath. It was what they'd uncovered beneath.

The workers had also removed layers of dirt to a depth of several feet, revealing a magnificent mosaic floor. Composed of what must be hundreds of thousands of tiny intricately patterned tiles, it depicted a scene of breath-taking detail and beauty.

Around the outside were all manner of mythical creatures, half-men and half-beasts, their bodies defined in a riot of colour and movement. Centaurs, their powerful equine bodies rendered in shades of ochre and sienna, galloped alongside satyrs, their mischievous grins frozen in time.

A fierce lion, its mane a blaze of gold and orange, stood midroar, its teeth bared in a silent snarl.

Flowers, their petals a masterpiece of swirling mosaic, bloomed around the creatures, their colours as vibrant as the day they were laid.

And, if all that wasn't enough, in the middle was a man, his face youthful and serene, strumming a golden lyre.

Greg edged farther into the room, his jaw practically scraping along the floor, his gaze darting from one detail to another, drinking it all in. "It's Roman." He waved a hand at the image of the man with the lyre. "Orpheus," he breathed. "Late second century. It's— It's—"

"Going to make us a fortune," Ray finished.

Orlando and Persephone remained by the archway, watching as Greg stumbled around the unearthed masterpiece.

"Hadfield Hall was built on top of a Roman villa." Liam, ever the picture of passive composure, was the last to enter the room, his voice calm and measured. "The workmen discovered it while repairing a section of the floor." He gestured above their heads at a series of thick lead water pipes that snaked across the ceiling, their surfaces dulled with age. On the largest, a newly repaired section was visible —the old lead replaced with gleaming copper.

"Is that why JT was here?" Ray asked Liam. "I thought it had something to do with that old church."

By "JT," Ruth knew he meant the famous archaeologist Clarence had mentioned before: Professor JT Wilson.

"Why on earth did Clarence and Winifred keep this from us?" Persephone demanded, her voice a mix of disbelief and outrage. "Wait." She glared at Orlando, her expression accusing. "You knew about this? Why didn't you say anything at our last shareholders' meeting?"

Orlando shook his head. "I only knew the work was expensive and time-consuming, but I had no idea this is what they were doing." He shrugged. "Grandmama only told me it was essential work, and to keep paying the bills."

"Never mind all that," Ray said. "Just think of how many people would pay to see this. Look at the bigger picture." He adjusted his parka. "We'll uncover as much as we can, set up a gift shop, guided tours, that sort of thing. People will come from all over the world to see this."

"The hotel is already at capacity," Helena retorted. "We couldn't possibly take on any more guests."

"We could give out day passes," Ray suggested in a low voice, his gaze still fixed on the mosaic floor. "An extra charge on top of park admission. Limited numbers, of course."

Ruth, though not immune to the allure of such a discovery, felt a surge of protectiveness toward the fragile beauty.

She empathised with Greg's awe, his wonder, something he'd inherited from his grandfather, and she also recognised the importance of preserving such a find.

Greg's anger at Ray's crass money-making comments was evident in the set of his jaw. He wandered off to the far wall of the basement and knelt in front. "It continues under here," he said, his voice echoing in the vast chamber. He ran his fingers lightly over the rough stone of the basement wall, careful not to touch the edge of the mosaic.

"It extends into the garden," Liam said. "Once the archaeologists and workmen are finished here, they'll continue their dig outside and see what else they can uncover."

Helena glared at him. "So, you knew about this."

Ruth scanned the rest of the large room. *Why has Clarence sent us down* here? Other than to cause conflict? *Or is that the whole point?*

Greg called out, "Hey. Look at this." He straightened up and pointed to a worn leather bag dangling from one of the old water pipes, its drawstrings tied around a rusty valve.

Ray untied the bag from the pipe, loosened the drawstrings, and peered inside. A slow smile spread across his face. "It seems we have a new puzzle." Ray removed a tarnished silver key.

"What on earth does that open?" Helena said.

Ray flipped the key over in his hand. "I have no idea. I've never seen it before."

Orlando furrowed his brow. "Why put it down here?"

Ray turned to Ruth. "What do you make of this, Mrs Morgan?"

She took the key, her fingers tracing its simple design. It wasn't ornate or intricate as one might expect from such an old house. The small key seemed unremarkable, with no inscriptions or clues as to what lock it might fit.

Ruth went to return the key, but Ray stopped her with a gesture.

"Keep hold of it," he said. "We were led down here for a reason. I strongly suspect we'll need that key in the third game."

"Clarence is obviously toying with us." Helena jabbed a finger at the elaborate mosaic floor, her face tight. "Don't you see?" Her eyes darted around the room. "When we win these stupid games and this house is finally ours, I'll—"

Orlando cut her off with a raised hand. "Clarence said he's handing over his shares in the park, not the house."

Ray frowned. "They're bundled together. The park and house. They always have been."

Orlando shook his head.

Ray's eyebrows shot up. "They're not?"

"Grandmama and Clarence owned the house equally." Orlando let out a breath, and his gaze fell to the floor. "When they turned it into a hotel, the covenant stated Clarence could live here for the rest of his life, but he signed full ownership over to Grandmama."

"What?" Helena shrieked. "Are you telling us Clarence owns nothing?"

"Only the park shares, and his magic collection," Orlando said. "He even signed over his cars to Grandmama. She tried to stop him, but he insisted. Told her to sell them, if she wished." He then murmured, "She did sell a couple."

Now Ruth understood where the early inheritance money had come from.

"When did this happen?" Ray asked, appearing to want to sound casual.

"A few months ago."

Ray stared at him. "Clarence and Grandmama have been at each other's throats for years. Why the sudden change of heart?"

"Clarence wanted to make amends," Orlando said in a low voice. "He's always felt terrible about what happened at the lake."

"What about it?" Ruth asked, unable to help herself.

Orlando glanced at her. "The way he didn't try to save her when they were kids."

"Grandmama almost drowned," Ray said, mistaking Ruth's stunned expression for confusion. "Clarence remained on shore, frozen, and she somehow managed to crawl out on her own. It was a close call. Never forgave him." He shrugged. "Guess the guilt finally caught up with the old fool."

Why did Clarence lie about that to me? Ruth thought.

She pocketed the silver key and glanced at Greg. He stared at Orlando and Ray with a mixture of curiosity and bewilderment. This casually revealed news put a fresh twist on things.

Liam, silent throughout the exchange, shuffled forward, his face betraying a rare sign of emotion: disbelief. He looked to Helena, as if expecting her to say something next.

What had his relationship with Winifred been like? He'd worked for Clarence for years; surely he was privy to their secrets. However, judging by his expression, these revelations surprised him too, and it was apparent he only trusted Helena.

Liam opened his mouth to say something, but she shot him a sharp, venomous look, so he retreated. He composed himself, and his face became an impassive mask once more.

Ruth's mind raced. This revelation about the house, this unexpected twist of ownership . . . *Does it somehow factor into the games and Winifred's murder?* She had assumed Clarence included the park shares as a grand prize to force them all to play, despite Winifred's death, and therefore reveal their skills.

Why didn't Clarence say something earlier?

18

In the damp, cold basement of Hadfield Hall, Ray rounded on his brother. "Grandmama is dead. If Clarence signed his ownership over to her, what happens to this place now? Does it go back to him?"

Orlando kept his gaze fixed on the floor. "No. It goes to me," he mumbled.

Helena's face contorted with rage. "What? How can— When those two die, everything goes to us. R-Right?" she sputtered, looking from Orlando to her husband. "The shares *and* the house."

Ray threw back his head and roared with laughter, the sound echoing through the basement. "Amazing." He clapped Orlando on the back hard enough to make him stumble. "Good for you, brother. Good for you."

Liam stared, his expression a mixture of resentment and jealousy, but it was gone in a flash.

Helena glared at Orlando. "You conniving little—"

"Enough." Ray stepped between them. "Leave it, Helena."

"He'll gamble it all away," she said, her voice tight.

Helena waved a hand at Orlando. "You know what he's like. He's pathetic. Has no control."

Ray chuckled. "So what? Who cares? We still have the park."

Ruth, however, distinctly remembered Ray's reaction during his conversation with Winifred the day before; the genuine concern in his voice about his brother's gambling addiction and the anger about him inheriting a large sum of money.

Why the sudden change of heart? Has Ray resigned himself to the inevitable? After all, his primary focus was acquiring those theme park shares so he could carry out his expansion plans.

"I'm sorry." Orlando's gaze moved to the mosaic floor. "I thought you knew." He met Ray's eyes. "Grandmama insisted. Said if anything were to happen to Marsh Park, at least Hadfield Hall would remain in the family. Clarence doesn't want anyone else to know. I only found out when I started on the accounts."

Ray stared at him, his earlier amusement gone. "You never told me. Why did they cut me out? What did I do to deserve this?"

"There appear to be a lot of secrets in this family," Helena murmured through gritted teeth, her gaze now fixed on Liam.

He shifted uncomfortably under her stare. His hands, usually clasped calmly behind his back, fidgeted at his sides.

Where does he fit into all this? Ruth mused. *Has Clarence promised Liam shares in one of the companies? For his years of service? And has this new piece of information now somehow affected that agreement? Is that why Liam forgave Clarence and puts up with all the nonsense?*

Ruth turned her thoughts to Clarence Marsh. Judging by

the interplay between the siblings, shareholders, and especially Helena, their resentment toward him was palpable, and it clearly went both ways.

She had only met the man briefly, yet Ruth could see how his manipulative gamesmanship would foster such animosity. For a moment, she regretted getting involved. He was like a puppet master, pulling strings, watching the drama unfold with cruel amusement.

But is there something else at play here? Something deeper, more sinister, than just sibling rivalry and a thirst for power?

"Come on." Ray clapped his hands, his voice sharp, cutting through the tense silence. "I've had enough excitement for one morning. We could all use a breather. I'll see if anyone else wants drinks in the sitting room." He marched out of the basement, leaving the others to follow.

Helena checked her watch. "I'll have a lie down before lunch." The colour had drained from her face. "I feel a migraine coming on." Her gaze lingered on Ruth for a moment, and then she left too.

"The third game starts this afternoon, right?" Orlando asked Liam, his voice subdued. "Usual time?"

Liam bowed his head. "Two o'clock, sir."

Orlando hesitated, mumbled something about needing a wash, and scurried off, apparently eager to escape the confines of the underground room and the weight of the revealed secrets.

Ruth approached Greg.

He had wandered back to the mosaic floor, his expression full of wonder. "This is really incredible."

Ruth smiled and placed a hand on her grandson's arm. "When this is all over, if Clarence is happy with the outcome, he'll honour his promise and put in a good word with Professor JT Wilson. You could work with him and the other archaeologists here." Her gaze swept over the ancient tiles. "I guess this is the reason Clarence knows him."

Greg's eyes lit up. "Do you really think there's a chance that'll happen?"

Before Ruth could answer, Liam cleared his throat, holding out an envelope. Surprised he hadn't left already, she took it from him.

Liam bowed his head. "Excuse me, madam." Without another word, he strode along the hallway and disappeared up the stairs, leaving Ruth and Greg alone in the basement.

Greg watched Ruth open the envelope and slide out a sheet of thick cream-coloured paper. The handwriting was elegant, almost calligraphic—definitely Clarence's.

Ruth read the message aloud, but only for his ears. "'One of the shareholders must have glimpsed Orlando's computer screen. They not only memorised the figures within the accounts but also realised there were discrepancies. I believe Orlando embezzled money from us, and the blackmailer took this evidence to Winifred. CM.'" She lowered her voice further. "The early inheritance. The blackmailer told Winifred what Orlando did, and she paid the money back into the business for him. Sold a couple of those cars and tried to cover his tracks."

"But it wasn't enough to stop them." Greg looked toward the stairs. "Does Ray know that's why Orlando got the inheritance money from Winifred?"

Ruth pursed her lips. "Not sure."

"Are you any closer to figuring out who blackmailed and murdered Winifred?" Greg's eyes darted to the stairs. "Can't be Belle, right?"

Ruth shook her head. "She was the first one to fail the memory game, and knew no Latin."

"Orlando?" Greg asked. "Ray? Do you think they seriously could kill their own family?"

"I don't know." Ruth shrugged. "Anything's possible." Her attention moved back to Clarence's note. Below the text was another crudely drawn map of Hadfield Hall, this time with Orlando's office circled in bold black ink. "That's near Winifred's office. I know the way." She returned the paper to the envelope and tucked it into her pocket. "Come on," Ruth said, already moving toward the stairs. "We have work to do."

"Grandma, it's almost lunchtime," Greg moaned as he trailed after her along the basement hallway. "Can't we do this after we've eaten?" His stomach rumbled for emphasis.

"Lunch is another two hours away," Ruth said. "I'm sure you can hold on for a while longer."

Leave it to him to prioritise his stomach over a mystery.

Ruth clenched her fists, determined to get a look at Orlando's office while most of the others were occupied in the sitting room. "We must figure out how someone saw his computer screen."

Besides, the ample time before the last game would give Ruth the opportunity to process the information she had gathered so far and see if any pieces of the puzzle fit to point to a potential culprit with any real certainty.

They climbed the basement stairs, and as they emerged from the tent, Ruth noticed the lights leading back to the house were now off.

How could anyone else know we found the key in the basement? It had to be Liam. This was another clue that he knew more about the games than he let on.

Is he a willing participant in Clarence's machinations, or is Liam being manipulated too?

Ruth was beginning to suspect Winifred's death was the tip of a very deep, very dark family iceberg.

Back in the house, they shed their coats and navigated the maze of corridors, their footsteps muffled by the thick runner carpets. The house was eerily quiet, the only sound the distant murmur of voices from the sitting room.

Orlando's office was larger than Ruth had expected, lined with shelves overflowing with leather-bound volumes. A faint layer of dust suggested they were more for show than actual use.

An oak desk dominated the middle of the room, its surface surprisingly tidy, as if meticulously curated to project an image of order. It was something Ruth hadn't expected from Orlando.

Perhaps he was a man who desperately wanted to appear in control, even when someone may have murdered his grandmother because of his recklessness with money.

"There's nothing here." Greg's voice broke through Ruth's thoughts. He shuffled over to the bookcase and pulled out a volume, squinting at the title. "*Ancient Tax Laws of the Byzantine Empire*. Riveting." He opened it. "The pages are blank."

That confirms it, Ruth thought. *Definitely for show.*

She made her way around the desk and sat in a large leather chair. The computer screen faced away from the door, which meant the only way for someone to have seen it would have been to . . .

Ruth spun in the chair and faced the window. It overlooked a compact walled garden with raised flower beds, several benches, and a vegetable patch. Ruth stood. "Hmm."

"What is it?" Greg joined her at the window.

"Someone must have been standing out there." Ruth pointed to a bench between rose bushes, positioned to offer a clear view of the desk. "It's the only way to have seen what was on Orlando's computer monitor."

The question was, who?

Greg motioned to the computer. "Or they got into it remotely."

Ruth considered this. "Do any of them strike you as a hacker?" She thought of the other guests, but none seemed likely candidates. "And wouldn't they need access to his computer? Or his passwords?"

Greg shrugged. "Could've hired someone. It's not as if they can't afford to."

"True," Ruth conceded. "But to do that, they would've needed to have suspected Orlando's embezzlement in the first place."

"Maybe they did," Greg said. "Orlando's gambling doesn't seem to be a secret."

Ruth pointed to the bench outside. "I think that's more likely. They caught a glimpse from there." She squinted. "It is close enough to make out numbers on his screen."

"But who?" Greg's brow furrowed as he scanned the gardens, as if hoping the culprit would magically appear.

Ruth leaned forward, peered left and right, and then pulled back. "No idea." She sighed. "It's a dead end. At least for now. Let's go." She turned to leave and froze.

Liam stood in the doorway. "What are you doing in here?" He glanced over his shoulder.

"Helping your employer figure some things out." Ruth motioned to the walled garden. "Who has access to that?"

Liam stared for a few seconds and then straightened his tie. "Master Ray, Master Orlando, Mistress Helena, and Mistress Belle. And Master Clarence, of course. The family."

"Not Persephone or Elias?" Greg asked.

Liam shook his head.

Given the winners of the games so far, if they eliminated Persephone and Elias, that only left Ray and Helena as suspects.

Could one of them really have murdered Winifred?

Ruth smiled. "Thank you, Liam." She went to leave, but he held up a hand, stopping her.

"Sorry, madam. I've just remembered, there is another person who has access to the garden. But—" He hesitated, looked over his shoulder, and swallowed. "I don't think I can say—"

"Mike the porter?" Ruth inclined her head. "Nadia?"

Liam stared, his lips parted.

Ruth lowered her voice. "It's okay. We know that business with her was all part of the game."

Liam seemed to gather himself. "Nadia is the one with access. She tends to the garden. It's her responsibility. She enjoys it. She asked Master Clarence if she could take on the responsibility a few months back." His eyes flitted to the window. "Is there a problem? She mentioned seeing—"

"What's going on in here?" a voice boomed, making them all jump. Ray strode into the room, looking between them. "An impromptu meeting?" He smirked. "Planning a hostile takeover of the Marsh empire?"

How long has he been standing there? And how much has he overheard?

"We were passing, and the door was open." Ruth thrust a thumb over her shoulder. "The little private garden caught my eye. It's delightful."

"Isn't it?" Ray's eyes narrowed.

"Yes, well." Ruth cleared her throat. "I need to check on Merlin." As she and Greg headed back along the hallway, Ruth wondered what the next game would entail, and whether it could help her gather definitive proof.

So far, and even though everything had been circumstantial and hearsay, she was satisfied the net was closing in
on suspects—Ray, Helena, or . . . Nadia.

Back in her suite, Ruth ensured Merlin had fresh water, a
clean litter tray, and a generous helping of his favourite food.
"There you go, you spoiled, midnight-furred ball of loveli-
ness." She massaged his ears, but Merlin seemed unimpressed
by her affections. "I know I've neglected you these past days,
but I promise to make it up to you once the madness is over."

As she washed, changed into a fresh outfit, and did her
makeup in preparation for the afternoon ahead, Ruth's
thoughts returned to Sonia and Nathaniel—the restaurant
owners from Hammersmith, London—and, of course, to the
poor murdered brunette.

Like Ruth at the time, the victim had been in her twenties, her life tragically cut short. Ruth couldn't imagine
having only lived a life one third the length of her own so
far. It seemed unfathomably cruel.

Back then, everyone assumed Sonia, the restaurant co-
owner and supposedly scorned wife, had murdered the
poor girl in a fit of jealous rage. Revenge for the affair with
her husband was motive enough.

However, Sonia's alibi checked out. CCTV footage
showed her working at the restaurant when the murder
occurred. The timestamps on the CCTV recordings backed
this up.

Her husband Nathaniel swiftly became the next suspect.

But that hadn't sat right with Ruth. People had always
known him as a placid man, unlikely to hurt a fly. Then

again, appearances could be deceiving. Killers didn't go around with "Murderer" tattooed on their foreheads.

Well, not all of them.

Often people looked normal, even charming. Which was what made some of the monsters even scarier—they blended in with society, their true nature hidden behind a mask of normalcy.

To complicate matters, the next day, someone had thrown a Molotov cocktail through the restaurant window. Luckily, a passing tourist caught the act on camera and reported it, preventing a major disaster.

The fire brigade extinguished the blaze before it caused significant damage. Only a few tables and chairs needed replacing, along with the window.

A coincidence? Someone attempting arson the very next day after the murder? Ruth thought not. It was too convenient, too calculated. There had to be a connection.

After the police checked the tourist's camera, the Molotov-throwing culprit had turned out to be the deceased woman's grieving brother, hell-bent on revenge.

It seemed like an open-and-shut case, but something bothered Ruth. She noticed a discrepancy in the time-stamps. The police had seized the restaurant's CCTV recording, but the footage supplied by the tourist had a different timestamp. They were two hours apart.

Sonia's alibi unravelled. She had killed the woman, returned to the restaurant, and tampered with the CCTV timestamps to show her working when in fact she'd been at the restaurant much earlier.

Unfortunately for her, she forgot to reset the time the next day, leaving all subsequent recordings with the same discrepancy.

That single mistake, that tiny oversight, was her undoing.

Ruth stared at her reflection in the bathroom mirror, her eyes unfocussed. She was searching for similar mistakes at Hadfield Hall, some oversight that could unravel the mystery of Winifred's death.

Several games were afoot at Hadfield Hall, some more obvious than others. Games orchestrated by Clarence, designed to reveal the killer. But the family and shareholders played their own games: manipulations, hidden agendas, and unspoken resentments simmering beneath the surface.

Clarence had put effort into the yearly games, but the others had made several remarks on the fact that this year's felt different in style, more intense.

Ruth shook herself, determined to focus. She strode from her suite and headed for the dining hall, her mind awhirl with unanswered questions.

To her astonishment, only Greg and Belle were present, tucking into salad and cold meats. And not any surprise at all was Greg's overflowing plate, piled high with seemingly every food on offer, threatening to scrape the ceiling. He waved vaguely at his grandmother, a bread roll clutched in his other hand, without interrupting his dedicated chewing.

"Hello, Mrs Morgan." Belle's voice came out a little raspy, and she was red and puffy around the eyes. "Nice rest?" Clearly, the day had taken its toll.

Ruth poured herself a large mug of tea, added five spoonfuls of sugar and at least half a dairy cow's worth of milk, before plonking herself down at the table. "Where is everyone?" She savoured its milky and, some would say, diabetes-inducing sweetness.

"Ray went back to Clarence's tower to talk sense into

him." Belle glanced over her shoulder and whispered, "Whatever that means."

Ruth raised an eyebrow. "And Helena?"

"I heard them arguing right before," Belle added. "She stormed off. I don't know where."

"Arguing about?"

Belle shrugged. "Not sure. They've been doing that a lot recently."

Greg, pausing his culinary assault, glanced at his grandmother. His expression suggested he knew the argument's subject, but he kept his thoughts to himself, returning to his lunch with gusto.

"And the others?" Ruth asked Belle, buttering two slices of bread and adding a generous slice of ham. "Where are they?"

"Orlando is in the drawing room." Belle sighed and nodded toward the closed door. "He said he wasn't hungry and wanted time to think." A worried crease formed between her brows. "I don't know where Persephone and Elias are. I haven't seen them since the tent, after Ray told us about Winifred's will and this house."

"How did they take it?" Ruth asked, cutting her sandwich into triangles.

Belle cringed. "Not well. Persephone especially. She looked ready to throttle someone."

"Are they staying here? Persephone and Elias?" Ruth took a bite of her ham sandwich.

Belle nodded. "Down the hall from us."

Ruth was about to enquire after Liam when he stumbled into the dining room, ashen-faced. He limped toward them, clutching his thigh.

19

S hocked by the sight of Liam staggering, Ruth leapt to her feet. "Greg."

Together, grandmother and grandson helped him into a chair.

"What on earth happened?" Ruth asked.

Liam slumped, gasping. "Accident. My fault. Really stupid of me." He lifted his hand from his thigh and winced.

Ruth knelt beside him, her gaze drawn to a tear in his trousers. A sharp blade, perhaps a knife, had sliced through the fabric and his skin. Although a shallow cut, it needed attention. "Who's the designated first-aider?"

Liam gave her a sheepish look. "That would be me."

"Well, you can't very well patch yourself up." Ruth stood. "Where's the nearest first aid kit?"

Liam gestured over his shoulder. "Reception office."

Greg was already halfway across the room. "I'll get it."

Ruth pulled up a chair next to Liam, examining the wound. Fortunately, stitches wouldn't be necessary. "What happened?"

Liam took a deep breath, then another. "It's really silly. Beyond stupid."

Belle handed him a glass of water, her brow creased with worry.

"Thank you." He took a sip.

Belle stepped back, wringing her hands as she stared at the wound.

Ruth had the distinct impression Belle was about to faint. "You should sit down."

Belle dropped into a chair at the table.

"I was unloading the dishwasher," Liam said to Ruth. "What with us being light on staff 'n' all, and then . . ." He swallowed, and a flush crept up his neck. "Like I say, it was stupid. I lifted out the cutlery tray"—he mimed the action—"turned around, and bumped into an open drawer. Dropped the whole lot." Liam winced again, glancing at his leg. "One of the knives caught me on its way to the floor. A freak accident."

Greg hurried back, carrying a large green first aid kit.

Ruth took it from him, set it on the table and snapped it open. "I need you to remove your trousers," she told Liam, pulling out antiseptic wipes and gauze pads.

He stared at her with wide, startled eyes.

Ruth sighed. "Liam, I can't very well dress your wound unless you remove your trousers."

His cheeks flushed crimson. "Right. Yes, of course."

"Do you want me to leave, Liam?" Belle giggled, her earlier anxiety forgotten. "I've seen your bare legs before, you know? Last summer, at the pool party. You wore those red shorts." She leaned over and lowered her voice. "Helena kept staring at you, like you were a prime cut of beef or something. Remember?"

Liam looked away and muttered, "No," as he slipped his trousers past his knees.

Ruth pulled on disposable gloves and inclined her head at Belle. "Did she really?"

Before Belle could answer, Ray strode into the room, his voice a low growl. "Has anyone seen Helena?"

Belle shrank into her chair, shaking her head.

Ray's gaze swept over the scene and landed on Ruth, now seated beside Liam, cleaning his wound. "What's going on? What happened?"

"Accident," Liam mumbled, his face no doubt matching the colour of the red shorts Belle had mentioned.

Ruth plucked a napkin from a nearby table and dropped it across Liam's lap. "Better?"

At that precise moment, Elias and Persephone chose to join the unusual gathering. Elias sauntered over to the coffee station, seemingly unperturbed, as though the sight of a half-dressed Liam in the middle of the dining room was a regular occurrence at Hadfield Hall.

Persephone, however, was a different story. She settled into a chair and poured herself a glass of water, her eyes never wavering from the scene. "How did this happen?"

"An accident in the kitchen." Ruth applied gauze and then bandaged Liam's leg. She mentally kicked herself. Taking Liam to the first aid kit would have been more discreet than bringing the kit to him, but she supposed also more painful for the poor guy.

Persephone's gaze, sharp as a hawk's, zeroed in on Ray. "And what of Clarence?" The question hung in the air, heavy with unspoken implications.

"Not answering." Ray huffed and settled into a chair. "Tried calling too." He snatched up a bread roll. "Silly old codger is playing us for fools." He bit into the roll and chewed, gauging their reactions. "I say we continue. Beat him at his own game. So to speak."

Elias poured a round of coffees and handed them out.

Helena glided into the room, but her step faltered when she laid eyes on Liam, and a small gasp escaped her lips.

"Accident. He's okay." Greg sat back at the table to finish his meal.

Concern flickered crossed Helena's features, but her usual hard-nosed expression quickly replaced it. She eyed the grandfather clock, and said in a loud voice, "Are we continuing?"

The door to the drawing room opened, and Orlando strolled in. "Of course. We must." His attention lingered on his brother.

Ray studied him, as though about to say something, then turned back to Liam, who was now hastily pulling up his trousers. "You should be more careful, old fellow." Ray accepted a steaming mug of coffee from Elias. "You're our host, after all." He took a sip. "Can't have you falling at the last hurdle."

Ruth rose and rested a hand on Liam's shoulder. "Try not to move too much. Take it easy." She pulled off the disposable gloves.

"Thank you." He looked down at the tear in his trousers. "I'll change into a new pair." Liam stood, staggered, and winced. "I think I must have twisted my ankle too."

"Greg, help him to his room, please," Ruth said.

He polished off the last of his meal and escorted Liam from the dining room.

"Poor Liam," Belle said softly. "I hope he'll be all right."

"In a household such as this," Elias said in clear amusement, "danger lurks around every corner." He waggled his fingers. "We'll all be ghosts soon enough."

"Can we show some respect?" Orlando sat next to his wife and took a coffee. "Grandmama only died yesterday."

"I loved Winifred as much as you, boy," Elias snarled, his jovial mask gone. "Don't ever question it."

Orlando glared back.

"We all did," Helena said in the least sincere tone imaginable. Her gaze drifted to the grandfather clock again. "Twenty minutes until game three."

"But without Liam to guide us," Belle said, "how can we proceed?"

"He hasn't exactly done much guiding this year." Persephone sniffed. "I'm sure we'll muddle through."

"I'll check on him." Helena pushed back her chair.

"No need." Ray waved her back down. "I'll do it." He stood, offered his wife a smile that didn't reach his eyes, and strode from the room.

"What's going on between you two now?" Belle blurted, voicing what everyone else in the room was thinking.

Helena sipped her coffee. "He's in one of his moods, that's all." She shot Orlando a look of annoyance. "After everything, is it any wonder?"

Ruth, however, wasn't convinced. The tension between husband and wife was palpable, and she had a feeling it ran far deeper than what had happened in the basement. Also, from what Belle had said before, they'd been at each other's throats for a long while. Something was amiss with the couple, something that extended beyond the events of the past few days.

Helena rose from the table, her movements graceful despite the tension radiating from her.

"Where are you going?" Belle asked.

"To powder my nose. I'll meet you in the hallway before the next game." And with that, she glided from the room.

Seizing the opportunity, Ruth addressed the others, keeping her voice calm and measured. "Why would Winifred cut Ray from her will? Was there a history of animosity between them?"

"Absolutely not," Persephone said, her voice firm. "Winifred loved both boys equally."

"Do we know that for sure?" Elias looked at Orlando, his expression sceptical. "Not to doubt you, old boy, but until probate starts and we see Winifred's will, it's hearsay."

"Whatever happens," Orlando said, "I'll sign half over to my brother."

Belle took his hand and squeezed it, her eyes shining with adoration. "That's why I love you. You're so kind."

Ruth sat back and rubbed her chin. It still didn't add up. *If Winifred treated her grandsons equally, why cut one out of her will?* As a mother and grandmother, Ruth couldn't imagine doing such a thing.

Persephone fixed her with a level gaze. "Is this the retired police officer in you speaking?"

Belle's jaw dropped. "You're a retired cop? Really?"

Ruth didn't need to ask how exactly Persephone knew. Either Clarence or Winifred had shared that information with her, which had first come from Ruth's sister. "Actually, I was sacked."

Belle laughed, then straightened her face when she saw Ruth was serious.

It wasn't a big deal, although it created unnecessary tension. Helena was trying to stir the pot, create suspicion. *But why? If Greg or I win the games, would that snatch away their chance at the shares?*

Elias cleared his throat. "You think someone pushed Winifred into that river, Mrs Morgan?"

Belle's hand flew to her mouth, while Orlando's expression remained unreadable.

Ruth chose her next words carefully. "That will be up to the police and the coroner."

"But it was an accident." Belle glanced at her husband, her eyes wide and uncertain. "That's what they said."

"To think otherwise would be absurd." Persephone shoved her coffee cup aside. "We mustn't start ridiculous rumours."

An uncomfortable silence descended, the only sound the ticking of the grandfather clock.

Ruth's phone vibrated in her pocket. She surreptitiously removed it and, keeping it hidden, read the display:

HADFIELD HALL
Calling

Ruth stared.

"Everything all right?" Elias asked.

Her head snapped up. "What? Oh, yes. Fine. Thank you." Ruth swallowed. "If you'll excuse me." She rose and hastily left the room.

As her phone continued to buzz, Ruth hurried from the dining room, through reception, and into the back office. She answered the call. "Hello?"

"Mrs Morgan," came a low, raspy voice, barely above a whisper and hard to make out. "Clarence Marsh."

"Oh. Hi. How are you?" Ruth dropped into the chair.

"I've been better." Clarence coughed. "I gather you're about to start the last game. I thought I would give you the next piece of evidence myself." There came a short pause, and then he continued in a hoarse whisper, "The person who murdered Winifred cheats at the Marsh Game. You'll see what it is. We play every Christmas. I never figured out how, or who did such a rotten thing, but someone among us had a large side bet with Orlando for the past two Christmases running. He refused to tell Winifred who it was. This is what forced Orlando to steal money from the business, getting himself deeper into trouble, unwilling or unable to ask for help. Cheating at the last game alone isn't enough to point a finger, I think several of them have cheated at one time or another, but combining the results from the previous two games with this next one should give you a definitive idea. The killer knew what they were doing and how he'd react. They played Orlando."

Ruth stared into space. "Orlando lost, both times, forcing him to dip into the family finances?"

"Precisely. I have the proof of what they did, but I still need you to figure out who the perpetrator is." Clarence hung up.

Ruth huffed out a breath, pocketed her phone, and composed herself.

The overlapping winners from the first two games were Ray, Helena, Persephone, and Elias. If she could focus on those four and figure out which one cheated, she'd know who the murderer was likely to be. After that, all Ruth needed was concrete evidence. Clarence claimed to have some, but she needed something more concrete.

Ruth strode back into the dining room and sat.

Persephone studied her. "Is there a problem?"

She forced a smile. "No problem."

Ten minutes later, Ray returned.

"How's Liam?" Belle said.

"Ask him yourself." Ray gestured over his shoulder.

With Greg's assistance, Liam hobbled into the room and sat next to Ruth with a sigh. He placed a sealed envelope in front of her. "Would you mind taking over hosting duties? I'll sit this one out. Offer advice, should you need it."

Ruth hesitated, then, quietly pleased she wouldn't participate directly in any further games, leaving her free to observe, nodded. "Of course." She slid a card out of the envelope and read. "It takes place in the ballroom." That was all the card said, and she wondered what fresh madness awaited them.

"This way." Ray strode from the room.

Orlando jumped to his feet, his eyes gleaming with anticipation. "It's nearly over." He offered his wife a hand up.

As they filed out after Ray, Greg assisted Liam, and they followed the others through Hadfield's labyrinthine corridors, the air thickening with anticipation with every step.

"Wait for me." Helena emerged from the kitchen doorway, falling into step beside them.

The deeper they went into the bowels of the mansion, the more oppressive the atmosphere seemed to become. Finally, they reached a massive set of oak double doors, at least ten feet high and equally wide. Intricate carvings of flora, fauna, and all manner of creatures adorned the panels.

"The ballroom." Ray pushed open the doors with a flourish.

Ruth stood rooted to the spot, her breath catching in her throat as her brain tried to process the scene before them.

"Well," Greg said. "That's not something you see every day."

She had to agree.

Even though they must be accustomed to the hotel's unusual brand of whimsy, the others seemed taken aback too.

The ballroom was undeniably grand and would have been impressive on any normal day, with its thirty-foot-high vaulted ceiling adorned with gigantic crystal chandeliers, each tier sparkling with hundreds of glittering crystals.

Floor-to-ceiling windows lined the opposite wall, their daylight obscured by plush velvet curtains. Oil paintings of idyllic countryside scenes and majestic horses graced the remaining walls, while the polished oak flooring beckoned guests to dance.

Yet, all this paled in comparison to the scene before them.

Greg scratched his head. "Bizarre."

A dining table stretched almost the full length of the ballroom, groaning under the weight of an eclectic collection of china teacups, bowls, and plates, alongside gleaming silver cutlery and sparkling crystal goblets.

Tureens and serving platters overflowed with everything from flaky pastries and croissants to succulent joints of beef and golden roast chickens. Bowls brimmed with vegetables and potatoes, while mountains of fruit and decadent desserts, like creamy trifles and rich chocolate cakes, completed the spread.

Ruth caught Greg eyeing the food and licking his lips. "Don't even think about it," she said. "It's all fake. Wax and plastic." At least, Ruth sincerely hoped it was. The waste would be criminal otherwise.

Although, knowing Greg's appetite, he'd probably polish off the entire spread in a matter of hours, with room to spare for coffee and mints.

Seated around the table, in high-backed chairs, were twenty mannequins. Each had a ghostly pallor and wore flowing garments crafted from gossamer-thin fabrics.

Hidden spotlights bathed them in hues of ethereal blue, green, and purple.

Unlike the static figures from the previous game, these mannequins were animated. They swayed to a jaunty tune, clinking wineglasses, raising cups in a toast, and miming bites from the delectable spread before them.

The air buzzed with the energy of lively conversations, all whispered in spectral tones.

"It's like something out of Alice in Wonderland, only they're all ghosts." Belle wrapped her arms around herself. "Creepy."

"I think it's magnificent." Elias looked to Liam. "Clarence has outdone himself."

"The Mad Hatter's tea party." Helena glanced at Belle. "It's supposed to be creepy. We're in a haunted house."

At the head of the table, perched precariously on a tower of books stacked head-high, sat a figure: the Mad Hatter himself.

He teetered back and forth, a mischievous glint in his eye. A patchwork coat of mismatched fabrics draped his skeletal frame, and a tea-stained top hat adorned with a riot of multicoloured feathers sat upon his head.

To his right, a regal ghost, her gown shimmering with an otherworldly glow, regarded him with a disapproving frown over a pair of half spectacles perched on the end of her nose. She sipped tea from a dainty china cup, her pinky finger outstretched in a display of practised etiquette.

More ghostly figures, shimmering and translucent, bathed in ethereal blue light, floated above their heads, weaving in and out of the chandeliers.

Ruth took a breath, taking in as many details as she could, but the scene overwhelmed her.

Her attention shifted to the other end of the table, where

a distinguished Victorian gentleman with a high collar sat rigid in his chair. He wore a monocle in his right eye and a stern frown etched upon his face, as if disapproving of the ghostly revelry.

Greg pointed. "Look."

A young boy, barely more than a wisp of spectral energy, zipped through the room, giggling mischievously as he chased after a runaway teacup.

Liam motioned to a chair inside the room, by the door. Greg helped him into it and then returned to Ruth's side.

She leaned in and whispered, "Stay close. I have a feeling this last game will be . . . interesting, to say the least."

Greg cocked an eyebrow at her. "And you think the other two games have been normal?"

Ruth swallowed and turned to the others. "Judging by your expressions, none of you have ever seen anything quite like this before?"

"Only in the park," Ray said. "Never here."

Orlando nodded in agreement. "Clarence orchestrated all this without our knowledge. The ballroom has been closed for the last couple of weeks, and I've seen ride technicians come and go." He glanced at his brother. "Now we know why."

Persephone's face fell. "Winifred." She pointed a trembling finger toward a spectral bride hovering in the air, staring at them with glowing eyes.

"No, she's from the haunted train ride," Ray said. "Although . . ." He squinted. "Someone has altered her appearance. She does look a bit like Grandmama."

Belle scrunched up her nose. "Why would Clarence do such a horrid thing?" Her eyes darted toward Liam.

"And *he's* from Captain Blood's Island." Ray nodded to a bearded ghost. "And that fellow over there." He indicated the Victorian gentleman. "He's from the Star Adventure ride. Normally wears a lab coat."

"Right." Orlando clicked his fingers. "Next to the control consoles. Has that helmet with the flashing lights." He turned to his brother, a nostalgic gleam in his eye. "He's been there since we were kids. A real fan favourite."

Ray nodded. "I hope Clarence has arranged to have them returned before the park opens Monday morning, or I'm in for a headache."

20

Persephone strode farther into the ballroom, and her gaze swept over the scene with a critical eye. "I see no murder victim. This charade is meant to distract us from our objective. Speaking of which . . ." She turned to Ruth. "What's the game?"

Ruth blinked. "Excuse me?"

"The host's card, Mrs Morgan." Ray smiled. "You're our new Liam, remember?"

Ruth pulled the envelope from her pocket and slid out the card. "It only mentions this location."

Liam beckoned her over and flipped the card in her hands.

She winced. "Ah." On the back was a list of detailed instructions. She cleared her throat and read aloud. "In this final game, you must work in pairs."

"But we're still working as a team, right?" Belle asked with a furtive glance at the others. "One pair wins, we all win?"

"Hmm." Ray rubbed his chin. "I'm not so sure. There's so much riding on this."

Persephone's eyes darkened. "I knew it. You never planned to divide the shares equally. It's winner takes all."

"What?" Belle stared at Ray. "You said—"

"And we fell for it." Elias shook his head. "It seems any one of us could still walk away with the keys to the kingdom."

Helena folded her arms, her lips pressed into a thin line.

"Don't say that." Belle looked to her husband. "We're in this together. Us against Clarence."

He gave a small shake of his head, silently telling her not to argue.

Her face fell.

"Master Clarence insists on teams for this game," Liam said, cutting through the tension.

"Although . . ." Elias looked between the brothers. "All your efforts in the last games could have been for nought, boys."

Ray smiled, seemingly unfazed by the challenge, and nodded to Ruth. "Please continue, Mrs Morgan."

She resumed reading from the card. "To ensure fairness, everyone must hand over their mobile phones. Even Greg and me, apparently." Although, Ruth thought, anyone foolish enough to try and pry Greg's phone away from him would be in for a fight. "This is a locked-room game," she continued. "With a thirty-minute timer. Fail to complete the tasks before the countdown ends, and you lose."

"Well, then . . ." Ray pulled out his mobile phone, insisted Helena do the same, and dropped both into a wooden bowl placed strategically in the hallway. "Seeing as I'm guaranteed to win, feel free to sit this one out, everyone." He rubbed his hands.

Orlando smirked and murmured, "Not a chance." He

took Belle's phone from her and dropped it into the bowl, along with his own.

With obvious reluctance, Persephone and Elias did the same.

Ruth considered lying about her phone, claiming she'd left it in her room. But something told her Liam would see right through her ruse. With a resigned sigh, she dropped it into the bowl and stepped into the ballroom.

All eyes moved to Greg.

He held up his hands. "I'm not playing."

"The instructions are clear," Persephone said, her tone cold.

"In the bowl, there's a good lad." Elias nodded to it. "You're holding everyone up."

For a fleeting moment, Greg looked mutinous. The thought of being separated from his precious phone was likely causing him physical pain. Ten seconds without contacting Mia was a fate worse than death.

However, one imploring look from Ruth was all it took to change his mind. He stomped over to the bowl, hesitated, and placed his phone inside. Greg glared at Ruth as he stepped into the ballroom, silently telling her if anything went wrong, it would be her fault.

With their phones secured, Elias shut the doors with a decisive click. A whirring filled the air as an electronic lock engaged, followed by the ominous ticking of a timer, counting down from thirty minutes.

Greg eyed the electronic keypad with a flicker of anxiety. "What if we need to get out? Like, in an emergency?"

"Don't worry," Liam said. "There's an override code: 999."

"I want to use it now." Belle clutched Orlando's arm.

"Don't be ridiculous." Persephone strode over to stand beside Elias.

Ruth continued reading from the card. "The game requires you to move counters on a game board." She paused and looked around the room. "Where is it?"

Liam pointed. "Over there."

Everyone circled the table.

On the floor, previously hidden by the sprawling ghostly tea party, lay a giant Snakes and Ladders board. Fifteen feet square, it was divided into a six-by-six grid of black and white squares, numbered one to thirty-six. Printed over the top of some were ladders—if a player landed on those, they'd climb up several rows. On other squares were snakes—having the reverse effect and sending players sliding back to an earlier square on the board.

To the side of the board sat three intricately crafted wooden animal figurines to be used as counters: a stag, a fox, and an owl.

Orlando groaned, while Ray beamed, his eyes gleaming with competitive spirit. Elias merely shook his head and tutted.

Ruth's gaze flitted from the board to the others' reactions.

"The Marsh Game," Helena said, her voice tight. "We're forced to play every Christmas."

"Snakes and Ladders?" Greg snorted. "A kid's game on a giant board? Seriously?"

Ruth had to admit, it did seem rather childish.

"It's not just Snakes and Ladders," Persephone said. "It has a twist. A Clarence and Winifred Marsh original. Winifred loved this game as much as he does."

"A mishmash of several games into one." Persephone

sniffed. "Far more complex and cunning than it first appears."

Ruth reminded herself to focus on Persephone, Elias, Ray, and Helena during this last game. All knew Latin and had passed the numbers challenge. If one of them cheated at this final game, Ruth would have her suspect. All she needed after that was hard evidence to back it up, but one thing at a time.

She glanced around. "Where's the wheel?"

"Over here." Elias pulled back one of the velvet drapes covering a nearby window. Behind it stood an upright wheel, six feet across, divided into fourteen colourful segments. Twelve of the sections bore the names of the players, appearing twice each, while the remaining two were blacked out. A pointer sat at the top.

Ruth scanned the card again. "There are no rules listed."

"They know the rules." Liam turned his attention to Greg. "Perhaps you'd be so kind as to operate the wheel?" He winced and clutched his leg.

"Ah." Persephone's expression darkened. "No doubt that's what Clarence intended all along, and we wouldn't want anyone cheating." She shot Ray a pointed look. "Not when so much is at stake."

He grinned. "I don't need to cheat."

Ruth's stomach clenched.

"We answer questions or perform tasks assigned to us at random," Orlando explained, mistaking her expression for confusion, and he gestured toward the giant Snakes and Ladders board. "Each correct answer earns the team six moves, as if we had rolled the maximum on a die."

"However," Helena added, "we are not obligated to move our counter forward the full six spaces."

"Right," Ray said. "We can choose to move fewer spaces

and . . . *gift* the remaining moves." A cheeky grin spread across his face.

"Gift them?" Greg's brow furrowed.

"To our opponents," Elias said. "It adds a certain tactical element to the game, wouldn't you say?"

Persephone pointed to a square next to a snake's head. "We may choose to send another team spiralling back down the board, or even boost them forward, if it suits us."

"Any team can give away up to five of their earned moves at a time," Ray continued, "divided among the others however we see fit, but, and this is crucial"—he held up a finger for emphasis—"we must keep at least one move for ourselves."

Elias rubbed his hands together. "It can get quite dastardly."

Ruth nodded as she absorbed the rules. By the sound of it, "*cutthroat*" might be a more apt description. Clarence had likely left such a game last on purpose—to also expose those very natures among the group.

After all, whoever had murdered Winifred must be cold and remorseless, driven only by greed.

Greg looked about the chaotic room. "What kind of tasks does this game require?"

"You're about to find out." Ray dropped into a chair at the ghostly tea party table and waved Greg on. "Spin the wheel, please. There's a good chap."

Ruth glanced at Liam, but he remained tight-lipped: a passive observer.

Greg did as he was asked. He grabbed the wheel with both hands and gave it a hard spin, the names blurring together in a dizzying kaleidoscope of colours, and everyone stared at it as if willing the pointer to choose them.

Helena stepped toward it, one hand in her trouser pocket.

Finally, with a clattering halt, the pointer landed on her name.

"Excellent." Ray clapped his hands. "Well done, Greg. You're a natural." With a triumphant grin plastered on his face, he spun in his chair and reached for a towering plate piled high with tempting hot cross buns. Then, with a theatrical flourish, Ray lifted it, and peered beneath. "As I suspected. Predictable, Clarence. Very predictable." He retrieved a red envelope from its hiding place, returned the plate to the table, and then jumped to his feet. He marched toward Ruth. "Ready, darling?" Ray asked his wife as he passed her.

Helena set her chin in an expression of steely determination.

Ray handed Ruth the envelope and stepped back.

She drew a fortifying breath, bracing herself for whatever challenge awaited. Greg wore a bemused expression.

Inside the envelope, a single question stared back at her from a rectangular card. "Who was the author of *Alice's Adventures in Wonderland*, and what was his real name?" At the very bottom of the card, written in tiny, almost illegible script, were the answers.

"Two questions?" Helena scoffed. She glared at Liam. "A tad unfair, wouldn't you say? We deserve double moves."

Ray, however, didn't miss a beat. "His real name was Charles Lutwidge Dodgson. Grandmama used to read all his stories when we were children." He glanced at Orlando. "And his pseudonym, of course, was Lewis Carroll. Who else? Everyone knows that."

"Correct." Ruth still struggled to see how this family

game could expose a killer. *How can they possibly cheat at general knowledge?*

Ray strode over to the giant Snakes and Ladders board. "We'll take the full six moves," he declared, "seeing as we can't send anyone back . . . yet." He picked up the stag figurine and moved it to the end of the first row.

Greg spun the wheel.

Persephone took a step toward it again as she watched intently, but this time, both hands were out of her pockets, her arms folded across her chest.

The wheel stopped on a blacked-out section.

"Spin again, dear fellow," Elias said.

Greg did as asked, and half a minute later, the wheel landed on Elias's name.

"I'm beginning to like you," Elias said with a toothy grin, and sauntered to the table. He selected a silver teapot, its surface polished to a mirror shine, lifted the lid, and peered inside. "Ah, there you are," he murmured, retrieving a rolled-up envelope. He handed it to Ruth.

She extracted the card and scanned it.

"Something wrong?" Persephone asked, concern in her usually sharp voice.

Ruth cleared her throat. "It's a riddle."

Ray threw back his head and laughed. "Oh my, this should be good." His voice dripped with sarcasm. "Good luck. You two can never solve them."

"Neither can you, brother," Orlando murmured.

Ruth read the riddle aloud. "I gleam with wealth, yet hold no coin, born from the earth, but never sown. I fill your mouth, but have no taste, used by the privileged, never in haste. What am I?" Unlike the previous question, there was no answer provided beneath. Riddles, Ruth had to admit, were not her forte.

"Please read it again," Persephone said, her voice tight.

"You only have two minutes to answer," Liam warned.

"Yes, yes. I know," Persephone snapped, waving away his reminder.

Twice more, Ruth read the riddle aloud, hoping the answer would magically reveal itself. It didn't. She looked up at Elias and Persephone, searching their faces for any flicker of recognition. They seemed as mystified as she was.

As the seconds ticked by, Elias and Persephone shifted uncomfortably from foot to foot, muttering to one another under their breaths, their frustration clearly mounting.

Liam's expression remained impassive, almost bored. "One minute remaining."

Belle gasped. "Wait. I know the answer."

Persephone spun, eyebrows shooting up. "You?"

Belle nodded. "The 'used by the privileged' part . . . I get it."

Ray's face fell. "You can't tell them."

"You know she can. It's in the rules." Persephone looked to Liam, but he remained tight-lipped. She let out a breath and returned her attention to Belle. "We'll exchange your answer for two moves."

"Two?" Orlando shook his head. "Without Belle, you'd have nothing. Four moves, or lose your turn."

"Thirty seconds," Liam called.

Persephone gritted her teeth. "Three. Final offer." She looked to Elias for support, and he nodded.

Orlando squeezed Belle's shoulder. "It's your call."

Belle bit her lip. "Hmm." Finally, she sighed. "Okay. Three moves. That's fair." She looked at Ruth. "The answer is a silver spoon."

Ruth reread the riddle, this time with Belle's answer in mind.

I gleam with wealth, yet hold no coin, born from the earth, but never sown. I fill your mouth, but have no taste, used by the privileged, never in haste.

She had to hand it to Belle; the girl possessed a sharp mind hidden deep beneath her timid exterior. The answer fit perfectly.

Despite the high stakes, Ruth found herself momentarily enjoying the game. She quickly reminded herself to stay focussed—*find the cheat.*

"I think you're right," she finally said.

Belle squealed and clapped.

"Well done, darling." Orlando beamed at her. "Three moves to us."

"We go first. It was our challenge." Elias stepped to the Snakes and Ladders board, picked up the owl figurine, and moved it forward three spaces. "That should do it."

Persephone, her expression unreadable, followed his every move as if checking for mistakes.

Belle, eager for her turn, reached for the fox figurine, but Orlando stopped her with a gentle hand on her arm.

"Hold on, darling." A sly smile spread across his face; his eyes, now sharp and calculating, flicked to Ruth. "We're only moving two spaces." He pointed to the board, where the second square sat conveniently at the base of a ladder. With a triumphant flourish, Orlando moved their fox up the ladder to the fifteenth square.

"And with our remaining move," Orlando continued, his tone casual, "we'll send my dear brother and his lovely wife back one space." He reached over and moved Ray and Helena's stag back to the number five position.

If they can give away moves, Ruth thought, *why didn't Elias and Persephone do the same? Are they trying to let Ray win? Is that where the cheating comes in?*

Ray, his face up until that point a mask of forced joviality, scowled but said nothing. He dropped into a chair at the table and folded his arms.

Perhaps he thought protesting would only give Orlando the satisfaction of knowing he'd got under his skin. Or, more likely, the players were used to how the Marsh Game operated.

Greg reached up and spun the wheel. All eyes followed the whirling pointer, a mixture of anticipation and determination on each face.

It slowed, finally coming to a stop on . . . Orlando's name. A collective groan rippled through the room, punctuated by Belle's delighted squeal.

Orlando chuckled and rubbed his hands together.

These challenges seem to have brought him out of his shell, Ruth thought.

He paced the length of the table several times before lifting a fruit bowl piled high with pears and apples. He extracted a red envelope from beneath it and, with a spring in his step, returned to Ruth.

She slid out the card, cleared her throat, and read in a loud voice, "What does the *drink me* potion do to Alice?"

"That's it?" Ray's voice dripped with indignation. "Why do they get such an easy question?" He threw his hands up. "This game must be rigged."

"Aren't they always?" Persephone muttered.

"It's only luck, brother." Orlando's eyes gleamed with amusement. "Lady Luck smiling on us for a change." He winked at Belle, and she giggled.

And then it hit Ruth. The shift in Orlando's demeanour, the sudden move from timid husband and brother to the almost manic glee in his eyes—it pointed to one thing: his love of gambling. This wasn't just a silly game for him; it was an opportunity to indulge in his vice.

Has Clarence engineered it that way?

Belle faced Ruth. "The drink potion makes Alice shrink. Drink, shrink."

"Correct." Ruth folded the card and stuffed it back into the envelope.

Ray ground his teeth, while Helena huffed and glared.

"Six whole glorious moves to us." Orlando studied the board.

Their fox sat on square fifteen, at the top of a ladder, with a few snakes to avoid from there on.

"We'll take all six." Orlando lifted the figurine and placed it on square twenty-one.

Two more rows to the finish.

Greg spun the wheel, and after landing on a black section for a second time, he spun again, and it stopped on Belle's name.

She squealed, this time with unbridled delight.

Ray balled his fists. "You have to be kidding."

Ruth frowned at the wheel. It looked normal, mechanical, and with Greg spinning it, there was no obvious way for Orlando to cheat. Besides, he wasn't her focus.

Belle skipped to the table, plunged her hand into a floral arrangement, and yanked out an envelope. Beaming at her husband, she handed it to Ruth.

As before, Ruth slid out a card and read. "Team charades." Below the title was the name of a movie. "The category is films."

Orlando groaned, but Ray punched the air, a triumphant grin spreading across his face. "Finally."

"Another chance to steal points," Persephone said in response to Ruth's confused reaction. "We play at the same time, all six of us, and the winners who guess first get the moves."

"I'll act it out, and you'll guess," Ray told Helena.

"Acting or guessing?" Persephone asked Elias.

He shrugged. "Matters not to me."

"You act, then," Persephone said.

"You too," Belle said to Orlando.

The three men stood with their backs to one another, forming a triangle. Helena, Persephone, and Belle then placed themselves facing their partners around the outer edge.

They all wore serious expressions, their faces etched with intense concentration. Greg, meanwhile, appeared bemused by their antics, whereas Liam seemed bored.

Keeping the card obscured, Ruth moved between Ray, Orlando, and Elias, showing each of them the film title.

Once they were ready, she stepped back. "Go."

21

I n Hadfield Hall's grand ballroom, the three charades actors erupted into a frenzy of motion. Orlando, closest to Ruth, leapt into action with such enthusiasm it bordered on manic. He flapped his hands, his face contorted.

Ray, meanwhile, had adopted a rigid posture, his arms outstretched, his fingers curled into clawlike shapes.

Elias seemed content to simply stand there and make the odd gesture, think for a while, and then try again.

This went on for a full minute, each partner shouting out guesses, their voices growing increasingly louder and more frantic as the seconds ticked by.

Greg, unable to contain his amusement any longer, moved beside Ruth and leaned in. "What are they trying to act out?"

The scene was chaotic, absurd.

She showed him the card.

It read, in bold black letters:

Night of the Living Dead.

Greg's eyebrows rose in obvious indignation. "Seriously?" He looked at the actors and stifled a laugh.

Orlando dropped to the floor, crumpled into a heap, and worked his mouth like a goldfish.

Belle's brow furrowed in concentration. "Dying?"

He rose, motioned for her to try again, and keeled over for a second time, squeezing his eyes shut and sticking out his tongue.

"*Night of the Living Dead*," Helena shouted, her voice ringing with triumph. However, she was no longer looking at her husband, who was making random gestures vaguely resembling a broken helicopter. Instead, her gaze was fixed on Orlando, sprawled on the floor like a particularly unconvincing corpse.

Could that be classed as cheating?

Orlando swore and clambered to his feet.

Belle winced. "Sorry."

"Not your fault." He pulled her into a hug that seemed designed to reassure them both. "Nice try. We'll do better next time."

"Six moves to us." Helena marched to the Snakes and Ladders board, Ray in tow. They conferred for a few moments, whispering in each other's ears.

Ray then grabbed their playing piece—the stag with intricately carved antlers. "We'll move two spaces." He dragged the figure to the base of a ladder on square seven, which took them all the way up to square twenty-eight, the second to last row.

Belle gaped at the board.

Smirking, Ray said to her with smug satisfaction, "And you two can take four spaces, going the other way, of course." He grabbed their fox and moved it back, negating their earlier progress.

Orlando sighed. "I really hate this game," he muttered, his earlier enthusiasm clearly extinguished.

"Only because you always lose," Elias said, his voice devoid of sympathy.

Ray sat back at the table and winked.

Greg spun the wheel. This time, it stopped on Persephone.

She perused the long dining table as though shopping in a posh antiques store. When she reached Ray, he waved her off. Persephone continued down the table before stopping at a silver tea caddy in front of the Victorian ghost, its intricate engravings glinting in the shimmering light. She lifted the lid, extracted a red envelope from within, and handed it to Ruth.

On the card was another riddle.

Ruth read aloud, "I perch upon an eye, though sightless I remain, a single lens to focus, on pleasure or on pain. I'm a circle held by metal, a dandy's delight, a glimpse of a world refined, with just a touch of might."

"A monocle," Elias said, as if stating a simple fact.

Ruth's eyebrows lifted. "Yes. That looks right. Well done."

If he was cheating, she couldn't see how. Elias hadn't even glanced at the card.

Speaking of which, having almost forgotten his presence, Ruth glanced over at Liam.

He now slouched in his chair, head tipped back, eyes closed.

"We'll take four moves." Persephone picked up their owl and carried it to the base of the same ladder Ray and Helena had used on their turn. She then placed it next to theirs on square twenty-eight. "And these can go back, I think," she added as she shifted the fox back to square twenty-six.

Interesting, Ruth thought, watching the interplay between couples. *It seems the alliances in this group are as fluid as the game itself.*

Greg spun the wheel again. It whirred, slowed, and finally came to a stop on ... Belle. Again?

She squealed. "Brilliant." Belle clapped. "You go this time, darling."

Orlando went to the table and picked up a plate, but found no envelope. He lifted a serving bowl, but there was nothing under that one either.

Ray pointed to an oversized gravy boat nearby. "Try that, dearest brother."

Orlando hesitated, then hurried over and lifted it from the table. "Thanks," he mumbled, and unstuck an envelope from its base. Then he strode across the room and handed it to Ruth.

She slid out the card. "It's an anagram."

"Concentrate." Belle screwed up her face and balled her fists. "We can do this."

Careful to cover the solution at the bottom, Ruth turned the anagram toward them.

They both leaned in, their heads close together as they scanned the letters.

The words were:

Here is the catch

Which Ruth thought was rather apt, given the hidden intent behind the games.

Orlando and Belle muttered between themselves and turned their heads back and forth, as if by doing so they could magically unscramble the anagram.

"Thirty seconds remaining," Liam said, now sitting upright, wide awake.

"I don't get it." Belle huffed. "It's meaningless."

Orlando clasped his hands behind his back and paced, muttering under his breath, but to no avail.

"Time's up," Liam called.

"Excellent." Ray leapt to his feet. "In that case, it opens to the other teams." He sauntered over to Ruth, peered at the card, and before Elias and Persephone had got look, he said, "The Cheshire Cat."

"Correct," Ruth said, surprised by his quick response. Her gaze darted to the table and the gravy boat, her suspicions piqued.

Ray laughed. "This game is too easy." He marched to the Snakes and Ladders board. After a moment of consideration, he said, "We'll give these jokers two forward moves." He grabbed Elias and Persephone's owl figurine and moved it to the head of a snake, sending them all the way down to square nine.

Persephone ground her teeth, her eyes flashing with anger. Elias, for his part, merely scowled, his expression unreadable.

"We'll take three spaces for ourselves." Ray moved their stag to square twenty-nine, now only one row from victory. "And, last but not least, this counter can go back one." He smirked as he picked up Orlando and Belle's fox and dragged it back to square sixteen. "That should do it." Ray lowered himself into another chair at the table, next to the ghost of a lady wearing a summer hat, looking thoroughly pleased with himself.

Helena nodded her appreciation for his play.

Orlando frowned. "That was a bit harsh."

"It's only luck, brother." Ray leaned back.

All eyes moved to the wheel.

Greg reached up and pulled down hard, giving it a vigorous spin.

And that's when, with everyone focussed on the spinning wheel of Marsh fate and fortune, Ruth finally spotted one player blatantly cheat: Ray leaned across the table with practised stealth. He lifted a serving platter with a plump roast chicken nestled among herbs, slipped an envelope from beneath, glanced at the card, and then returned it, all within seconds.

"Sly," Ruth murmured, her eyes narrowed. She looked away as he glanced in her direction, and then surreptitiously peered back at Ray a few seconds later.

Obviously thinking no one was currently watching him, with the other players' backs turned from Ray as they concentrated on the game, he slid a mini smartphone from his sleeve, did a quick search, and returned it before the wheel stopped.

The two magical Davids—Blaine and Copperfield—would've been proud of Ray's level of practised skill.

He had a spare phone the whole time.

Ruth wasn't entirely surprised. Ray struck her as a man who planned for every eventuality, especially if it involved cheating his own family out of an inheritance.

Ruth glanced in Liam's direction, but he had his eyes closed again, head tipped back, as if asleep. She refocussed on the wheel as it settled on Helena's name, playing right into Ray's hands.

He laughed without mirth.

Greg leaned behind the wheel, examining it as if looking for signs of tampering. After a moment, he shrugged at Ruth.

She kept her expression neutral, though her stomach

did backflips and her mind raced. As far as she could tell, the wheel hadn't been tampered with, but Ray certainly knew how to cheat at the Marsh game. However, cheating didn't automatically make him a murderer.

Helena, flushed with excitement, reached for a bowl of trifle, but Ray stopped her. "I've got this." He lifted the chicken platter again, slid out the envelope, and approached Ruth with a Cheshire Cat grin.

For the briefest of moments, Ruth considered calling him out. It would be satisfying, watching the smug expression melt from Ray's face. *But what good will it do?* Clarence's games only pointed a finger. She needed hard evidence that Ray had blackmailed Winifred, then silenced her.

But how could he? she thought as he strode toward her. *His own grandmother . . . Surely no amount of money—*

Ray stopped before her. "Here you go, Mrs Morgan."

She took the envelope, hands trembling, and extracted the card. "Who is Haigha? A name that first appears in Lewis Carroll's *Through the Looking-Glass*." Ruth didn't know the stories well enough to improvise a different question.

"The March Hare." Ray swaggered to the Snakes and Ladders board and moved their stag figurine forward five spaces to square thirty-four, two spaces from victory.

Square thirty-five held a snake's head. If another couple won the next spin, they could send Ray and Helena plummeting back to twenty-one.

Ray obviously realised this, and his smile vanished. He used the remaining move to send Persephone and Elias forward to space ten, which saw them sliding down a snake head, all the way back to square six. Then he sat back at the table, anxiety creasing his brow.

Despite his cheating, winning wasn't a certainty. The wheel, at least, seemed bound by the laws of chance.

Greg spun it hard.

The silence from the players was absolute, broken only by the clatter of the pointer. Finally, it slowed, coming to rest on ... Orlando's name.

Ray and Helena groaned in unison.

Orlando sauntered to the table, grabbed a sugar bowl, and extracted a rolled-up envelope. He avoided his brother's eyes as he handed it to Ruth.

She cleared her throat. "In which month and year was *Alice's Adventures in Wonderland* first published?" She glanced at Ray, who sat with his arms folded.

Both Orlando and Belle's faces fell.

"Do you know, darling?" Belle asked, her voice small and uncertain.

Orlando shook his head.

"Not even the year?"

He shook his head again.

Belle's shoulders slumped. She looked at Persephone, her eyes pleading, but Persephone only sighed.

Elias scowled at the floor.

"Do you want to have a stab at it?" Ruth asked Belle, a pang of sympathy gnawing at her insides.

"I know," Ray said. Of course he did, he'd probably just looked at his phone. "I'll trade the answer for two moves."

Belle frowned at the board. "You'd win."

Orlando let out a slow breath. "And if we forfeit, the question opens up to the other teams." He looked to Persephone and Elias. "And you really don't know the answer?"

"He might be wrong," Belle said, her chin lifting. "Ray could be guessing."

Ray chuckled. "I could be."

He's not, Ruth thought, and it took every ounce of strength not to scream "*cheat*" at the top of her lungs.

Ray's charade was ridiculous. But she needed the game to play out. The sooner the better. Then she'd speak to Clarence, get the evidence, and be done with this family and their bizarre inheritance games.

"Fine. We forfeit," Orlando huffed.

"November, 1865." Ray rose from the table and walked to the Snakes and Ladders board.

He was, of course, correct.

Belle gaped at him, slack jawed. "How did you know that?"

"It's general knowledge." Ray moved the stag to the finish. "That was fun. Commiserations to the losers."

A click sounded from beneath the board, as though the figurine had depressed a switch. A claxon blared, the lights dimmed, and the ghosts froze. A spotlight illuminated a flower arrangement in the middle of the table.

Ray lifted the flowers and revealed a silver box inside the basket. It was twelve inches square, ornately engraved with roses. "Needs a key." He looked to Ruth. "Mrs Morgan, if you please?"

Ruth retrieved the silver key from her pocket and handed it to him.

"A simple document signing everything over to me would have sufficed." Ray unlocked the box. "Instead, Clarence has to go overboard with the theatrics." He smirked at his wife, lifted the lid, and his face fell. "No. It's— It's not right." He shook his head. "What does he think he's playing at?"

Helena took a step toward him. "What is it?"

Ray's face twisted with anger. "I've had enough." He stormed across the room, his gaze fixed on Liam. "Did you know about this?"

Liam didn't respond. He merely stared back at Ray, his expression passive and unreadable.

Ray punched 999 into the keypad, threw open the door, and stormed out.

"Come back," Elias called after him. "Screaming at the old man will do you no good."

But Ray ignored him and vanished around the corner.

Ruth beckoned Greg over.

Everyone remained rooted to the spot for a few seconds, stunned into silence, before Persephone approached the table and peered into the box.

"It's empty." She looked up. "I don't understand. Clarence was clear that whoever won would—"

Elias laughed, a sharp bark that echoed in the vast room. He sank into a chair. "Good old Clarence." He waved a dismissive hand at Orlando. "He had you boys fighting for nothing. The old man has absolutely no intention of handing anything over. Probably never did. You'll have to prise those shares out of his cold, dead hands."

"But why?" Belle asked, her voice small and lost.

Persephone paced. "Precisely. Why even say he would sign his shares over if he had no intention?" She balled her fists. "It doesn't make sense. Clarence always keeps his word."

Orlando stared at the floor, his shoulders slumped. "I don't get it either."

Belle looked to Liam. "Do you know what this has all been about?"

"I only do as I'm told, madam."

As always, Ruth couldn't believe him.

Belle's gaze moved to Helena, but she seemed stunned into silence.

If Clarence had asked Liam to tweak the games at the last minute, surely he must have had an inkling as to why.

Can Liam truly be ignorant of his employer's motives?

Ruth leaned in to Greg, her voice a low murmur. "Let's see what Clarence has in mind for an endgame. And hopefully, what other evidence he has."

Greg rolled his eyes. "Please, not another game."

"Where are you going?" Helena called after them as they headed toward the door.

"To check on my cat," Ruth lied. She wasn't sure why she bothered. These people had more on their minds than a guest and her pet.

She and Greg snatched their phones from the bowl, and then hurried through Hadfield Hall, up the stairs, and to the spiral staircase.

At the bottom, Ruth hesitated. Something felt off. She turned to Greg. "Stay alert. Watch your back."

"Sure."

"I mean it."

"I know," Greg said, his voice taking on a rare serious tone.

Ruth was about to step onto the first stair when Ray rushed down, his face pale, and barged past, almost knocking her off balance.

"Hey," Greg shouted at Ray's retreating back.

The older Marsh brother didn't acknowledge him or slow down.

Greg faced Ruth, his eyebrows raised. "He's the one, right? The killer?"

"We still only have circumstantial evidence." Ruth took a breath. "It's true, Ray could be the one who murdered Winifred, but we need facts. Hard evidence. We'll start by getting whatever Clarence has been holding back and work from there."

Greg nodded. "Right."

They headed on up the spiral staircase and into the vestibule. Ruth stopped dead. The door to Clarence's rooms stood ajar.

The hairs on the back of her neck bristled.

"Stay here." She took a deep breath and entered the sitting room. It took a few seconds for her eyes to adjust to the gloom. Sprawled before the cold fireplace was Clarence's lifeless form.

22

Ruth rushed over to Clarence, her heart pounding. She knelt and, careful not to touch the body, turned an ear to his mouth.

Nothing.

He's gone.

Ruth clambered to her feet.

There were no obvious signs of what might have killed him. *Could he have succumbed to his illness?*

"Greg. Call the police." She looked back at her grandson, who stood frozen by the door, his face ashen. "Don't leave. Stay right outside." As he stepped into the vestibule and shakily pressed the phone to his ear, Ruth scanned the room. Nothing seemed out of place from their prior visit.

Her gaze shifted to the magic cabinet.

She hesitated, knowing she shouldn't touch anything, but had to check if Clarence had left more evidence against Ray.

She raced to the cabinet and opened it.

Empty.

"The p-police are on their w-way," Greg said, obviously doing his best to avoid looking at the body.

"What was the trick to opening this?" Ruth motioned to the cabinet.

"Twist the handle half a turn clockwise."

She closed the door, did as he said, and opened it again.

This time, a manila file lay inside.

Ruth lifted it out and rifled through its contents. It was all there. The proof of the Latin page, the financial records, and extra evidence of blackmail, including threatening letters and printouts of Orlando's embezzlement.

But . . . it was still mostly circumstantial.

She glanced at Clarence's lifeless form. The police would have her eyewitness account of Ray's behaviour, plus there had to be forensic evidence here too. Ruth and Greg needed to leave before contaminating it.

Having replaced the file, she closed the cabinet, turned the handle the other way, and checked the file had vanished before straightening. "Let's go."

As they headed down the spiral staircase, Greg said, "Ray did this? You think there's enough evidence?"

"For an arrest, yes," Ruth said. "But for a conviction?" She sighed. "I'm not sure a jury could be swayed."

"So what happens now?"

"We wait for the police, tell them what we know, and it's up to them." Although she couldn't rule out natural causes, given everything, Ruth suspected foul play, and the police would too.

She and Greg raced through the house and down the stairs.

Raised voices echoed from below.

"What do you mean, he's dead?" Elias's voice boomed over Belle's sobs.

"No," Persephone said. "That can't be right. You must be joking. Is this still part of the games? You're lying."

"Go up there and see for yourself," Ray shouted back, his voice frantic.

Ruth rounded the landing, with Greg close behind, and hurried down the stairs.

Everyone had gathered in the reception hall. Liam sat in a chair by the front door, his posture ramrod straight, his gaze fixed on Ray.

Ray Marsh's eyes, wide and manic, met Ruth's. "I found him like that."

Everyone watched her, their expressions a mixture of shock, grief, and suspicion.

Keeping her face neutral, despite feeling trapped by the others, Ruth strode past them, and opened the front door wide, allowing the cool air in.

She took in a slow, calming breath, and let it out. Her cleithrophobia eased. "Police are on their way," Ruth said to Liam, and motioned for Greg to stay close.

"I didn't have anything to do with Clarence's death, Mrs Morgan." Ray looked between the others, his face flushed and sweaty. "He was ill. Everyone knows that. I only went up there to have it out with him, to find out what he was playing at." Ray took a juddering breath. "Would never hurt the old man. Fed up with his games. That's all."

Persephone folded her arms. "And yet you were happy to play them when you thought there was something in it for you. You expect us to believe he merely keeled over from pneumonia? Despite the fact he was getting better? How do we know you didn't take advantage of his weakened state?"

Belle sniffed. "It's horrible. Winifred too."

Ray looked to Orlando, his eyes pleading. "You have to believe me."

Orlando stared at the floor, jaw clenched.

Ray stepped toward Helena, but she backed away, her expression shuttered. He turned back to Ruth. "If I murdered Clarence, why would I still be here?" He thrust a finger at the front door. "I should be long gone. I wouldn't be hanging about if I was guilty."

"Maybe that's what you want us to think," Elias growled.

Belle's voice cracked. "How— How could you?" She buried her head in Orlando's shoulder.

Ray didn't take his focus off Ruth as police sirens wailed in the distance, growing louder by the second. "Does it really make sense? Why would I come down here and tell you he's dead if I'd killed him?"

He had a point, but killers were rarely rational.

Ruth tried to piece together the sequence of events. She had to be methodical. "Clarence called me right before the last game. He sounded tired, like before, but he seemed okay at that point."

"I didn't kill him. How could I?" Ray pointed to Greg and then Liam. "I was with them the whole time. Waited while he got changed into a fresh pair of trousers, and we came straight back down here."

"That's true," Greg said. "He didn't leave."

"See?" Ray's voice held a note of desperation. "How would I have had time to do in the old guy? I only went up there to have it out with him."

Ruth nodded slowly, wanting to believe him, but trying to remain objective. After all, Ray could've clubbed Clarence over the head and ran away. However, she looked for other opportunities among the group and her attention moved to Helena.

"Don't look at me," she said. "I didn't kill Clarence. I was in the bathroom."

"But you came from the kitchen," Ruth said.

"There's a servant's bathroom off the kitchen." Helena pointed. "Go check, if you don't believe me."

Ruth didn't need to. Even if Helena lied about where she was, she couldn't have run up to the tower, murdered Clarence, and returned within the space of a few minutes, and certainly not without being spotted.

"What about the staff?" Ruth asked Liam.

Ray's face twisted in confusion. "What staff? I thought they'd all gone home."

Liam shuffled uncomfortably in his chair. "They have. Call them to check, if you like."

"The police will," Persephone said, her tone clipped. "You can be sure of that."

As the sirens grew louder, Ray became increasingly agitated, and paced back and forth. "I didn't do it. They'll prove it was the pneumonia. You'll see. Has to be. The only logical explanation. A coincidence."

"What about Nadia?" Ruth asked Liam, ignoring Ray's frantic rambling.

"She's in hospital," Ray said.

"And Mike was arrested," Orlando said. "What do they have to do with anything?"

Elias' eyes narrowed at Liam. "All very strange happenings in only a couple of short days."

Liam hesitated, then hung his head. "It was— It was part of the game."

This resulted in several gasps.

Ray balled his fists. "What are you talking about?"

Liam let out a breath. "With Master Clarence unwell . . . Let's just say he felt I needed extra help. To manage the household, the guests, the games."

"The person operating the stick puppets," Belle said.

Liam looked to Ruth. "Nadia went home straight afterward. You can check."

"What about Mike?"

"He left before the fake arrest. He had no idea." Liam winced as he shifted his weight. "The security cameras outside will back up what I'm saying."

On top of any CCTV footage, the police could speak directly to both Mike and Nadia.

It was Ruth's turn to pace, her hands clasped behind her back. Her mind raced to piece together the events leading up to Clarence's death, searching for anything she may have overlooked.

She glanced outside as the trees lit up with overlapping flashes of blue. "We played the last game. Together. All of us. No one left." Ruth pursed her lips. "Which means, there was only a small window of opportunity where someone . . ." She looked at Ray. "Where someone could have reached Clarence. Right before Greg and I made it up there just now."

Ray's eyes darted to the front door and then to the hallway.

"Don't even think about running," Elias snarled.

Tyres crunched on gravel as several police cars slid to a halt outside. Officers jumped out, their movements swift and practised, and raced up the steps, streaming into the house.

In the lead were the two officers from Ruth's questioning —Inspector Jane Harlow and Sergeant Nick Pierce.

Inspector Harlow, her gaze sharp, looked around. "Is this everyone? Who found the body?"

Ray raised a shaking hand into the air.

"Can you show me?"

Ray swallowed. "I—"

"We will." Ruth gestured between Greg and herself. "We found him moments after."

Inspector Harlow considered Ray as he avoided eye contact, and then she addressed Sergeant Pierce. "Get everyone seated. We'll need statements." She then motioned for Ruth to lead the way, and two police officers fell into step behind.

The five of them made their way up through Hadfield Hall into the tower vestibule.

Ruth stopped short of Clarence's door. "In there."

Greg lowered himself into one of the armchairs. Ruth followed suit, her heart heavy.

Inspector Harlow entered the rooms, one officer right behind her.

Ten minutes later, she reemerged, talking on her phone, explaining the layout, and how to find them.

When she hung up, Ruth cleared her throat. "You'll want to start with us."

Inspector Harlow glanced about. "Is here okay?"

Greg rose from his chair, clearly making a deliberate effort not to look into Clarence's room, and stood on the other side of the vestibule, next to the officer.

"Thank you." Inspector Harlow took out her notepad and pen, and sat. "Start from the beginning, Mrs Morgan."

Ruth took a deep breath and explained everything: their initial meeting with Clarence, his accusations of blackmail, murder, and treachery, the games, the family and shareholders, their constant bickering, and finally, the evidence pointing to Ray Marsh. "There's a file in the cabinet. It has all the details Clarence had gathered."

Inspector Harlow looked to the officer.

Greg told them how to open the trick cabinet while

crime scene examiners filed up the stairs and into the rooms, followed by a doctor.

Ruth's stomach clenched.

Now they were about to find out if it was murder.

The officer in turn explained to a crime scene technician, who disappeared into Clarence's rooms and emerged moments later with the file, carefully placing it into an evidence bag.

Ruth continued, outlining the timing of Clarence's murder, how she'd spoken to him right before the third game started, and showed the call time to Inspector Harlow. The inspector took pictures and bagged Ruth's phone for evidence.

After asking her to recap the events again, making sure she left out no details, Inspector Harlow then took Greg's statement.

Greg finished by describing how he'd been with Ray and Liam.

Inspector Harlow's brow furrowed. "He cut his leg?"

"In the kitchen," Ruth said. "It was an accident."

Sergeant Pierce appeared at the top of the spiral staircase, bent double, breathing hard. "They're no joke." He straightened, wiping his brow with the back of his hand. "Mr Marsh scaled these every day?"

"There's a lift." A crime scene officer appeared at the door and motioned over her shoulder. "Hidden behind one of the cabinets."

Ruth and Greg exchanged startled glances.

"Where does it go?" Inspector Harlow asked.

"I'll find out." The officer stepped back inside.

Inspector Harlow then studied Sergeant Pierce. "Is there something wrong?"

He shook his head. "We have the family in the sitting room. They've been asked not to confer, but we've posted two officers in there." He took a deep breath. "Meanwhile, other officers are sweeping the house. So far, it appears empty."

Inspector Harlow nodded. "I gathered."

"That's not all, ma'am," Sergeant Pierce continued. "A staff member showed up at the front door. He's quite insistent he speak to someone. I have him waiting in reception."

Ruth sat upright, her interest piqued. "Who is it?"

Sergeant Pierce read from his notebook. "Mike Thomas. A porter. He's concerned about his fiancée, Nadia. Said she was supposed to be home hours ago."

Ruth's mouth dropped open, and her mind raced.

Nadia didn't go home?

That means Liam lied?

The doctor appeared at the door. "I'm finished here," he said to Inspector Harlow. "The coroner can move the body when your officers are ready." He headed toward the stairs.

"Doctor?" Inspector Harlow called after him.

He turned back. "Oh, right." He responded to her raised eyebrows. "Preliminary examination is inconclusive. Records show Clarence Marsh has been very poorly with pneumonia, but an autopsy will be needed to confirm a cause."

Inspector Harlow glanced at Ruth and back. "Estimated time of death?"

The doctor consulted his notes. "A little over forty-eight hours."

Ruth's blood ran cold. "No. That's . . ." She shook her head, trying to comprehend.

"It's impossible," Greg said. "We saw Clarence yesterday." He waved a hand at Ruth. "Grandma spoke to him earlier today."

Ruth stared at the floor, her mind spinning. "That doesn't make sense." She gasped. "Unless . . ."

Ruth and Greg, followed by Inspector Harlow and an accompanying officer, marched along the tunnel beneath Marsh Park. They entered the room filled with costumes and makeup tables, their surfaces cluttered with brushes, lipsticks, and half-used palettes.

Ruth turned on the spot, eyes scanning the rows of hanging costumes, heart pounding.

Inspector Harlow observed her with obvious suspicion and impatience. "Why are we here?"

Ruth pointed to the maid's outfit on a wire hanger, its pristine white marred by splatters of fake blood. "Yesterday, we thought Clarence and Liam staged an elaborate charade, which initially had us believe Nadia's boyfriend attacked and seriously harmed her. We thought she was rushed to hospital, and Mike was arrested for attempted murder."

"The gentleman who showed up earlier?" Inspector Harlow asked.

"Yes, but I don't think Mike had anything to do with it," Ruth said. "He wasn't here when Nadia faked the attack. Or that's what I think the CCTV will show."

"I don't understand." Greg scratched his head. "Why go through such elaborate lengths to hide Nadia? We knew it was her working behind the scenes."

"We had our suspicions," Ruth corrected. "We didn't know for sure because we never saw her at the house during the games. We only later took Liam's word for it." She took a breath. "We have no proof Nadia was operating those puppets."

Greg frowned. "Then who was?"

Ruth turned to Inspector Harlow. "Please have one of your officers go to the music room. There's another smaller room off to the side. In there, they'll find a raised turntable and box. The left-hand side of the box holds a puppet theatre. Look underneath and report back."

Inspector Harlow stared at Ruth as though she were mad, but got on the radio and relayed the instructions.

Then, while they waited, Ruth paced the room, her brow furrowed, trying to piece the events of the previous couple of days together.

"You saw Nadia take the puppets from the theme park," Greg said.

Ruth faced her grandson. "Let me ask you, what difference did it make if we knew she was helping with the games?"

Greg shrugged. "Don't see it makes any difference at all."

"Precisely."

He opened his mouth to say something, but the police radio crackled.

An officer then relayed their findings—underneath the puppet theatre was a complicated system of interconnected gears, pulleys, and circuit boards, and no room for someone to crouch. All animatronics. Not human operated.

Greg gaped. "No one was under there?"

Ruth shook her head. "I think Nadia staying behind was a last-minute change. Someone made up some excuse to keep her there. Asked for help with the games." Aware of Inspector Harlow's impatient glare, she added, "I'm betting Nadia saw something earlier she shouldn't have."

"Like what?"

Ruth's gaze fixed on the bloodstained costume. "Something before the games began. Someone convinced her to play the victim, by telling Nadia it was part of the fun. They tricked her into making us all believe she was injured."

Inspector Harlow folded her arms. "Go on."

A cold certainty settled in Ruth's stomach. "Must have fed her some elaborate story, convinced Nadia to play the part. Mike had already gone home by that point." She shook her head. "No, someone wanted Nadia to stay, to wrongfully think she was involved in the games, where they could take care of her later."

"Who?" Greg asked.

Ruth recalled the raised voices coming from the drawing room the previous day. Nadia had argued with someone. "They wanted her to remain here," she murmured, her voice barely above a whisper. "Wanted to make sure they could silence her when the opportunity arose." Ruth's gaze shifted back to the bloodstained costume as the disjointed events slotted into place one after another.

And then the memory of Nadia in the bedroom next to the spiral staircase popped into Ruth's mind—the moment they'd seen her after their visit with Clarence, and then on her errand into the park.

Ruth spun on the spot, searching, and that was when she spotted the picnic hamper under a cloak. She gasped and looked at Inspector Harlow. "Someone asked Nadia to fetch the puppets, but I'm betting she never made it back to Hadfield Hall." She pointed to the hamper. "They intercepted her, which means . . ."

"Nadia is still here," Greg finished, his eyes widening.

Ruth rushed past the makeup benches and racks of costumes. She stopped at a door marked "Store Room" and threw it open.

Nadia lay on the floor, her hands and wrists bound, her

mouth gagged. Her eyes were bleary, filled with terror, but at least she was conscious.

Ruth hurried to her side; her fingers fumbled to remove the gag. "It's all right. You're safe now."

Nadia groaned, relief flooding her features.

Ruth leaned down. "You saw someone. That's what the argument was about in the drawing room." Then she pictured the room upstairs where Nadia had been cleaning the windows—it sat directly under Clarence's bedroom. "You saw someone step out of the secret elevator that goes up to Clarence's tower. Is it hidden behind something?" An image of Winifred's room flashed into her mind. "A bookcase? Wardrobe?"

Nadia hesitated, gave a single nod in reply, and then her eyes rolled into the back of her head.

Inspector Harlow barked orders to her officer. "Radio for paramedics. And get the team down here to dust for prints."

23

B ack at Hadfield Hall's sitting room, tension hung in the air, a suffocating blanket of suspicion and fear. Ruth, flanked by Greg and Inspector Harlow, faced the assembled family and friends. Their faces were a tapestry of shock and apprehension, as five police officers filed in and took up positions around the room.

Helena sat with her arms folded, while Belle appeared utterly bewildered and fearful. Elias fidgeted in his seat, his brow furrowed with worry. Persephone, her lips pressed into a thin line, emanated an aura of barely controlled fury. Orlando stared at the floor, and Liam watched with passive interest.

Ray, his face ashen, rose to his feet, and his voice trembled. "Are— Are we under arrest?"

Inspector Harlow waved him back down. "We have a lot to discuss." She turned to Ruth, a silent invitation to begin.

They'd discussed her conclusions on the way back to Hadfield Hall, and the inspector had agreed to let her take the lead, under close supervision, drawing out the guilty party.

Ruth pulled in a steadying breath, and her gaze swept the gathered faces before her. "Clarence believed, and had some evidence to support his claim, that one of you was blackmailing Winifred."

Helena's eyes darkened.

"Blackmail?" Elias's eyebrows shot up. "What about?"

"As if you don't know," Helena muttered.

Ruth's gaze settled on Orlando, whose shoulders slumped, guilt etched onto his face. "They threatened to expose a secret, one that would ruin your reputation."

"Oh please. If this is about his gambling," Persephone scoffed with a dismissive wave of her hand, "everyone knows—"

"It wasn't only about gambling," Ruth interrupted, her voice firm. "It was more to do with the money he stole to fund his habit."

A collective gasp went through the room.

Orlando hung his head, his silence speaking volumes.

Ray glared at him.

"From the business?" Elias's face contorted in disbelief. "You stole from us? The shareholders? From your own family?"

When Orlando didn't respond, Ruth continued, "Someone, with access to the private garden outside Orlando's office, saw a page of company accounts through the window. Not only did they memorise the figures, but they worked out what Orlando was doing—covering his tracks."

Persephone shook her head at him, her face a mask of disappointment. "Embezzlement? How could you? After all the support we've given you."

Belle blinked. "What support? All of you tried to pretend it wasn't happening."

Helena scowled at her.

"It appears the blackmailer was subtle at first." Ruth paced the room, her hands clasped behind her back. "Determined to keep it between themselves and Winifred. They sent her a page of Latin text, knowing she would understand the message hidden within."

"What message?" Elias asked. "Hold on. Latin? Numbers?" His eyes then widened in dawning comprehension. "This year's games."

Ruth looked at Ray. "You said Winifred and Clarence had been at each other's throats for years." Her gaze shifted to Orlando. "And you pointed out Clarence recently wanted to make amends. That's why he signed over his share of Hadfield Hall to Winifred." Ruth sighed. "That was his intent. I assume he realised his health was failing and he was short on time. I also think he wanted Winifred to have his shares in the theme park."

Elias's brow furrowed. "How do you figure that?"

"Winifred was supposed to win these games," Ruth said. "Clarence designed them that way—the Latin books in the library, all her favourites; the music box with her favourite tune, the one she made you play so often; the wheel with the blacked-out sections, where her name once resided; and then the puppet show . . ."

Persephone shook her head. "I don't believe it."

"Going back a step," Ruth continued. "Orlando embezzled money from the firm. Someone figured that out. Winifred, desperate to protect him, tried to cover his losses. It's likely she even paid off the blackmailer, hoping it would end there."

"But it didn't," Belle whispered, her voice barely audible.

Ruth stared through the window to the garden beyond. "Clarence discovered what was happening and tried to intervene. He spoke to Winifred, but she refused his help.

He even hired a private investigator to uncover the black-mailer's identity." She paused, letting the weight of her words sink in. "Meanwhile, Winifred likely tried again to reason with the blackmailer, but they—"

"Murdered my friend." Persephone clenched her fists, and her voice shook with fury. "They threw Winifred off that bridge, knowing she couldn't swim." Her eyes, cold and furious, darted around the room, settling on each of them in turn. "Which one of you was it?" Her gaze moved over Helena and landed on Ray.

However, Ruth's attention moved to Elias. "Winifred wasn't sure who to trust, so she had you followed."

His face fell.

Ruth pulled the memory card from her pocket and handed it to Inspector Harlow, before facing Elias and Persephone. "Both of you."

Persephone stared back, unblinking.

Ruth resumed pacing, gathering her thoughts. "Winifred had proof that you conspired with Ray to force the park expansion."

"That's true," Ray said. "Although, we weren't conspiring. We were planning. There's a difference. And we can't force anything. That's the whole point."

Ruth stopped pacing and clasped her hands. "Please explain."

"Grandmama and Clarence have controlling votes," Ray said. "Our hands were tied. So, we were about to attempt another go at persuading them a park expansion is in everyone's interest." He sighed. "I spent hundreds of hours working with investors, developers, planners, and architects, putting together a foolproof presentation."

Elias sighed. "We made the mistake of not involving Winifred from the start."

"We were going to tell her before the meeting," Ray said in a defensive tone. "We only wanted to put a proposal together first. Something neither of them could ignore."

Persephone nodded to Ray. "He's the one most desperate to expand. That's all he's talked about for the last year."

"The park won't survive without it," Ray snapped. "We've gone over the finances. There's no other way. Winifred's idea about franchises and selling land won't generate enough income. It will push the business deeper into trouble."

Ruth pressed on. "I was told the supposed blackmailer cheated in previous years' Marsh Games." She looked at Orlando. "You placed large bets on the outcomes and lost."

Orlando's eyes darted to his brother before falling back to the floor.

"So what?" Ray's voice was defensive. "I admit we had a wager or two, and I won. Private bets, nothing more. What do they have to do with anything? I've got nothing to hide. Neither does my brother." Then his jaw dropped, and his head snapped toward Orlando. "That's what all this was about? You stole from the business to pay me?" He rose from his chair. "Knowing the park was in trouble? Are you insane? Why didn't you say something?"

Inspector Harlow waved him down.

Ray dropped back into the chair. "Answer me, Orlando."

"Winifred also asked whom the bet was with." Ruth focussed on Orlando too, her voice calm but insistent. "You wouldn't tell her. Already drowning in debt from previous gambling losses, you . . . you stole the money to pay him."

"This is insane." Ray balled his fists. "We're brothers. Why didn't you tell me?"

"Because you would never let him hear the end," Belle shouted, making everyone jump. "All your lives you've put him down." Her face twisted with anger. "Treated him like he's inferior. You're horrible. If Orlando had told you he'd gambled all his money away and couldn't afford to pay you, you would've held it over him forever."

"I—" Ray swallowed. "I had no idea."

"Why would you?" Belle snarled. "You're always too wrapped up in yourself to care about anyone else." Her eyes shot to Helena and away again. "It would also mean admitting how bad Orlando's addiction has become."

"I was going to pay it back," Orlando mumbled, his voice thick with shame. "Grandmama insisted I get help. I've been seeing a therapist for a while now. Making real progress."

Belle took his hand. "There's no point defending yourself to these people."

Helena merely scowled at them both.

Ray's eyes dropped to the rug. "I'm— I'm sorry."

"When someone murdered Winifred"—Ruth glanced at Inspector Harlow—"I agreed to participate in the games, to observe you all, to try and determine who was responsible, to link a set of skills to the evidence." She took a deep breath. "The games were supposedly tweaked to expose the killer, but I now know Clarence finished the games weeks, if not months, ago with only Winifred in mind." She looked at Belle. "You mentioned they've always been rigged, designed to shift the advantage to a predetermined winner each year."

Orlando frowned at his wife. "What are you talking about?"

Belle shrugged. "I thought it was obvious."

"Hold your horses." Elias shifted in his seat, his face creased in thought. "Ray won this year."

"Someone else tweaked the games to make sure he did," Ruth said. "The original winner was supposed to be

Winifred, where she'd receive Clarence's shares as the prize, but the killer changed the games enough to have Ray win instead." Ruth studied their faces as this information sank in. "Some of the accompanying evidence I was given was fabricated. Manipulated to create the illusion of a genuine investigation. All designed to make it appear the games would expose Winifred's killer, but in reality, it was all orchestrated to frame Ray."

Ray shot to his feet, his face contorted with rage. "Which one of you did this?"

"Sit down, sir," Inspector Harlow said in a firm voice. "Let Mrs Morgan explain."

Ray hesitated, then slumped back into the chair.

"If the true blackmailer is behind the plot to pin the murder on Ray," Elias said to Ruth, "why have they revealed the whole situation involving Orlando and Winifred?"

"Because they wanted to pin the blackmail on me too," Ray said.

"And if Clarence found out, anyone else could have," Belle said.

Ruth continued in a level tone, "I never met Clarence. Unfortunately, someone murdered him days ago."

Stunned silence greeted this revelation.

Helena sat bolt upright, Elias's brow furrowed in confusion, while Belle simply blinked at Ruth.

"Then . . ." Belle swallowed. "Who did you meet?"

Ruth resumed pacing as she thought it through. "The killer must have overheard Winifred and Clarence talking about me, about my past as a police officer. Maybe there's an email exchange. Either way, the killer saw an opportunity." She glanced at Inspector Harlow as she passed her. "The killer wanted me to gather false evidence to present to the police, along with the planted forensic evidence they no doubt left behind at the murder scenes." She looked at Ray. "They'd have a case for your conviction."

"If you didn't speak to Clarence," Persephone interjected, her voice sharp, "then who was it?"

Belle stared at Ruth, her eyes widening. "No." She gasped, and her gaze shot to Liam. "It was you."

Liam, his face pale and drawn, stammered a denial, but his words were lost in the uproar that followed.

"What?" Persephone and Elias shouted in unison.

Ray erupted from his seat again and lunged past Helena. "I'll kill you." He wrapped his hands around Liam's throat and roared, "You murdered them."

Officers sprang into action, pulling Ray off a sputtering Liam.

Inspector Harlow, her face grim, wasted no time. "Arrest him."

Sergeant Pierce dragged Liam to his feet and cuffed him. "You're under arrest for the murders of Clarence and Winifred Marsh . . ."

As they led Liam away, his protests echoing through the hall, Ruth drew a deep breath, willing herself to remain level-headed. Pieces of the puzzle were still falling into place, but a nagging unease lingered.

"I can't believe that scumbag," Elias said through gritted teeth. "It feels so unreal. He murdered our two dearest friends? I hope he rots in hell."

Persephone looked ready to leap up and go after Liam.

Ray gripped the arms of his chair, his face contorted with a mixture of hurt, anger, and exhaustion. "Why did he do it?"

Orlando stared at the floor, muttering, "It's my fault. It's all my fault."

Ruth cleared her throat.

All eyes turned toward her.

She waited for the tension to ease enough for them to listen. "Greg and I had never met Clarence before this weekend. That's why he allowed us into his private rooms, when all others were barred, why he was so willing to share his suspicions." She paused, took a breath. "If anyone else had entered those rooms, they would have realised it wasn't Clarence at all."

"That's why it was so dark?" Greg's shoulders slumped. "Why he kept us on the other side of the room." He groaned and buried his head in his hands.

"Belle mentioned Liam does a good impression of Clarence," Ruth continued. "It may not have been convincing enough to fool anyone who knew him well, but it worked on us." She pictured all the costumes and makeup benches under the park, and then the bedroom below Clarence's rooms. "Nadia saw Liam coming out of a hidden elevator, right after his meeting with us. I believe when she's well enough to talk, she'll say he was disguised as Clarence." Ruth took a breath. "Liam must have made up some elaborate excuse to placate her at the time, explained his actions away, convinced Nadia Clarence was fine and this was part of the games. Even so, worried she'd run off and tell someone, he had her stay under false pretences. Liam persuaded her to play a part in the games, all so he could deal with her later." Ruth scanned their shocked expressions. "I overheard an argument. Perhaps Nadia had second thoughts, but in the end, Liam won. He sprayed her with the fake blood, and she lay on the floor."

"Back up," Elias said, his brow furrowed. "Clarence called you. Right before the third game. I remember it clearly. He was alive."

"No, he wasn't, and no, he didn't call." Greg looked up at

Ray, realisation dawning on his face. "Liam went to the bathroom to get changed, remember? He must have phoned Grandma then and pretended to be Clarence."

"I'm afraid we'll need statements from everyone," Inspector Harlow said to the group.

"Now?" Belle asked.

"While it's still fresh," Inspector Harlow said.

"While it's raw, you mean," Persephone muttered.

Inspector Harlow faced Ruth. "We have your statement, and will be in touch. You're free to leave."

Ruth glanced around at the family, and then left the sitting room with Greg, that deep unease still in the pit of her stomach.

24

I n her suite at Hadfield Hall, Ruth zipped up her suitcase, and then ushered Merlin into his box, all the while an unsettling feeling gnawed at her insides.

Greg leaned against the doorframe, watching her pack, his suitcase by his side. "What first gave Liam away?"

"When he was pretending to be Clarence, he spoke of Winifred with such affection. It turned out there were also discrepancies in the frozen lake story, when Winifred almost drowned as a child." Ruth shook her head. "But according to the family, their relationship was strained, distant. They barely tolerated each other."

Greg slowly nodded. "You're saying Liam wanted us to believe Clarence had a strong, credible reason to find the blackmailer and therefore the killer?"

"Precisely." Ruth fastened the clasps on Merlin's box and checked the air vents were open. "If we'd known the truth, that Clarence and Winifred were at odds, I might have questioned his reasons more." She stood. "Liam needed us to think Clarence was obsessed with finding Winifred's killer, that he was paranoid and suspicious of everyone.

That way, when Clarence was found dead, it would seem like a natural progression of events. Like the killer had finally got to him."

"Liam was playing a long game," Greg said. "He was setting Ray up from the start."

"He knew Ray was desperate to expand the park," Ruth said. "That Ray was frustrated with Clarence and Winifred's resistance. Liam used that frustration, that ambition, to his advantage. He manipulated Ray, played on his emotions, and made him the perfect patsy."

"And Winifred?" Greg asked. "Do you think she went to that bridge, refused to pay any more blackmail money, and that's why he pushed her into the river?"

"Liam probably chose the bridge, knowing Winifred was afraid of water." Ruth pictured them standing there, in the dark. "He made it look like an accident, hoping no one would immediately suspect foul play."

"But why kill Clarence too?" Greg rubbed the back of his neck. "I mean, wouldn't it have been easier to frame Ray for Winifred's murder and leave it at that?"

"My guess is Liam was afraid Clarence would figure it out," Ruth said. "He knew Clarence was suspicious, that he'd hired a private investigator. Liam couldn't risk Clarence uncovering the truth. He had to silence him."

"But why go through all the trouble of setting up the games?" Greg pressed. "I don't get it. Why not just kill Clarence and make it also look like an accident?"

"That would be too much of a coincidence."

It's sad, Ruth thought, *because Clarence was trying to make amends with Winifred. The games, and signing across ownership of Hadfield Hall, prove that.*

Liam had needed what he considered a soft target, someone they could manipulate into investigating, and had assumed Ruth fit the bill. He'd thought he had the perfect puppets and—

Ruth gasped and staggered back a step as the last piece of the puzzle finally clicked into place. "That's it."

Greg's brow furrowed. "What?"

Back in the sitting room, Ray gritted his teeth. "I can't believe this is happening. Why did he do this to us? It feels like a nightmare."

"I'm afraid it gets worse." Ruth strode into the room. "What was Liam's motive?" She looked round at them all.

Inspector Harlow frowned at her.

"Revenge for what Clarence did to him?" Ruth continued. "For his lies? For ensuring Liam lost his chance at working as Lord Montague's personal assistant?"

"Money," Elias said. "Pure and simple."

Ruth shook her head. "Not so easy. Upon their deaths, Winifred and Clarence's shares are divided among all of you, not Liam. How could he gain?" She turned her attention to Persephone. "You knew I was a former police officer. How?"

A crease formed on her brow, and her eyes darted to Helena. "She told me."

Ruth faced Helena. "Right. And how did you know?"

Helena's gaze flickered nervously between Ruth, Persephone, and Ray. "I—I don't recall. Someone must have mentioned it. I'm not sure."

"Oh, I think you know," Ruth countered. "Clarence and Winifred were the only ones who knew that information. And I doubt they would have had any cause to share it freely. After all, I was only here to help with the kitchen."

She paused, letting the silence hang heavy in the air. "That leaves only one possibility. Liam told you."

Ray whipped his head around to face his wife, his eyes blazing. "What is she talking about?"

Helena shifted under her husband's stare. "I must have overheard. That's all."

An image of Liam eavesdropping on Winifred and Ray's discussion flashed into Ruth's mind.

How often has he done that over the years? And how much of what he's caught has he relayed to Helena?

Ruth glanced at Inspector Harlow and then addressed Ray. "As I said, Liam wouldn't benefit from Winifred and Clarence's deaths, or from you going to prison. Not directly." She took a steadying breath, steeling herself. "But with you behind bars, serving a lengthy sentence for their murders, Helena would be free to file for divorce."

"And walk away with half of everything he owns," Elias finished, his voice heavy with disgust. "That prenuptial agreement you have would lend less weight under such circumstances."

"She'd immediately sell those shares," Persephone added. "Would finally be free of him, but still live in the style you're accustomed to." Persephone looked about ready to commit a murder of her own. "You know the business is floundering, and were afraid you'd lose everything if it goes under. You wanted to act now, before it's too late."

"What was the plan after?" Ruth inclined her head at Helena. "You and Liam moving abroad? Living happily ever after? Or splitting your spoils and going your separate ways? Is he just a . . . puppet?" She clicked her fingers. "Perhaps you planned on disposing of him once the money was in your account."

"You were going to let me take the fall for you?" Ray's

voice was dangerously quiet as he studied his wife's reaction. "Just so you and your side piece could run off together?"

Belle gasped. "You knew they were together?"

Ray shook his head. "I suspected. Didn't want it to be true."

Helena finally met his gaze. "This is all complete fantasy. I would never—"

"What about the house?" Belle asked, her brow furrowed. "The ownership going to Orlando?"

"We can't be certain," Ruth conceded. "But maybe Winifred suspected where this was leading, that Helena was somehow involved in the blackmail, so she—"

"Signed it over to me," Orlando said. "To protect it." He looked at his brother with a mixture of sadness and guilt. "She needed to shield the family legacy."

"But if Winifred suspected Helena, why didn't she say something?" Elias asked.

"Unfortunately, she uncovered the blackmailer's identity too late." Ruth's gaze fixed on a point beyond the family, to a glorious oak tree outside. "I believe Winifred went to the bridge that night to confront them, to try and reason with the blackmailer, and hoped to finally reveal them."

"Was that you, Helena?" Ray asked, his face a mask of pain and anguish. "What happened on that bridge?" He leaned toward her, his eyes pleading. "Tell me you didn't kill Grandmama. It was Liam, right? He pushed her?"

The officers near Ray tensed, ready to restrain him if needed.

Helena, however, remained unflinching. Finally, she shrugged, a chillingly nonchalant gesture that spoke volumes.

Ruth pictured Winifred receiving a late-night phone call

from Helena, agreeing to meet her on the bridge, and the resulting tussle as she shoved Winifred over the railing.

"It's all true?" Elias breathed.

Helena sneered at him. "Should've had Liam take care of you before all this started." Her cold gaze shifted to Persephone. "And you."

Ray's face fell. "No." He shook his head. "It can't be true. It's not real. Please, Helena?" He reached for her hand, but she pulled away. "You're in love with Liam?"

"He's twice the man you are." Helena leapt to her feet and lashed out at Ray as he rose too, but he stumbled back.

His expression flipped to rage. "You're a monster," he roared. "If money is all you care about . . ."

Officers pounced, pulling Ray back and restraining Helena, but she fought against them, teeth bared, and spat at her husband.

"That's enough." Inspector Harlow stepped forward, her voice firm. "You are under arrest for the murders of Winifred and Clarence Marsh. You have the right to remain silent . . ."

While the officers handcuffed Helena and then led her away, Ray dropped back to his chair, breathing hard, the pain of his wife's betrayal etched onto his features.

Orlando, his face pale and drawn, squeezed Belle's hand, and his voice choked, he said, "It's my fault. If I hadn't—"

"Don't," Belle whispered. "You couldn't have known this would happen."

As Ruth watched the broken family before her, she couldn't help a pang of sympathy. Orlando may have been foolish, reckless even, but he hadn't set out to hurt anyone. In the end, he was as much a victim of circumstance as the rest of them, and it would take the brothers a long time to heal.

Ruth strode toward her motorhome, away from Hadfield Hall and the wreckage of the Marsh family. The weight of the previous days' events pressed down on her.

She adjusted her grip on Merlin's box.

One of her biggest takeaways from this ordeal was to never take people at face value again. Her grandson was right: Ruth was a sucker for a sob story.

Greg waddled along beside her, a suitcase in each hand.

"Oh no." Ruth's step faltered.

Greg flinched, and looked back at the house. "What's wrong now?"

She sighed. "Professor JT Wilson. The archaeologist. Clarence— I mean, *Liam*, promised you'd get to work with him."

"Oh. I don't mind," Greg murmured.

Even so, Ruth vowed to leave it a couple of weeks and then drop an email to Ray. Given all this weekend's shenanigans, he owed her.

They reached the motorhome, the familiar sight a welcome comfort after the chaos. Ruth was about to grab the door handle, but Greg gasped, making her jump.

He dropped the suitcases. "We can't leave."

Ruth's eyes darted to the house. "Why not?"

"We have unfinished business."

Ruth's mind raced. "We do?"

Greg bobbed his head. "You and I agreed, if you investigated anything while we were here . . ." A cheesy, Cheshire-Cat-sized grin spread across his face. "You have to go on a roller coaster with me."

Ruth stared at him, every muscle tensed.

"It's okay, Grandma," Greg said, nonchalant. "I wouldn't do that to you. Not with your cleithrophobia."

Ruth relaxed. "Thank you. That's very kind of—"

"We'll go on a haunted train ride instead." Greg winked.

Thank you for reading!

To be notified of FUTURE RELEASES in the Ruth Morgan series, click on the author name "Peter Jay Black" at Amazon, and then "Follow" in the top left of the author profile page.

If you've not yet read the Ruth Morgan series prequel:
MURDER ON THE OCEAN ODYSSEY
OUT NOW

We would be incredibly grateful if you could leave a star rating or review. Your invaluable support is vital to the Ruth Morgan Mystery Series' success and can make all the difference.

PETER JAY BLACK
BIBLIOGRAPHY

DEATH IN LONDON
Book One in a Fast-Paced Crime Thriller Series
https://mybook.to/DeathinLondonKindle

Emma leads a quiet life, away from her divorced parents' business interests, but when her father's fiancée turns up dead in her mother's warehouse, she can't ignore the threat of a civil war.

Unable to call the police, Emma's parents ask her to assist an eccentric private detective with the investigation. She reluctantly agrees, on the condition that when she's done they allow her to have her own life in America, away from the turmoil.

The amateur sleuths investigate the murder, and piece together a series of cryptic clues left by the killer, who seems to know the families intimately, but a mistake leads to the slaying of another close relative.

Now dragged into a world she's fought hard to avoid, Emma must do everything she can to help catch the culprit and restore peace. However, with time running out, could her parents be the next victims?

"Pick up Death in London today and start book one in a gripping Crime Thriller Mystery series."

***

DEATH IN MANHATTAN
Book One in a Fast-Paced Crime Thriller Series
https://mybook.to/DeathinManhattanKindle

When someone murders New York's leading crime boss, despite him being surrounded by advanced security, the event throws the underworld into chaos. Before anyone can figure out how the killer did it, he dies under mysterious circumstances and takes his secret to the grave.

Emma's uncle asks her to check out the crime scene, but she's reluctant to get involved, especially after the traumatic events back in London. However, with Nightshade's unique brand of encouragement, they figure out how the killer reached one of the most protected men in the world. Their lives are then complicated further when another member of the Syndicate is murdered, seemingly by the hands of the same deceased perpetrator.

Emma and Nightshade now find themselves in way over their heads, caught up in a race against time, trying to solve clues and expose a web of deception, but will they be quick enough to stop a war?

URBAN OUTLAWS
A High-Octane Middle Grade Action Series
mybook.to/UrbanOutlaws

In a bunker hidden deep beneath London live five extraordinary kids: meet world-famous hacker Jack, gadget geek Charlie, free runner Slink, comms chief Obi, and decoy diva Wren. They're not just friends; they're URBAN OUTLAWS. They outsmart London's crime gangs and hand out their dirty money through Random Acts of Kindness (R.A.K.s).

Others in the series:
URBAN OUTLAWS: BLACKOUT
mybook.to/UOBlackout

Power is out. Security is down. Computers hacked. The world's most destructive computer virus is out of control and the pressure is on for the Urban Outlaws to destroy it. Jack knows that it's not just the world's secrets that could end up in the wrong hands. The secret location of their bunker is at the fingertips of many and the identities of the Urban Outlaws are up for grabs. But capturing the virus feels like an almost impossible mission until they meet Hector. The Urban Outlaws know they need his help, but they have made some dangerous enemies. They could take a risk and win – or lose everything ...

URBAN OUTLAWS: LOCKDOWN
mybook.to/UOLockdown

he Urban Outlaws have been betrayed – and defeated. Or so Hector thought when he stole the world's most advanced computer virus. But Hector will need to try much harder than just crossing the Atlantic if he wants to outsmart Jack and his team ...

URBAN OUTLAWS: COUNTERSTRIKE
mybook.to/UOCounterstrike

The Urban Outlaws face their biggest challenge yet. They have to break into the Facility and find the ultimate weapon – Medusa – before Hector does. But there are five levels of security to crack and a mystery room that has Jack sweating whenever he thinks about it.

URBAN OUTLAWS: SHOCKWAVE
mybook.to/UOShockwave

The Urban Outlaws have been infected! Hector Del Sarto used them to spread the deadly Medusa virus and now the whole of London is in lockdown. Only Hector and his father have the antidote. Can Jack, Charlie, Obi, Slink and Wren work together to bring down the Del Sartos once and for all? The whole city depends on them!

GAME SPACE
Kids' Space Adventure
Jumanji Meets The Last Starfighter
mybook.to/GameSpace

Trapped Inside Alien Game. SEND HELP!

When Leo moves to Colorado, he uncovers a crashed UFO with an alien game on board. Forty years ago his grandmother fell into the virtual world and vanished.

Now determined to solve the mystery, Leo goes inside, believing he'll captain a spaceship and bring her home, but he finds himself surrounded by a decimated fleet and in real danger.

To survive, Leo must adapt quickly, win over new friends, and blend in. That won't be easy because one of them is deeply suspicious of him. Leo faces impossible challenges where the smallest misstep could mean losing his family, and his life.

STAR QUEST
(Game Space Book Two)
Gone Back Inside Alien Game. NEED HELP!
mybook.to/GS2StarQuest

Leo finishes writing about his previous space adventure and is ready to return to the game world. Once there, he'll complete a secret mission and convince his grandmother to finally come home. However, Grandpa John goes inside alone, and when he doesn't return in an instant, Leo knows something has gone horribly wrong.

ARCADIA
A Game Space FastRead
Kids' Space Adventure
mybook.to/ArcadiA

When her brother falls into the secret world of an alien arcade game, mystery-obsessed Kira must go in and rescue him. However, a simple task turns complicated as she finds herself in a universe filled with aliens, diverse creatures, and puzzles to solve.

In order to save her brother and the people of ArcadiA, Kira must make new friends, face her fears, and confront enemies, but time is running out.

ArcadiA is set in the Game Space universe, with new characters and locations.

**Print Length is approximately 97 pages (23k words) + Game Space sample chapters.

peterjayblack.com

Printed in Great Britain
by Amazon

49461425R00169